THE PEARL RIVER

THE
PEARL
RIVER

Mark Butterworth

MARK BUTTERWORTH

Matador
Unit E2 Airfield Business Park,
Harrison Road, Market Harborough,
Leicestershire. LE16 7UL
Tel: 0116 279 2299
Email: books@troubador.co.uk
Web: www.troubador.co.uk/matador
Twitter: @matadorbooks

ISBN 9781803135892

British Library Cataloguing in Publication Data.
A catalogue record for this book is available from the British Library.

Printed and bound in Great Britain by 4edge Limited
Typeset in 10pt Adobe Garamond Pro by Troubador Publishing Ltd, Leicester, UK

Matador is an imprint of Troubador Publishing Ltd

To Gemma and Julia

The Pearl River is a work of fiction based on true events that happened in the Far East in 1948–1949. 28 Squadron was a real RAF squadron operating in Malaya, Singapore and Hong Kong around this time. Various other features of the book are based on true events but have been adapted for the purposes of the story. All characters are fictitious. Some of the places mentioned are real, while others are imaginary.

ONE

Malaya, February 1949

"Just keep everyone low, Daines, and quiet. Let's hope we can find a way through the CTs and we can get out of here before full light." Captain Hind's voice was controlled and confident.

"Yes, sir. But we're seriously outnumbered and it looks like we're trapped in this gorge. The CTs have been moving round us during the night. We *must* move soon or—"

"Grenade, grenade!" The shout was followed by a crashing red explosion that blinded Hind momentarily, but he found his rifle and called his support team. "To me, 1st Recon, to me! Fire at will!" he called. "Sergeant Daines, take 2nd Recon over to the right and give covering fire. I'll take my section to the left to get a clear view of the bastards."

"Captain! Enemy to the front and right! We can't move out." A volley of machine-gun rounds ripped through the trees above Hind's head, and he realised they were in serious trouble. In the growing morning light, the enemy were closing in. Hind's Australian reconnaissance team of twenty men was in danger of being wiped out.

The Communist Terrorists had better jungle tracking and movement skills, but the Aussies were far better at weapons handling and firing. They were also trained to give fire support to each other and identify and take out a target.

"All ranks, find your man. Shoot to kill!" Hind's order was hardly needed. The overconfident terrorists had exposed their position – and Hind's troops opened fire. Hind watched with a shivering satisfaction as his men cut down the first dozen enemy troops. The CTs behind saw the attack fail and cowered down before melting back into the jungle. One of the wounded terrorists was screaming in pain, but after a couple of minutes he fell as silent and still as his dead comrades.

The Aussies could take a breather and reform their defences.

"Captain Hind, sir, Smithson has taken a hit. It's not good." The calm, experienced voice of Sergeant Daines dealt with the facts, not the emotion behind them. "The medic is with him now."

"Where is he?" said Hind. "If he's the only casualty, we've been very lucky."

"Yes, sir. This way."

Twenty yards to their left in a small clearing two men were crouched over Smithson, who lay on his back, his feet shaking like a madman.

"Corporal White, how is he?" said Hind.

"Grenade shrapnel wound to the neck, sir. The piece went straight through. Windpipe's OK, but he's losing a lot of blood."

Hind could see for himself the rich red stain across Smithson's neck and left shoulder. "Can you fix him up?"

"Morphine given, sir. I'll try to dress the wound."

"Do the best you can. We'll need to have him ready to move out before the CTs return."

"He might not be fit to move, sir. He's in a bad way."

"Well, do the best you can. Sergeant Daines, get the radio operator here – we're going to need air support."

The young radio operator seemed to have read Hind's mind. He immediately dropped the set down beside Hind and handed him the mouthpiece.

"Mayday, mayday! Come in, Battalion HQ, this is Captain Hind, 1st Recon patrol. Request urgent air cover, over." There was an unnerving silence for a few seconds, then the radio crackled to life.

"1st Recon, Battalion HQ receiving you. State your position and situation, over."

"We're in the western col, between Hills 33 and 35, trapped by a CT force. We cannot withdraw. We forced back the initial attack but the CTs have significant numbers and weaponry. Request air attack on the north side of the valley to open up an escape route for us. Over."

"Stand by, 1st Recon."

"Sir! CT movement to our front – they're setting up for an attack." Sergeant Daines' voice had risen an octave and Hind could see the concern in his face.

"Set the men up in a defensive line, Daines. Make sure they stop any further incursion up the valley."

"1st Recon? Army cooperation officer here, Lieutenant Gower. We are scrambling 28 Squadron's Spitfires. They should be overhead in fifteen minutes. Make sure you smoke the CTs with white – I repeat, white – Very flares."

"Roger. Understood, Gower, white flares it is. Get those aircraft here as soon as you can! Out."

"That's good, sir, but what firepower do those Spits carry?" said Sergeant Daines.

"Cannons, machine guns, and let's hope rockets. They need to give the CTs hell if we're going to get out of here."

***

The dispersal room at RAF Penang came to life. The sound of the scramble bell had the pilots and ground crew racing for the Spitfires. Two sections of three aircraft each were started up, already armed and fuelled. Red Section, led by Flight Lieutenant Adam Devon, was the first to taxi to the runway. He jabbed the radio button. "Rolling take-off, Red Section. Follow me!" Devon turned his Spitfire from the taxiway to the runway threshold and, without stopping, pushed the throttle lever forward. The Griffon engine roared, the tailwheel rose off the ground, and the aircraft climbed rapidly into the air. Devon glanced to his left and saw Flight Sergeant Bryant levelling next to him. Pilot Mills was already on his right wing. "Circle the field, chaps, and wait for the others to join us."

Flight Lieutenant Fitzjohn was climbing away from the airfield, leading Pilots Corrigan and Jameson in Blue Section. The six aircraft took up two V formations and turned to head north-east across the dense Malayan jungle. When they had completed their climbing turn the Spitfires levelled off and the ground radio operator cut in.

"Penang field to Spitfire patrol. Adjust magnetic heading to 030 degrees. Approximately twenty-eight miles to target. You're looking for the Aussie 1st Recon patrol trapped in the upper valley south of Hill 33. Look for white smoke. Good hunting, out." The radio operator turned to Lieutenant Gower, who sat beside him.

"I didn't know we had Australians in the area, sir. What are they up to?"

"It's an advance reconnaissance party – some of their best forces on a special mission to identify supply interception routes. If the Aussies come into the conflict full-on, they will need people experienced in the terrain. The team will definitely have a good appreciation of the country they'll have to fight in after this little party."

The Spitfires were soon over the expected area, but the pilots could not immediately identify the right valley: the terrain was a carpet of thickly forested hills and valleys stretching as far as the eye could see.

"Fitzjohn, if you see the white flare signal, go in first with your section. Use cannons and rockets. Red Section, stay with me, maintain 1,000 feet," Devon ordered.

"Captain, look – Spitfires!" On the ground, Sergeant Daines pointed to the east side of the valley.

"Right, Sergeant, stand by with the Very pistols. Let's not give the CTs time to evacuate their positions. Now, keep your aim low. Fire!"

Four booms reverberated across the valley as the Very pistol flares buried themselves into the jungle among the CT troops. Columns of white smoke ballooned through the tree canopy.

"Can you see the smoke, Corrie?" Flight Lieutenant Fitzjohn called over the radio.

"Yes, sir, off my starboard wingtip. Breaking now." Fitzjohn watched as Corrigan, on the right of the three Spitfires, banked and dived towards the ridge of the southern hill ahead of the east–west valley, where columns of white smoke rose into the air.

The other two Spitfires followed, 200 yards apart. Corrigan's approach to the target looked perilously low as he fired cannon shells and two of his rockets at the enemy positions. But the grey-white tracer smoke of the rockets showed that the weapons shot harmlessly a hundred feet above the enemy. He pulled up in a steep climb, his heart missing a beat as he cleared the treetops on the northern ridge by a couple of feet.

"Sod it, that was close!" he muttered. He glanced to his left to see Jameson's rockets scream over the heads of the enemy and explode behind them.

"Tally-ho, chaps." Fitzjohn's confidence rang through his words as he dived towards the southern hill. He left it too late to fire; his shots tore into the jungle, still overhead the enemy. "Bloody impossible to get a shot on target. Let's get back to Penang. All aircraft break off," Fitzjohn ordered as he climbed away. He felt empowered to give the order as he was the senior officer in terms of service.

"Negative! Bryant, Mills, have a go. I'll follow you in," Devon snapped.

The first two aircraft followed the same diving approach with the same result, missing the target high. It was clear that the Australian ground troops were in a mess; Devon had to hit the target if they were to get out of there alive. He pushed the stick forward and set his gunsights for the white smoke. But as he approached he could see he would miss, so he pulled up early without firing. He spoke calmly over the radio. "This is hopeless. I'm going to try something else."

Devon circled the target and commenced his second dive as the others had done, across the valley but further east, apparently off-target. Curving round, he suddenly saw red tracer bullets rising from the white smoke – the terrorists had sighted a machine gun on him. Devon ignored the danger. As the white smoke came into view on his left he banked the Spitfire at a 90-degree angle and loosed his four high-explosive rockets and a five-second burst of cannon and machine-gun fire. The aircraft shuddered under the recoil. When Devon saw the rockets, shells and bullets rip through the CT's position he pulled back the control column, rolled the plane level and made a vicious straight-ahead climb to take him up the valley. A twang-twang from the left wing made Devon flinch. There were bullet holes near the wingtip. Devon shook off his fear, as the damage was minimal, and focused on getting out of the valley. But as he approached the far western ridge he knew he was too low – he would fly straight into the trees. Throttling back and pulling up the Spitfire's nose, Devon was able to slow the aircraft to achieve the maximum angle of climb without stalling. This only gave him a few feet of extra altitude. The sickening fear that he was not going to make it flooded over him.

At the last moment, Devon reapplied power to get the aircraft's last ounce of lift. With a crashing judder the Spitfire flew into the high branches of the trees on the ridge. As he emerged through the other side of the trees, Devon realised that the damage to his aircraft was not catastrophic. He was able to fly on. "Red Section, form on me. Let's get back to Penang. Slow cruise speed, chaps. I don't want to put any further strain on my Spit."

From the ground Captain Hind saw the awful effect of the cannon fire and rockets exploding among the terrorists. A bloodied leg cartwheeled through the air and men were launched twenty feet from the ground. The Aussies reacted quickly.

"Daines, get the men ready for a fighting withdrawal down the valley to the east," called Hind. "And assign a couple of men to carry Smithson."

The unit required no further encouragement. Each man crouched, ready for the order to move.

"Right, move out!" Without hesitation Sergeant Daines led his men safely across the open clearing that five minutes earlier would have been a killing ground. No fire came from the CTs; Devon's attack had given them other things to think about.

***

"Bloody good shooting, sir!" Bryant jumped down from his Spitfire's wing and pulled off his flying gloves. "Mind you, your aircraft is a bit of a mess."

"Thanks, Bryant, it's just superficial damage. Let's hope the Aussies got away," Devon said, walking across to the intelligence office to file his report. Blue Section had already landed and Fitzjohn was in the office. He spoke first.

"That was a pretty stupid risk you took, Devon. Trying to kill yourself, eh? And you know it's an offence to endanger your aircraft." Fitzjohn sounded annoyed.

"Nonsense, Fitzjohn. Sure, the angle was tight, but the Spit's more than capable of handling it." Devon knew that Fitzjohn was cross that he had achieved what Fitzjohn had failed to do. Devon tried to be nonchalant and hide his irritation with Fitzjohn. He couldn't deny that his actions had endangered both his aircraft and himself.

Fitzjohn's outburst had not gone unnoticed.

"Reports, please, gentlemen. You can settle your flying differences in the Mess," said the intelligence officer.

Devon completed the interview and paperwork then returned to his quarters and called his orderly. "Coffee, please, Young."

"Yes, sir, straight away. Good mission, sir?"

Devon smiled inwardly. "Yes, I think so. We'll have to see if everyone agrees."

"Difficulties, sir?"

Devon could see that Young sensed something was wrong. "Possibly. You can't please everyone, can you? Now, let's have that coffee, Young, nice and strong."

"Yes, sir."

Devon threw his flying helmet and flight plan onto his desk and looked in the small mirror above it. A stranger might think he had Scandinavian blood: he had pale blue eyes and blond hair, left long on top and neatly cut around his ears and neck. He took a towel and patted his face dry. He was medium height, slim and lean, his muscular frame kept in good shape through distance running and his use of free weights in the gymnasium. He pondered the morning's action and smiled to himself. It had gone well.

TWO

Two hours later Devon was starting to feel the after-effects of the mission. When adrenaline dissipates from the system, stress comes to the fore and the body reacts with fear, panic and sometimes terror. Devon recognised the reaction. He'd experienced it after many previous missions where he knew he had killed the enemy on the ground, and he realised what he was going through. As he ran in for his final attack on the communists, anger flowed through his system. He had no regrets; the enemy were killers who had to be stopped. Devon knew he had to give himself a few hours' rest to manage the mental images of the mission. He felt nauseous. But they had been terrorists. It had to be done. Devon had never taken any pleasure in killing the enemy, but today he felt huge satisfaction in knowing that he had prevented harm coming to his own men. He was a natural flyer, not a natural killer, and the work was essentially abhorrent to him, as it was to most service personnel. Having a purpose or cause to fight for was essential to his motivation, it gave reason and legitimacy to what he was doing; it was right.

A knock at the door and Young entered with more coffee, accompanied by Beresford, the commanding officer's adjutant.

"Flight Lieutenant Devon, you are asked to attend Group Captain Franks' office at 1400 hours." Beresford's clipped, authoritative tone indicated that the message was not a request but an order.

"Understood, sir. Please let the CO know I will be there." Devon knew he would have no chance to rest for a while. After Beresford had left, Devon turned to Young. "Get over to maintenance, please, Young and find out what the true damage to the Spit is. Then come back and let me know."

***

With five minutes to spare, Devon stepped into the CO's anteroom. Beresford stood in front of a green metal filing cabinet, a thin buff cardboard file in his hand. "He's ready to see you straight away." Beresford went to the CO's office door, knocked and entered without waiting to be asked.

"Devon, come in." Group Captain Franks sat behind an impressive mahogany desk – doubtless commandeered from the Colonial Office. To his right stood Squadron Leader David Porter, Devon's immediate boss. His expression did not augur well for the meeting. Devon glanced around the room and was surprised to see Fitzjohn standing in the corner. The CO noticed his look. "I have asked Flight Lieutenant Fitzjohn to join us as he had a clear view of this morning's operation. I have already read his report and now I would like to hear from you."

"Yes, sir. The approach to the target was so steep that our attacks shot over the heads of the enemy. Direct attacks were not effective, so I banked left over the valley, fired the rockets and cannons, then climbed away. The Mark XVIII has an excellent rate of climb, as you know, if well handled. I clipped the trees on the way out but the damage was minor, apparently, and just a couple of rounds through the wing. I hit the target – a very satisfactory ending to the mission, I believe."

"I beg to differ, Devon! I think you will find the damage to your aircraft is such that it will be in maintenance for a week. You recklessly exposed the machine and yourself to unnecessary danger. Aside from the damage caused by colliding with the trees, a bullet could easily have hit the fuel tank, not the wing, and ended in disaster. You will also be aware that this is potentially a court martial offence." The Commanding Officer's face reddened as the volume of his voice increased.

"But sir, these were exceptional circumstances. The ground troops were trapped."

"Devon, you were advised to return to Penang by Fitzjohn here."

"I know that Flight Lieutenant Fitzjohn wanted to call off the attack as the other pilots had had no joy, sir, but I felt we could get at the enemy across the line of the valley."

"And in doing so your aircraft was severely damaged…" Fitzjohn pressed the point home.

"I got the job done, Fitzjohn, and you know it! There's minimal damage to the air intakes and wings, and the bullet holes can be easily repaired. And I got the aircraft home safely," said Devon.

"*Enough,* Devon!" The CO got to his feet. "Count yourself lucky that you are only getting a serious warning. This will be noted on your record. Any further flying misdemeanours and you'll find yourself back in the UK in double time."

"Sir, I must protest! Is a warning sufficient?" Fitzjohn stepped forward. "Flight Lieutenant Devon's antics set a very bad example to the pilots. We cannot allow showmanship into our flying. A less experienced man might try his own luck next time and kill himself."

"Alright, Fitzjohn. I'm aware of the implications of this morning's events, as is the squadron leader. You are both dismissed."

"But sir…"

"Dismissed, I said, Fitzjohn. That will be all."

Devon stepped into the heat of the afternoon Malayan sun, looking forward to a period of downtime. Some music or reading, he thought – anything to shake off the depression caused by the CO's reaction to his attack on Hill 33.

"Bad luck, old boy," called Fitzjohn, his voice mocking. "Shame the CO gave you such a rollicking."

"Get lost, Fitzjohn."

"Temper, temper! How about a drink in the Mess? I'd be happy to buy a drink for the hero of the day."

"I'll pass on that. And you might be better occupied studying the Spitfire's handling manual. You could learn something."

Devon watched Fitzjohn storm away in the direction of the Officers' Mess. Squadron Leader Porter came out of the CO's office and approached Devon. "The old man's right, you know, Devon. You broke all the rules. But off the record, well done. Looks like the Aussies all got out OK. Nice work."

"Thank you, sir. I'm very pleased to hear that." Devon strolled across the tarmac to his quarters. An afternoon of music, he thought. Yes, Grieg, 'In the Hall of the Mountain King'. Ha! Very appropriate.

THREE

On a chilly late-winter morning, after a ten-minute walk from Liverpool Street Station in the City of London, Hannah Shaw found she had time for a cup of coffee before her appointment. On the northern side of Eastcheap she found a Kardomah café. It was busy with commuters stopping for a quick breakfast or to meet friends before going into the office, but she went in and ordered a drink from the counter. She noticed a spare chair at a table occupied by one other person – a smartly dressed, petite, elegant woman in her forties – to Hannah, the image of an executive secretary. She sat down and the two exchanged a brief smile.

The older woman left within a few minutes, leaving Hannah to ponder the task ahead of her. She wondered if a job in a bank would make the most of her physics degree. Would it suit her? Would she fit in to the hurried, impersonal life that the City seemed to offer? She had a vague feeling for 'the City', the mysterious world of finance, share dealing, insurance and banking, but admitted that she already liked the buzz and the sense of purpose that seemed to prevail.

She glanced at her watch. It was 8.45 a.m. The café was clearing as people went off to their offices. Her interview at the bank was at 9.15 so she had some time to relax. She gave some thought to the questions she might be asked at the interview – about her background, of course, but she had a well-rehearsed story that she could recite to deflect any probing enquiries into her past. She concentrated on the role she was applying for in marketing. She had some ideas she had picked up from a university friend who was already working in the sales team of an insurance company. Hannah told herself that an interview was just a simple meeting, nothing to be concerned about.

But a sudden shiver of nerves made her collect herself and look again at her watch. She had fifteen minutes to go. She knew her destination was five minutes away, but she decided to leave the Kardomah anyway. She wanted to make a good first impression. The job would be important to her: she needed a good salary to fund her share of the small flat she hoped to rent in London with Sophia, a friend from university. It would be foolish to be late. She put on her tan leather gloves, brushed imaginary dust from her handbag, straightened her silk scarf and left, full of renewed self-assurance.

She walked north through Rood Lane, then cut across to Lime Street. The doors of the Grapes public house had just been opened, and the aroma of stale beer and cigarette smoke wafted out. The shops in Leadenhall Market were already open, and boxes of supplies were stacked outside restaurants, ready for the lunchtime trade. When she arrived at Leadenhall Street she had to wait for a string of London buses to pass before crossing the road and stepping into the entrance hall of the bank.

A uniformed commissionaire saluted her. On hearing that she was attending an interview, he asked her to wait. He went to make a phone call, giving her time to look around and take in the impressive interior of the building – all designed to entice wealthy clients, she imagined. Five minutes later she was in the interview room, relaxed and confident.

FOUR

For the next month, army patrols in the north of Malaya were stepped up as the fighting on the ground continued. Despite the gruelling heat and humidity in the jungle, the British and Commonwealth troops' fighting skills and spirit started to overpower the communists. The army's reconnaissance patrols became more successful in identifying enemy movements and targets for attack. Using camouflage techniques honed in the Second World War, attack troops painted their faces green and black, used foliage woven into their uniforms as camouflage, and were not averse to sinking into filthy ditch water to set an ambush. There was no time in the jungle for squeamishness about snakes and insects. The presence of the Spitfires usually meant that the terrorists kept their heads down; only occasionally did the army ask for rocket and cannon fire. The core of the communists had originally been trained by the British Army during the Second World War to resist a Japanese invasion but the rest were keen amateur soldiers. Often young and inexperienced, but they had a cause to fight for, and that made them dangerous.

The Communist Terrorists wanted to gain independence from British colonial power. The British government was very motivated to resist this aim: to set an example to other countries under British rule, and to protect the British economic assets in Malaya. British-owned rubber plantations and tin mines were being targeted by the communist forces. The government declared the situation to be an 'Emergency', but never actually referring to the conflict as a war. There were suggestions that the situation was driven by economic priorities – insurance underwriters covering the plantations, rubber mills and mines excluded paying out for damage that happened during a war but could not apply this exclusion to claims for damage caused by rebellious factions with political ambitions, where no war had been declared.

Pilots and other service personnel were allowed short periods of leave for rest and recuperation, and on these occasions they often took one of the regular trucks or buses into Kuala Lumpur. KL offered entertainment, bars, and the chance to meet local girls. The men were even able to go and watch Malaya League football matches, bringing back fond memories of Saturday afternoons back home. Cinemas ran the latest English language films and the men could see what was happening in the wider world on the Pathé newsreels. They watched reports on the likely outcome of the next general election. Opinions varied on which party was considered most likely to maintain the colonial stance of the UK, ensuring an ongoing role for operational squadrons. More of interest to many servicemen was news on FA Cup matches.

All pilots reported back for duty on Sunday evening, allowing them time to sober up before Monday morning's regular briefing.

"Gentlemen, please take your seats. Group Captain Franks will be addressing us in a few minutes." The adjutant, Charles Beresford, held the rank of squadron leader. He wore an immaculate uniform, despite the heat, which told everyone present that he was a stickler for detail. His job was to ensure that all administrative matters were taken care of for the station commander. The adjutant's role was often derided for 'flying a desk', but Beresford was admired and respected by all who came into contact with him.

The group captain walked forward. "Good morning, everyone. You will be briefed this morning on a change to the squadron's role, and the logistics for our next posting will be outlined. Squadron Leader Beresford will provide the details. But before we move on, let me offer my congratulations for the hard work and excellent flying you have all shown during our deployment here. Reports from HQ Army Command have all been positive. We must show constraint, but also at times our offensive attack capabilities. Your work has been exemplary."

The CO knew the pilots were keen to hear what the immediate future held for them. Most of the men feared that the squadron would be disbanded and all ranks repatriated to the UK. Not something the crews had signed up for.

"Squadron Leader Beresford, over to you."

"Thank you, sir." Beresford removed his cap to reveal perfectly groomed and Brylcreemed brown hair. His voice spoke of privilege and the establishment. His self-assured style gave confidence to the assembled men.

"After a highly successful tour here at RAF Penang, 28 Squadron is being assigned a defence role in Singapore. We shall be a reserve squadron, with ground attack capabilities maintained, should we be required as a result of any escalation of the Emergency." Beresford paused while the pilots absorbed the implication of his news. The challenge and excitement of front-line flying was to be replaced with a cosy training deployment. It was better than being sent home, but what would their future career options be?

Beresford continued. "Next month, the squadron will fly south to RAF Changi. The planned departure date is currently 4 May. The engineering ground crews, armaments and fuelling teams will transfer by sea and transport aircraft in stages to ensure that we maintain full operational capability. Many of you know the field but, for those who do not, it is situated on the eastern tip of Singapore Island, giving immediate access to the Straits and the South China Sea. We will also be on call for a return to Malaya, should the situation in the Emergency deteriorate. You can expect some intense exercises with the navy and army to hone our skills. Please don't worry that you will have too little to do!" Beresford paused. His gentle smile helped to reassure the pilots. "I will now hand back to Group Captain Franks."

"The longer-term strategy for Army Cooperation squadrons is under consideration by Air Vice-Marshall Whitlock in the UK. We expect more details in the next three months or so." Not such positive news. "As you know, future home defence will be carried out largely by jet aircraft, with Vampires and Meteors already in service. Naturally, our more advanced Spitfire version will continue to operate, particularly in support of ground forces, as fighter-bombers and in a reconnaissance role. So, get yourselves ready for the redeployment. RAF Changi is one of the most attractive stations in the Far East – indeed, the service as a whole – and you can look forward to the cultural and social delights of Singapore!"

The men laughed quietly.

Pensively, Franks added: "But stay sharp, and maintain the high standard of flying you have achieved here. Now, Squadron Leader Beresford has further comments for you."

Beresford stood up slowly and walked forward. "I can now advise you all of a key change to the command of the squadron. Squadron Leader Porter will soon be retiring from the Royal Air Force."

A ripple of subdued gasps went around the room. The news did not come as a shock to the more astute members of the squadron, who had suspected that it wouldn't be long before the skipper moved on. All the pilots knew of Porter's excellent record from the Battle of Britain through

D-Day and to the Far East. Everyone appreciated that he would be an excellent civilian pilot in whatever role he took on.

"Squadron Leader Porter will be leading a new and exciting function at British Overseas Airways Corporation – the exploration of new destinations and services around the world," Beresford went on.

Spontaneously the pilots applauded, and there were calls of "Bravo!"

Group Captain Franks held his hand up to restore order. "Thank you, gentlemen. You will have the opportunity of congratulating the squadron leader properly when you are established in Singapore. If there are no questions, you are dismissed."

On their way out, Devon asked Porter, "Is this the beginning of the end for the squadron, sir?"

Their good working relations and mutual friendship allowed Devon to ask the question of the squadron leader.

"No, certainly not, Devon. Have faith in our front-line role. The CO is serious about us maintaining operational excellence and being ready to redeploy at a moment's notice. But being stationed at Changi is one of the best deployments in the world. We should enjoy it while we can."

FIVE

A week after their arrival in Singapore, Squadron Leader Porter was buying the drinks in the Officers' Mess. He wanted to mark his forthcoming departure from the squadron, but not to have a formal celebration. After more than ten years of flying in the RAF, it was time to return to England and take up his new role as development director with BOAC. It wasn't as exciting as being on an operational squadron, but it would still allow Porter to travel the world, test-flying potential new routes for the airline.

"Cheers, David. Wishing you all the best for the future," said Group Captain Green, the Changi Commanding Officer. Porter wondered what the man really thought – probably that he would be bored stiff and would regret his decision within a month.

The pilots grouped in threes and fours, mainly debating their plans for the rest of the evening, but discussion soon turned to the future of front-line fighters. The groups merged into one large circle. Porter heard Fitzjohn become more vocal.

"I'm definitely applying for a transfer to a home defence squadron and retraining on jets. That's the future. It's going to be a couple of years before this squadron gets Vampires, if ever, and I can't wait for that."

"But aren't the latest variants of Spitfire as good? And they have a multifunctional role." Pilot Officer Tyler Anderson chipped in.

"Nonsense, man. Our machines are the tops here in the Far East, and that's fine if you have no ambition."

Anderson didn't respond to the implied criticism.

"Spits give us excellent tactical army support – we have proven that they're more than capable of doing the job in Malaya," Flight Lieutenant Devon said.

"Look, old man…" Fitzjohn gave Devon his most derisive look. "The RAF will only be the best air arm in the world if it has the best kit, and that's jet fighters. And the best pilots, of course." Fitzjohn's demeanour clearly implied that he meant himself, naturally.

Squadron Leader Porter stepped forward. "Let's not criticise any part of the service – all squadrons and all aircraft types have a role to play. Spitfires have undoubtedly had their day as the number-one fighter and they're now being overtaken by jets. But there's no prejudice to a pilot enhancing his career by staying with prop-driven aircraft."

"Quite so," mumbled Fitzjohn.

"But how would they cope with Russian MiG-9s, sir?"

"They couldn't, of course, Anderson. Any serious jet opposition would be devastating for Spitfires. But that's why we have Vampires and Meteors and better aircraft in development."

"And the Americans have the F-86 Sabre, one of the best jet aircraft around." Fitzjohn reinforced his argument.

"In the meantime, gentlemen, we have the pleasure of flying the world's most beautiful aircraft!" Porter calmed the increasingly tense mood and the group broke up, with some of the men discussing the best bars to meet girls in Singapore.

***

"David, could I have a word, please?" Group Captain Green guided Porter to a quiet corner of the bar. "You know you still have the opportunity to delay your resignation – a couple of months, perhaps, give yourself time to think. I'm not convinced you really are ready to quit the service and take a civilian flying job. You are key to this squadron and it will be a challenge to find a replacement for you."

"Sir, I'm not sure that's the case. No doubt the Air Ministry is considering who my replacement might be from the UK, and we have two talented flight lieutenants who are ready for promotion to squadron leader."

"Fitzjohn and Devon?" asked Green.

"Yes, sir."

"Fitzjohn is a very good man, but seems to be putting more emphasis on flying jets than concerning himself with promotion. And what of Devon's record – that business up in Penang? Nearly got himself court-martialled. Doesn't that scupper his chances?"

Porter looked quizzically at his superior. "With respect, sir, I should say not. That was a fine piece of flying, by all accounts, and the other pilots recognise his quality. Saved a group of Aussies from a very tight situation. No, I hope you would agree that a touch of resourcefulness marks a man out as a leader. As for Fitzjohn, he's also a skilled pilot. I suggest we meet the two of them to gauge their interest. Would you like me to arrange interviews?"

"Yes, do that, Porter. Let's get on with it."

***

A few days later Devon was enjoying Bach's 'Prelude No. 1' in his quarters when there was a knock at his door.

"Message from the adjutant, sir. The governor wants to see you tomorrow morning, 9 a.m.," said Young.

"It's the CO to you, Young. Any indication what it's all about?" Devon always preferred to know why he was being called to the station commander's office.

"Um, nothing official, sir."

"Spit it out, Young, what do you know?"

"Rumour has it, sir, that the CO is thinking about replacing Squadron Leader Porter with one of our very own flight lieutenants. Can't say I know more than that, sir." Young pursed his lips in a knowing way.

***

Devon presented himself at the CO's office right on time and was shown in. He saluted to Group Captain Green and the squadron leader, also in the room, and said a "good morning, sir," to each of the officers.

"Sit down, please, Devon," said Green. "We want to have an informal talk with you about your future in the RAF, your ambitions and so on. As you know, Squadron Leader Porter will be departing soon and we need to appoint his replacement. You have a fine record – well, mostly unblemished, put it that way – and the time is coming for you to make some important decisions. I see from your record that you joined the RAF as a trainee pilot in 1945. What made you want to fly?"

"We're all pilots here, sir, and I think we all have the same feelings on that: the strong desire to get airborne, the thrill of flying, the sheer exhilaration, particularly in the Spits."

"And do you see yourself staying in the service as a career professional?"

"Essentially, sir, yes. I am very keen to keep flying and I believe my experience as a flight commander is the right platform for me to be considered for squadron leader, particularly of a Spitfire outfit. But I'm not certain in my mind yet, sir. Transferring to a jet squadron might also be an option – subject to selection, of course. And there are also opportunities outside the RAF that I'm attracted to."

"Oh yes? And what are they?"

"Sir, you may be aware that I attended technical college before joining up, and my particular interest lies in radar. I may be able to build a career in the development of more advanced radar and intruder identification systems, on the ground and in the air. I think I would be a good test pilot for new systems."

"Are you really more interested in technical matters than front-line flying, Devon? As I said, we're looking to replace the squadron leader here, and if you wish to be considered then you must be one hundred per cent committed to flying."

"Yes, sir, there's no doubt about that. Flying is my number-one career ambition, and commanding a squadron would be a fantastic opportunity to show that I can both fly and lead a team. My thoughts about other career possibilities are second to flying, and options I might consider at some time in the future."

"Well, Devon, you certainly have the credentials for the role. Squadron Leader Porter has testified to your skills and believes that you are well respected as an officer and in leading your flight." Green sat back in his chair and studied the fountain pen he held. "Thank you for being so open about your plans, Devon. We will be discussing the way forward over the next couple of weeks and will come back to you. In the meantime, if you have any questions, please do let me know."

The two senior officers stood up and Devon did the same. After saluting, Devon turned to leave the office, then halted and turned back to face Green. "Sir, may I ask, do you feel I would be successful if I applied for jet conversion training?"

"It's a very tough selection process, of course, but there's no reason why you shouldn't be successful. But Devon, you need to think about commanding a Spitfire squadron – that's what we're here today to discuss. If that doesn't appeal to you then you must say so." Green looked indignant, and Devon realised that his question could have undermined the CO's support for his potential promotion to squadron leader. But what was said couldn't be unsaid, even if Devon wished it could.

***

"A very good man, Porter. I'm not sure he has the resolve for leading a squadron, though. Your opinion?"

Squadron Leader Porter chose his response carefully. It was always a risk opposing the view of a senior officer, particularly on matters of promotion, where decisions might be influenced by class and background. Green came from a wealthy family, as did Fitzjohn, while Devon was the son of a tradesman, even if his father was an electrician working on advanced aircraft.

"We all have to learn our profession in stages. Devon is one of the best Spitfire pilots around and is well liked by the men. Sometimes a senior appointment is the fillip required to spur a good man on. I would not hesitate to fly wingman for him if he commanded a squadron. In short, sir, I believe he could be an excellent asset to us as 28's next squadron leader. I am aware you disapproved strongly of the Hill 33 incident, but it was an adroit piece of flying that got the job done and inspired the rest of the squadron."

"Yes, as you say, he most definitely has notable attributes, but let's see what we have with Fitzjohn. A very self-confident young man, I know, but let's assess his leadership qualities. Have the adjutant bring him in, please."

"Yes, sir," said Porter in a resigned tone.

***

"Good morning, Fitzjohn. Come in." The officers saluted each other, then Green leant forward to shake Fitzjohn's hand. Green didn't see Porter frown at the informality.

"Now Fitzjohn, tell me, why do you want to be considered for promotion to command the squadron?" Green maintained a faint smile and sat back.

Fitzjohn immediately looked at ease and smiled at Green. The two men could have been members of the same golf club having a beer at the nineteenth hole.

Henry Fitzjohn was of medium height and substantial build – not muscular but well-rounded and perhaps a touch overweight. He had a round, well-suntanned face, brown eyes and tawny hair that was longer than RAF convention, combed over from his left eye to behind his right ear. His classic RAF moustache was kept trim – he avoided the stereotypical handlebars. His image was of a suave, sophisticated matinee idol.

Fitzjohn regarded himself as a natural leader. His family home, Park Castle, near Saffron Waldon in north Essex, included 22,000 acres of prime farmland, fishing rights and game-shooting grounds. The house was built more than 300 years ago. Although it wasn't a castle at all, it featured faux battlements and a lookout tower. Much of the land was tenanted, providing a secure and vast income that had supported the Fitzjohn family admirably for generations. Fitzjohn's father, Sir Charles Fitzjohn, had been the chair of the local National Farmers' Union branch before the war. Fitzjohn had two older brothers who managed the tenants and oversaw the estate – something young Henry had no intention, or desire, to do, other than in the stables. He loved to ride, and commanded a team of trainers, grooms and stable lads who kept the horses in excellent condition.

"Thank you, sir. Yes, I would very much like to be considered for the promotion. I think it's fair to say that I'm more than ready for the job. Whenever Squadron Leader Porter has been away, I have taken the position of leader of my own volition – taking the initiative, one might say."

Green smiled a satisfied smile.

"I know you will be aware, sir, that I made the initial application for training on jets, but that went no further than the written application stage. I am not sure I really wanted to take the jet conversion route but one has to look into these things, doesn't one?"

Green knew, but ignored the fact, that Fitzjohn's application had been rushed; he had hardly troubled himself to do a good job. Perhaps it was due to laziness, or perhaps he had wanted to be rejected. On second thoughts, Green concluded that Fitzjohn was not the type to accept rejection easily.

"I'm not sure the jet training people quite understood my flying background, sir, or how I could demonstrate my leadership," added Fitzjohn, a between-you-and-me smile playing round the corners of his mouth.

"Yes, quite. And going forward, Fitzjohn, what are your ambitions over the next, say, five years?" asked Green.

"I'm absolutely committed to flying, sir. I know some people are giving thought to other options as the air force reduces in size – I've heard of chaps looking for roles in Canada, executive flying in the goldfields of South Africa, and commercial flying at home. With due respect, sir." Fitzjohn glanced at Porter. "But for me, I want to lead this squadron. I feel very much that I'm the man for the job, and I will do well. I hope you agree, sir." This time he looked squarely at Group Captain Green.

"I'm sure that's the case, Fitzjohn," said Green, although not wholly convincingly. "Our next steps are to liaise with the Officer

Commanding, Far East Air Force, and provide details of candidates and input from myself and the squadron leader here. The OC Far East will, of course, be considering other options outside of the squadron. We expect to hear the outcome in the next few weeks. Any questions?"

"None, sir, but thank you for your time, and yourself, Squadron Leader. I shall look forward to hearing the outcome of the selection process." Fitzjohn stood smartly to attention, saluted and left the room.

SIX

Hannah settled in quickly to the routine of working life. She enjoyed the work and liked the people in her department. Very soon after starting her job at the bank she moved to London, sharing a flat with Sophia on the top floor of a large townhouse by Clapham Common. She found the half-hour commute on the Northern Line from Clapham South to Bank irksome, but it had to be tolerated. She always picked up a newspaper at the Tube station – she had a strong interest in political and social affairs. The changing world after the war, seen through the eyes of *The Times* correspondents, gave Hannah a sense of excitement and made her believe that she was a part of the new generation, engaged in building an exciting future, although she was troubled when she read about the struggles of people around the world seeking the freedoms they believed in.

Her room in the flat was bright and airy, with a large picture window that looked out across the common. Sophia had a wide range of friends, mostly in their early to mid-twenties, and every weekend they hosted parties, dinners or music evenings at the flat. Hannah tended to take a step back in organising gatherings, happy to leave most of the arrangements to Sophia, who was a natural socialite. Hannah enjoyed seeing her university friends and hearing about their promising careers. Some people had secured jobs in the civil service, their working lives mapped out right through to retirement, while others, who were more inclined towards the arts, worked in theatres, art galleries and museums. Hannah's job at the bank was enjoyable, but she had a faint sense at the back of her mind that she could feel stifled by office work.

Some of the guests were free with their political opinions, and impromptu debates on how society was developing after the war often led to heated arguments. Hannah liked to listen and consider, rarely commenting herself, even if she disagreed with a viewpoint. Late one Saturday night, after a particularly lively session, she strolled into the tiny kitchen to get one last glass of wine. A tall bearded man about her own age followed her in.

"Hannah, isn't it?" he said.

"Yes, hi…"

"I'm Uri. My sister is Judith – she's training to be a nurse with Sophia at St Thomas's."

"Ah, yes, I met her earlier," Hannah said. "What do you do yourself, Uri, workwise?"

"I'm a freelance journalist."

"Really? Sounds like fun. You seem to have strong political views, given the arguments just then."

"Yes, I'm not keen on the growing threat from the Soviets, and I don't believe that communism, or even socialism, is the way forward for the new world order." Uri's voice became louder, making Hannah flinch.

"Oh, sorry," Uri said. "I'm going on too much, I know."

"That's OK, it's no concern of mine. What do you believe in?"

"Freedom of expression, opportunities for all, doing away with inequality."

"Are you sure you don't favour communism?" Hannah smiled at Uri to show she was pulling his leg.

"No, but I do feel that we all have a part to play – we must all take responsibility for building a world not ruled by despots and dictators."

"I wouldn't disagree with that." Then Hannah heard a voice from behind Uri.

"How are you two getting on? Championing the tired, the poor and the huddled masses, no doubt!" It was Judith, leaning against the kitchen door, an empty wine glass in her hand.

"Not quite, sister, just getting to know each other."

"Good, good. It's important that we build new friendships, new connections…"

Hannah smiled and went to leave the kitchen, but Judith stepped in her way. "Yes, we must get to know each other. After all, I'm sure we have many interests in common. Tell me about your family, Hannah."

Hannah wondered if Judith was drunk. Had the alcohol made her tired, or was she just being aggressive?

"My parents live in Cambridge – I have a brother still at school there. What about you two?" Hannah turned to look at Uri, feeling she should involve him in the conversation as a way to avoid Judith's forcefulness.

Uri looked pleased to be asked. "We're from Stamford Hill in North London. Grew up there. I got a job as a junior reporter at the *Daily Telegraph* and went out on my own last year."

"Well, this is a very nice gathering."

Hannah was glad to see Sophia squeeze her way into the kitchen. "I hope my lovely friends are not boring you, Hannah, but they were very keen to meet you. Uri here knows one of the managers where you work."

"Oh, really? At the London and Hong Kong Bank?"

"Yes, his name is John-Paul Cohen. He has a great job, heading up the commercial client division. Pretty good for someone not yet thirty," said Uri.

"I don't think I know him. I've not been at the bank long. And anyway, he sounds very senior."

"John-Paul has been there less than a year. His family have strong connections at the bank and probably got him the job!"

The group all laughed and Sophia and Judith quietly withdrew from the kitchen, leaving Hannah alone with Uri.

"Expect to hear from John-Paul, Hannah. He has something to discuss with you that I believe you will find interesting."

Before Hannah could respond to this strange statement, Uri turned and rejoined the party.

SEVEN

"Squadron Leader Porter, come in, sit down. How are you, David?"
"Very well, sir, thank you."

Group Captain Green's bonhomie was as transparent as the blue sea. Porter knew there was something up that would demand his cooperation.

"I have asked you to come and see me as I have a very important task for you. We have been challenged to a cricket match by Sir James MacIntyre, the recently installed governor of Singapore. He wishes to see closer links with the military and in particular the RAF. Wants to get to know us better, that sort of thing. I too would welcome a positive relationship with the civil service types, and what more pleasant way than a cricket match? I would like you to organise affairs from our side and liaise with the Governor's XI captain, Mr Gerald Greaves at the Colonial Office. I have already spoken to the secretary at Singapore Cricket Club, and they would be delighted to host the match at the Padang. How do you feel about this, David?"

Knowing he could not dispute the value of the idea, and the group captain's obvious personal keenness, Porter said, "I would be honoured to pull together a team, sir."

"Got some good players, David? It's important we win, you know – wouldn't want the office clerks embarrassing the air force and damaging our reputation, would we?"

"No, sir, clearly not," said Porter, secretly thinking, who the hell cares about who wins and who loses if the purpose is better liaison? "I will put up an open invitation to the men, to find out who plays cricket. There's a corner on the far side of the airfield where we can get some practice in and select our best eleven. I will extend the invitation to all ranks."

"Well, yes, quite right, David. Can't have the affair limited to officers, can we? Do you play yourself?"

"Yes, sir – I'm something of an all-rounder with a slant towards batting. Do we have a date set?"

"Yes – Sunday 26 June. So you have about three weeks."

"Excellent, sir. I will trawl the station for those who are keen to play and organise our first practice for this weekend."

***

Saturday mornings usually had a less frenetic ambiance at RAF Changi. It was a period of rest and relaxation, when the men had time to themselves. A mile-long walk outside the camp led to a curved, sandy beach with lapping waves and cooling breezes. Many of the men sought out the company of women from the WAAF, the nurses and administrative staff. Naturally, many of the women sought out the men. Most female staff were from the UK, but an increasing number of Malay and Singaporean women worked at the station too. Romance was never far from the thoughts of the station's complement.

Squadron Leader Porter's call for volunteers for the station cricket team promised a welcome diversion from the usual. A self-conscious group of eighteen men waited outside the No. 1 equipment hangar. One woman, noticeable in her white shirt and blue trousers, approached from the women's quarters and stood quietly at the edge of the group. Some of the men glanced furtively towards her, perhaps wondering if she understood what the gathering was about. Porter approached the group with his orderly, who was carrying two large cricket bags that were overloaded with bats, stumps, pads and gloves.

Porter noticed Aircraftman Tony Jones approach the girl. "Good morning, ma'am, do you realise that we're here for the cricket team selection?" he said.

"Yes, of course. I am hoping to get into the team and open the batting." Her wry, friendly smile indicated that she was approachable and confident. Jones held out his hand. She returned the gesture with a good, firm handshake.

"I'm Barbara Blake – Senior Nurse, Queen Alexandra's, at the station. I arrived in Singapore a couple of months ago. I used to play back home in Kent." She was tall and athletic, her black hair cut in a short bob.

"Local school team, was it, or perhaps university?"

"Both of those, but I also played for Kent County Ladies. You may have seen newspaper coverage of the exhibition match last year when we played an Australian XI in Canterbury?"

The question didn't need an answer. "Well, Miss Blake, I'm sure you will outshine this ragged lot!" Jones cast a glance over his shoulder at the group, most of whom were watching the pair, amused at Jones' bravado.

Porter called the players together. "Good morning, everyone. Thank you for giving up your Saturday morning and turning out today. I think you know Simon Harrington here – he will distribute the kit. We will start by setting up a couple of wickets, splitting up into two groups and sharing some bowling and batting practice. Airfield Maintenance have mown a pitch of sorts for us just past the hanger. Flight Lieutenant Devon and Pilot Officer Mike Smith will captain the teams for the time being. Now, does anyone have wicketkeeping experience?" A couple of hands went up, and Porter assigned one man to each team captain. "A show of hands, please, for batsmen. Join Flight Lieutenant Devon, please. Now, bowlers, join Smith."

Then Porter noticed Barbara Blake at the back of the group. He smiled at her. "Good morning, ma'am. I'm sorry I didn't see you there. I know all the men, but we haven't met before. Do you have a preference for the bat or the ball?"

"Batting, sir. And it's Senior Nurse Barbara Blake. I hope it's in order for one of Queen Alexandra's to be part of the team."

"Oh yes, Nurse Blake, you are very much part of the station and I'm happy to field a mixed team. Please join Flight Lieutenant Devon."

Before the group started to move off, Porter added, "Listen in. We will have a couple of hours' practice today and tomorrow I will post the selected team, plus reserve, on the general noticeboard outside the Officers' Mess before chapel. Enjoy the morning, gentlemen. And lady."

Very quickly the squad got to it, reliving their sporting lives in the UK. Their enthusiasm grew as each player found old talents that had been buried away, and some skilful batting shots were made. Bowlers too showed that they could find an edge or beat the bat. Porter found it was going to be tough selecting a team of twelve.

The next morning at 7 a.m., as the sun rose, Harrington posted the team sheet on the station general noticeboard.

Singapore Governor's XI v. RAF Changi Cricket Match
The Padang
Sunday 26 June 1949, 2 p.m.

RAF Team (shown in batting order)
Pilot Stephen Archer
AC Anthony Jones
Sq. Leader David Porter (Capt.)
AC Peter Selfridge
Fl. Lt Adam Devon
Snr Nurse Barbara Blake (Miss)
PO Mike Smith
Fl. Lt Henry Fitzjohn
Fl. Sgt Jack Cooper (Wkt)
AC Richard Waite
Pilot Rupert Knight
12th man: Sgt Alex Bridge

The keener candidates got to the noticeboard soon after and were either pleased or disappointed with the squadron leader's selection. Most felt the chosen team was fair and reflected the skills that had been shown on the practice morning. No one person or rank was seen to be preferred. Later that morning Flight Lieutenant Fitzjohn knocked on Porter's office door, then entered. "Do you have a moment, sir?"

"Yes, come in, Henry. What can I do for you?"

"It's the cricket, sir." Fitzjohn sounded annoyed. "I'm not sure you have ordered the batting correctly. If I may, sir, with your permission, I should like to bat higher up. Not to open, of course, but surely above the ... er, the nurse? "

"I'm sure you understand, Henry, that team choice is a difficult job, but you're a useful bowler. I'm sure you will get some overs in. And there's every likelihood you will get to bat."

"I'm sure *you* understand, David. I'm not against women cricketers, of course not, but I'd like to show what I can do." Fitzjohn's serious expression took nothing from the insolence in his repetition of Porter's words.

"My decision is final – the team is as posted."

"Now, David, just a moment!"

"That's all, Fitzjohn!" Porter managed to be firm without losing his temper. Fitzjohn might be a senior pilot, but that didn't give him special treatment.

"Yes, sir." Fitzjohn spun on his heel and left the squadron leader's office with a face like thunder.

Porter reflected on Fitzjohn's growing self-importance. He was worried. It's always dangerous to have a player in a team, or a pilot in a squadron, who pursues his own interests first.

***

Squadron Leader Porter's driver steered the car slowly into the narrow approach to the Singapore Cricket Club. When Porter stepped out the white-painted frontage was dazzling, reflecting the light and heat of the sun. Porter glanced up at the twin columns of the impressive portico supporting the arched entrance. The sheer size of the building, which was more like a country house than a cricket club pavilion, never failed to impress. The red-brown terracotta roof tiles and tall, shuttered windows gave the place a look of wealth and achievement, and the Union flag flying above the entrance completed the colonial style. It was easy to see why the Japanese army of occupation six years earlier had made the club their headquarters and an exclusive watering hole for Japanese officers.

The largely Malay staff were on hand, immaculately uniformed in white jackets and black felt songkok hats, directing visitors through the glistening marble sanctuary of the ground-floor lobby.

A friendly murmur of chat flowed from the main clubroom, where pre-match drinks were being served. Players, umpires and supporters milled around, smartly dressed, the men mostly in pale cream trousers and blue sports jackets and the women in dresses of pink, lilac or light green. The Colonial Office people were easy to identify, with their pale skin – the result of living at a desk and avoiding the sun. Some had tucked their boaters, complete with university colours, under their arms. Senior RAF officers headed by Group Captain Green wore Far East uniforms of tan jacket and trousers, shirt and tie. The governor stood smiling benevolently with his entourage of trade secretaries, clerical civil servants and diplomats.

Porter had met his opposite number, the Colonial Office's captain, Gerald Greaves, before. He spotted him looking out across the playing field. "Good afternoon, Gerald. A lovely day for cricket!"

"Ah, David. Yes, indeed – somewhat warm, but such an inviting field to play on. Are you ready to go down to the pitch with the umpires for us to toss the coin?"

Porter clapped his hands." Certainly – let's do that now."

The formalities took only a few minutes. The RAF team won the toss and elected to bat. Returning to the reception, the two captains called their teams together, and they made for their respective changing rooms. The crowd at the ground had swelled to a couple of thousand, with Singaporeans and expats alike relishing the spectacle.

At 2 p.m. a hush descended on the cricket ground as the Governor's XI opening bowler started his walk back, looking committed to the task.

The first ball of the day rocketed down the pitch. Archer, opening the batting with Jones for the RAF, played a steady defensive shot. He took his time getting his eye in before trying anything more expansive. The fourth ball allowed a firm push to mid-wicket and a single run was taken to a polite round of applause. Gradually the RAF batsmen gained confidence and made some fine strokes before Archer mis-hit a cover drive and was caught out for just eight runs from a total of twelve. Archer was not happy with his performance, and even Squadron Leader Porter's, "Well played" as he came out to bat only vaguely lifted his spirits.

The Governor's XI had a couple of excellent bowlers, so Porter knew that his RAF team had to take some chances if they were to build a good total. Porter himself scored a respectable twenty-five before being bowled but Jones batted on, even if his run rate was rather slow. Selfridge showed that his batting skills were a touch rusty and on his third ball was bowled for a duck.

Adam Devon took the crease as the civil servants changed their tactics to a right-arm spinner around the wicket. Steady defensive play was required to assess the movement of the ball on the pitch, but soon Devon read the ball's flight and hit a solid boundary. They were scoring runs steadily when Jones walked down the pitch between overs for a quick chat with Devon on tactics.

"It's taken twelve of our thirty overs to get to fifty, sir. Should we have a go at increasing the run rate?"

"Yes, good idea, Jones. Do your best!"

Jones trotted back to the crease. The new approach worked well, and they took ten runs in the next over. In the following over Jones let himself get too confident and, with a mighty swing of the bat, missed the ball completely for a simple stumping by the governor's wicketkeeper.

Many members of the crowd stood to applaud Nurse Barbara Blake as she pulled on her gloves and took up position at the bowler's end. A single from Devon gave her strike and she took her guard at middle and leg. She eased herself in with a couple of gentle shots, but then a short ball rose invitingly on her off-side. Her lifting strike sent the ball over the heads of the slips for four runs.

Devon was then inspired to try some adventurous shots, but came unstuck when an unexpectedly slower ball clipped his inside edge and the ball was played on to the wicket. Smith followed with a steady twelve runs before Fitzjohn came out to bat.

With only three overs of the innings remaining, Fitzjohn was keen to show his batting talent and to score well. He took a couple of singles, and on his third delivery he swept the ball to square leg and called Blake to run. But the fielder had the ball and was drawing back his arm to throw it to the wicketkeeper.

"Go back, go back!" she shouted, but Fitzjohn ignored her call. His sudden stop was too late. Behind him, the cry of "Yes!" told him he had been stumped. Visibly angry, Fitzjohn marched back to the pavilion.

"Bad luck, Henry." Jack Cooper, coming out to bat, was being polite, considering it had been Fitzjohn's mistake; Blake had every right to make the call. At the end of the innings, the RAF team had chalked up a good score of 148 for 8: a challenging, but not impossible, target for the Governor's XI.

A cricket tea interval should be taken in a relaxed and convivial atmosphere. On this occasion, the teams waived the tradition of taking their own tables and chose instead to share each other's company. While they touched on their performance on the field, the team's main discussions centred on the future of Singapore as the key port in Asia, the Malayan Emergency, and the role of the RAF in the Far East. Sir James MacIntyre was delighted that his get-to-know-you plans were working so well. Only Fitzjohn failed to engage with the civil service people: he seemed to be dwelling on the mistake that had led to him being run out. He was the sort of person to be all the more determined to impress now.

Keen to get back to the game, the Governor's XI opening batsmen slipped away to pad up. A warm welcome from the crowd greeted the teams as they took their places on the field. With Waite and Knight to open the bowling for the RAF, both very capable fast bowlers, Squadron Leader Porter was confident that they could secure wickets early and play through to a comfortable win.

Croft, opening batsman for the Governor's XI, soon showed that he could easily handle the RAF's best bowlers. Supported by Freeman at number 2, they quickly notched up thirty-two runs without loss. Porter decided to throw the ball to Cooper, who had shown some skill as a spin bowler at the training session. They achieved the breakthrough they were looking for. First Croft was caught behind, then two balls later Freeman went to a well-taken catch at second slip. As new batsmen arrived and made steady scores, so the wickets fell. Cooper took two wickets and Fitzjohn one, which did a little to restore his bruised pride. After playing 28 overs, the Governor's XI had scored 135 for 5. With two overs to play and five wickets in hand, they could afford to go for the fourteen runs they needed to win.

Porter backed his fast bowlers, but the RAF conceded eight runs in the next over. There was only one over left, and what looked like an easy six needed to win. Waite had other ideas, however, and put in a couple of accurate yorkers that were defended without score.

Four balls to go, six runs required. Waite lost his eye a touch: a ball down the leg side was pushed for one, and a single was also taken off the next ball. By dint of focused concentration, Waite's next delivery was fast and direct. It could only be pushed to mid-wicket without score. One ball left, four required to win. The crowd had cheered and applauded the batting and bowling all afternoon, but now utter silence fell upon Singapore Cricket Ground.

With nothing to lose, Poulson, the Governor's XI batsman, took a sweeping cut at Waite's last ball. A great connection sent the ball at a ninety-degree angle off towards the boundary, with Fitzjohn chasing after it like a madman. Cheers and shouts of, "go on, Fitzjohn!" spurred him to greater effort. At last he dived on the ball. But he was too late – the ball had crossed the rope under his arms and the Governor's XI had scored four runs. Since they were on the far side of the field, the players and umpires couldn't see if the ball had crossed over or whether Fitzjohn had stopped it in time, and nor could the crowd as the ball was underneath him.

"Did it cross the boundary, Henry?" Porter called out.

Sportsmanship dictated that the only response should be the truth, but Fitzjohn's ego needed the accolades of his team.

"No, sir, I stopped it just in time!"

The Governor's XI batsmen had run two runs, and achieved a total of 147, one short of a draw.

The RAF players congregated around Fitzjohn, slapping him on the back and congratulating him on a fine piece of fielding. Fitzjohn was revelling in the praise and offered commiserations to the Governor's XI batsman. Everyone had seen a great effort from Fitzjohn – except one man. Devon had been running in from the left and had clearly seen the ball cross the boundary for four runs. Fitzjohn had patently cheated.

Post-match drinks were served in the cool of the pavilion. As the sun set, the men began to discuss the prospect of an evening celebrating in one of Singapore's nightlife districts. It fell to Fitzjohn, as the hero of the day, to seek permission from Squadron Leader Porter, as he was about to return to Changi.

"Sir, a number of the chaps would like an extended pass to take a stroll down to Clarke Quay. Would that be acceptable? Everyone will be back by midnight. Good to have a spot of R&R, wouldn't you say, sir?"

"Very well, go and enjoy yourselves." Porter smiled. "But remember, you have a strict curfew of midnight. I shall see you in the morning at the station. Don't forget we have a flight planning meeting in my office at 9 a.m."

"Excellent, thank you, sir." Fitzjohn returned to the salon and gathered the RAF men around him to announce his achievement.

"I had to call in a favour, of course, but the squadron leader gave in readily to my request." Fitzjohn paused to allow all present to absorb his talents and status. "We're going to walk down to Clarke Quay, pick up some street food and have a couple of drinks. You never know who we might meet!" He looked around the group. "Not really a thing for ladies, is it, Nurse Blake?" His tone was condescending.

"That's alright, Flight Lieutenant, I shall be returning to the station. I'm on duty tonight."

"Good show. OK, let's not waste any more time. Follow me, chaps!"

Clarke Quay was a melting pot of trade, entertainment and more than a few seedy bars and gambling houses. The bustling godowns that fronted the Singapore River and the myriad bumboats and lighters vying for mooring space gave a chaotic first appearance, but all the boxes of fruit, spices, exotic fabrics and commercial goods found their way to the right warehouses and shophouses along the riverbank. As night fell, candles were lit on most of the vessels along with small oil burners, on which the lightermen made their food. Mah-jong boards were brought out, along with small musical instruments that chimed and whistled gently across the water. The crowded river was matched on the banks with tightly packed terraces of buildings, two and three storeys high. The calmness of the early evening gave some relief to the godown labourers, who took the opportunity to visit their preferred bars for cheap beer and raw spirits. The pale grey smoke of cocaine smokers drifted lazily across the quay.

Some drinking establishments made an effort to attract more upmarket European customers, such as the shipping agents, dealers, Lloyd's insurance agents, lawyers and accountants who supported trade in the Singapore port. The Golden Sun was a favourite venue of servicemen. As the cricket team approached the door, a Malay waiter in a clean white outfit, undoubtedly originally a Cunard Line steward's uniform, put on a wide smile. "Come in, please, gentlemen! Nice drinks, good food, best place. My name Jonny, we look after you swell!"

Fitzjohn waved his hand to gesture the group in. "Come on, chaps, this way."

The bar was sparsely occupied, so the RAF men had room to sit and debate what they would drink. This didn't take long; they all wanted a beer.

"Bring us a bucket of cold Tigers, Jonny, that will get us started," Fitzjohn called.

The laughter and banter in the group steadily increased in volume, with the cricket victory uppermost in the men's minds. Fitzjohn revelled in the praise he had received but noticed the sullen look on Devon's face. He stood and announced he needed a breath of air and invited Devon to join him on the quayside. The warmth and humidity of the night gave little relief.

"What's on your mind, Devon?" Fitzjohn's tone was arrogant.

"I'm sure you know."

"I don't know what you're talking about, old boy. Tell me, what grieves you?"

"You and I both know that ball crossed the boundary." Devon's voice was calm and quiet.

"Absolute rubbish, man. I hope you don't have any ideas about spreading such slander!"

"It's a bit too late now, but do me a favour – get off your pedestal. I won't say anything, it would reflect badly on the squadron, but don't expect any praise from me."

***

The cricket match had the desired effect. The squadron was welcomed to the colony and a series of social gatherings, football and athletics tournaments, nights out in Chinatown and more than enough Singapore Slings at Raffles Hotel reinforced the idea among the airmen that a posting to Singapore was a treasure to be savoured. A swimming gala at the local beach attracted all ranks, male and female, together with the expat community, and the picnic that followed was laid on by Malay and Singaporean cooks from the air station. In the warmth of the early evening, in the quiet corners of the beach, close friendships were formed.

The squadron's fighting capability was maintained with regular training missions and classroom debates on tactics. Contingency plans were drafted and rehearsed, should a sortie up into Malaya be required to support the ground troops. The squadron flew regular patrols out to sea, crossing the Singapore Strait to set up mock attacks on Bintan Island and Batam Island. Unlike in Malaya, the political situation in Singapore was calm, with a planned reduction in the role that Britain played and a phased handover to national self-determination. But the politicians and colonial administrators would not take any chances – if subversive forces should emerge, a powerful military response was available to them, on the ground and in the air.

Such risks were considered remote, but experience from the war in Singapore – when the colony had been overrun by the Japanese – meant that no potential extreme circumstances were ignored. There were no hostile forces in the area but the armed conflict in neighbouring Indonesia, which was looking certain to achieve independence from the Netherlands, meant that the secret service kept a careful lookout for the potential importation of revolutionary ideals.

A high alert was maintained, but this didn't stop life from being a social whirl. A tropical landscape, wonderful food, people from all walks of life to befriend and romance, in the loveliest sunny weather. Everyone knew it was a dream posting from which they would one day wake up.

EIGHT

"Everyone, listen in!" Station Warrant Officer Wilkinson barked the command across the Officers' Mess. The urgency in his voice made the pilots stop and look up. It was unusual for the WO to get so excited on a Sunday afternoon.

"All pilots to report to the squadron ops room at 1400 hours. Group Captain Green will be briefing you on a new operation. All pilots to attend, no excuses. Same instructions to all pilot ranks."

"What's the flap about, sir? Pilot Officer Matthew 'Matt' Black took the initiative to cheek the warrant officer, but his wisecrack fell flat. Wilkinson was a long-serving officer and had seen and heard it all before.

"You'll see soon enough, Mr. Black, and the rest of you. 1400 sharp."

As Wilkinson quick-marched himself out of the Mess, the pilots glanced at each other.

"Bloody unlikely to be anything big. There's sod all happening in the peninsula," said Pilot Officer James Taylor.

***

The short walk from the Mess building to the ops room across the sun-heated tarmac was stifling. The soft breeze off the sea did little to cool the air. Dressed in the regulation Far East working kit of shorts and open shirt, the pilots did not relish the briefing in the oppressive atmosphere of the Nissen hut, where there were only ceiling fans to ease the humidity.

As the pilots filed in, Wilkinson was standing on the briefing platform. "Sit down please, everyone. You will shortly be provided with details of the operation."

As he spoke, Group Captain Green strode into the ops room, accompanied by a man the pilots had never seen before, dressed in a mid-grey suit and white shirt.

"Gentlemen, let me introduce our colleague from military intelligence. You will know him simply as Mason. Mr Mason will provide the background to a mission assigned to us and I will follow with detailed operational instructions."

Mason stepped to the front of the stage. "Thank you, Group Captain. My role here is to describe some disturbing developments in East Asia that require us to put on a show of force. If necessary, we will deliver that force. Corporal, the first map please." His voice was calm and clear.

The corporal unseen in the wings carried in a five-foot-high board showing a large-scale map of eastern China and South East Asia.

Mason glanced at the map and turned back to the pilots. "Our concerns focus on mainland China just to the west of Hong Kong. Chinese communist forces have strengthened significantly in the past month and our intelligence sources on the ground have observed the arrival of heavier equipment, more personnel and enhanced ammunition supplies. In short, we believe the Chinese may be thinking of having a go at invading and holding Hong Kong. As you know, Hong Kong is a dependent territory and its harbour is vital to our trade and naval operations throughout the region. Our American friends are also very anxious not to lose the base to a communist regime. Your mission will be to bolster the Hong Kong defences and discourage the Chinese from considering an invasion. Make no mistake: if required, you will be ordered to engage the Chinese forces to prevent any incursion. Our sources tell us that the communists do not have aircraft that come anywhere near to matching your Spitfires, but they do have heavy machine guns that have anti-aircraft capability." Mason paused to let that thought sink in. "Any questions at this stage, gentlemen?"

"Mr Mason, can I ask…" It was Black again, this time with a serious demeanour. "Do we not have an army defence garrison in Hong Kong that would deal with the threat?"

"Not entirely. The garrison is small and has no air support. While we know the Chinese have little capability in the air, we want to have strong army support from the RAF. We can't take any chances. Your air–ground armaments could be crucial in disrupting any land or sea assault. They will know that, of course, hence the deterrent factor in your operational presence." Mason picked up a pencil from the desk to use as a pointer. "If we look at the map of the Hong Kong colony we will see that we have Hong Kong Island, of course. Facing the island on the mainland is Kowloon, and that's where RAF Kai Tak airfield is. Behind Kowloon is the region known as the New Territories, which borders China itself. Any land-based invasion would come across the border and then down to Kowloon and through the Pearl River estuary. This would be a disaster as the enemy would then take hold of Victoria Harbour, where our naval operations are based.

"RAF Far East Command have assured the army senior officers that 28 Squadron has the capability of attacking enemy tanks, artillery and armoured vehicles. You are also highly proficient at attacking waterborne insertions. Air-to-air combat is not expected, although you will of course continue to train for this eventuality."

This time Devon put up his hand. "We also have a photo reconnaissance capability, Mr Mason. Will we be able to overfly mainland China to gather intelligence?"

"No, that is not planned, in the absence of an invasion. In fact, you will all be instructed not to do anything to antagonise the Chinese, and to keep strictly to Hong Kong airspace. I hope that is clear to all pilots. I will now hand over to Group Captain Green, who will brief you on the flight operations from Singapore to Hong Kong."

"Thank you, Mason. Corporal, the second chart, please."

When the new map was put up on the briefing stand, some pilots let out a low whistle and someone mumbled, "What the f…?" under his breath. The map focused on the South China Sea, to the east and north-east of Singapore. A thick red jagged pencil line drawn on the map showed the flight paths for each section of the journey from Singapore to Hong Kong.

Green continued. "Here's the planned route. All fifteen of 28 Squadron's Spitfires, the squadron of twelve plus three reserves, will depart at 1100 hours on Tuesday morning in formation and take an easterly heading initially." Green indicated the first red line on the map with a baton. "205 Squadron have been tasked with assigning one of their Catalina flying boats to transit ahead of us with the maintenance team and aircraft spares. Armaments and reserve fuel will be taken by cargo ship – this will depart tomorrow. We will be flying with drop tanks to provide the extra fuel capacity but, to reduce weight, all Spitfires will be unarmed.

"As you see, we will start our journey to Hong Kong by taking an easterly heading across to Sarawak, where we will land to refuel at Kuching. Then a further stretch to the north-east to Kota Kinabalu and an overnight stop. Both these airbases have good-quality runways and reliable servicing. This might not be the case for our next landing, at Puerto Princesa on Palawan Island. The base here was built during the war using perforated steel plate for the runway. Currently we do not have intelligence on the condition of the PSP. However, whatever the condition, we must land there. There is sufficient fuel cached on the island to see us through the next leg, to Manila in the Philippines. Any questions so far?"

Silence. Each pilot probably had a list of concerns but didn't feel this was the time to air them. Green turned back to the chart. "So, from Puerto Princesa we track 025 degrees up to the southernmost tip of Luzon and continue north to Manila. We refuel there, stay overnight, and plan for the flight from Manila to Hong Kong. As you can see from the map, this is a significant sea crossing, perhaps the longest you will experience in a single-engine fighter: approximately 600 miles. Now, as you may know, 88 Squadron is already operating their Sunderland flying boats from Hong Kong. Two of these aircraft will be patrolling our route across the sea. If any Spits get into trouble and have to ditch, the pilots will be picked up by a Sunderland. All being well." Green widened his eyes, indicating to all the pilots that he recognised the challenge of a sea landing in a Spitfire, then being able to climb out to await rescue. "Questions?"

Pilot Anderson raised his hand. "Sir, why are we taking the long route?"

"A more direct route, of course, would be north through Malaya and Siam, and then transiting French Indo-China. If we were able to get to Hanoi, we would still have a sea crossing to Hong Kong," said Green.

Mason stepped forward to deal with the political issues. "We would need to have French support to allow us to fly over Indo-China airspace and to land and refuel. Our relationship with the French is excellent, of course, but they have their own problems with the Chinese communists. Landing in Indo-China is not an option available to us at this time."

"Can't they be persuaded, sir? Surely we would assist if the positions were reversed?"

"Don't concern yourself, Anderson," Group Captain Green interjected. "Just accept that the current political circumstances require us to take the Philippines route. That's all you need to know."

"Yes sir, of course, sir."

Green faced the assembled pilots. "Let me tell you that secrecy is paramount – you are now in lockdown. We will assemble in this room at 0700 hours on Tuesday morning – we have less than forty-eight hours to prepare. All leave is cancelled and you are restricted to Changi Airfield. No letters home, no discussions with girlfriends in town, and most certainly no sad goodbyes. Do I make myself clear?"

All pilots murmured their assent.

"Squadron Leader Porter's retirement from the RAF has been put on hold. He has already been briefed and will command the lead flight. The remaining flight leaders are Fitzjohn and Devon. These pilots, please remain where you are. Other pilots are dismissed. Use the time to prepare thoroughly, but remember the security situation."

With a shuffling of feet and a banging of chairs, the pilots departed. The flight commanders sat at the front of the ops room, notebooks perched on their knees. Porter leant against the briefing desk. "Well, gentlemen, there's some serious flying ahead. As you heard, we will be leaving Changi the day after tomorrow with the first flight, led by me, taking off at 1100 hours. We will circle the airfield. Each flight will depart at half-minute intervals and we shall form up at 5,000 feet approximately five miles down-route."

There was a knock on the door. "Come in, Charlton."

The civilian weather forecaster came in, carrying a rolled chart that she clipped across the map on the briefing board.

"Flight Lieutenant Devon will be the nominated Met officer for the mission. Miss Charlton is here to give us the regional synopsis and outlook. Go ahead, please."

The young meteorologist turned to her chart. "Thank you, sir. The overall situation for the lower South China Sea is stable, with good visibility, generally three oktas cloud with a base of 12,000 feet, wind speed moderate from the north-east. We expect this to continue in this area for the next three days. So, good flying conditions to start. However, we are concerned about a developing low pressure system that will worsen into a typhoon and give you trouble after you depart Manila. We think the system will be centred to the north-west of Hong Kong, but it's difficult to predict at the moment."

"Very well, Charlton. Please liaise with Flight Lieutenant Devon over the next forty-eight hours and assess any changes, particularly the development of the typhoon. Thank you, Charlton."

"Thank you, sir. But could I add, if the centre of the typhoon forms even within fifty miles of Hong Kong the weather will be treacherous. And there will be no diversion airfields available."

"Yes, that's understood, Charlton. All the more reason for us to monitor the situation."

When Charlton left the ops room, everyone turned to look at Devon. He was responsible for assessing the weather from a pilot's viewpoint – and the Spitfire's capabilities in hazardous conditions. "I will liaise with Miss Charlton to assess the potential conditions in the Hong Kong area, sir. Looks like the aim will be to get into Hong Kong with the typhoon as far away as possible," said Devon.

They spent the rest of the afternoon packing essential personal equipment. "Young, would you ensure that my gramophone and records are safely packed ready for the cargo ship? Plus all my clothes and necessities, of course. You will be on the Catalina so we'd better get on with the packing," said Devon.

"Certainly, sir." Young grinned then turned to leave. "That bloody gramophone and those classical records – what does he see in them?" he muttered. "Not a swing, jazz or even big band among them. Heaven help me if they get broken!"

NINE

Devon had little work to do in his role as Met officer for the first leg of the mission to Hong Kong. Unusually for a region that has high humidity and murky conditions, the day dawned with crystal-clear skies and a moderate easterly wind. Near perfect conditions for flying.

The Spitfires were fully fuelled. The aircraftmen servicing them had worked through the night to ensure they were all in optimal operational readiness. Water bottles were tucked under the pilots' seats. They were taking a long flight in a part of the world close to the equator where the atmosphere is stifling, even at the altitude they would be flying. Kitted out in white overalls and wearing a Mae West lifejacket, the pilots would feel the heat.

Squadron Leader Porter was the first to taxi out, followed by the four other aircraft in his flight. To avoid wasting fuel and to help cool the engines, they got airborne immediately. Fitzjohn's flight followed suit, then Devon called his pilots forward to the runway threshold. Within minutes the squadron had levelled out at 5,000 feet and had formed into three groups of five aircraft, flying in a broad V formation.

The first leg would take more than two hours, flying directly east over the South China Sea. For most of the flight there was little to see other than a few small uninhabited islands. The sea changed from a light aquamarine blue in the shallower depths around the islands, over reefs and rocks, to a deep turquoise green further out. Above the squadron a few small white clouds broke up an otherwise clear blue sky. These beautiful views were not on the pilots' minds as they carefully managed their aircraft to ensure they minimised fuel consumption and maintained good formation discipline. They kept a close eye on engine performance, oil temperature and pressure. Engine failure and having to ditch into the sea was a prospect no one relished.

After nearly two hours, the western coast of Borneo came into view. The tell-tale pile of high cumulus clouds gave away the location of the mountainous island. Squadron Leader Porter commanded the three flights to skirt the coast to the north-east before turning to the right to approach the airfield at Kuching. Porter transmitted his coded security signal to the ground station so that there would be no misunderstandings about who was approaching the field.

The runway was relatively short, but the surface was good. The pilots knew how easy it would be to break an undercarriage leg, so landings had to be skilfully and gently executed. Porter went in first and landed without difficulty. Others followed, but Pilot Officer James Taylor in Devon's flight came in too fast, held off landing and was in danger of crashing off the end of the runway. Taylor applied full power and went round to approach again. This time he made a textbook short-field landing.

A lunch of boiled fish and potatoes followed by fresh mango was served by the small British contingent at the airfield. They also explained the growing strategic importance of Kuching and wanted to show the pilots the terminal building that was under construction, but the squadron could not afford the luxury of socialising and staying any longer than necessary to eat and to refuel the aircraft.

Once airborne again, the squadron hugged the north coast of Sarawak through to Kota Kinabalu. Engine failure on this route would not be welcome but the chances of making a successful forced landing were good, with rough landing areas available in fields or on beaches. Fuel management was again vital.

The reception they received at Jesselton Airfield in Kota Kinabalu was equally as warm as it had been at Kuching. The maintenance team had already arrived and immediately set to work on the Spitfires, carrying out essential checks and servicing. Alongside the airstrip a line of a couple of dozen tents had been erected for the airmen's overnight stay. After eating, everyone headed to their tents and hit the sack. Sleep came easily, despite the challenge of the next day's flying – into the unknown at Puerto Princesa in Palawan.

The morning's weather was not so benign, with a low mist all along the Sarawak coast. This made navigation difficult, but visibility improved as they left Borneo behind. Within half an hour they could see the southern tip of Palawan Island. The pilots could see how narrow the island was – around 25 miles at the widest point but 260 miles long. It was considered one of the most beautiful islands in the world. Lush green jungle tumbled down hillsides to white sandy coves and beaches, and colourful fishing huts clustered around idyllic harbours.

The airfield at Puerto Princesa was about halfway along the island. They knew it had been built during the war by American POWs for the Japanese. Porter had been told it had fallen into poor condition. Holes and gaps in the runway had been repaired with old sections of perforated steel plate and wooden planks. This could give a good surface if laid evenly, but any raised edge could rip through a Spitfire's tyres.

Porter again went to land first, ordering the other pilots to wait for his report on the state of the runway. First he carried out a flypast over the airfield at a low height to look at its condition. There was no tower or traffic control, so no help would be given on runway status from the ground. Porter could see the dangerous patchwork repairs, but a clearer section to the right of centre line looked more promising. On his final approach to the runway all looked well and he descended to land. Given the shortness of the runway, he aimed right at the threshold. Dipping steeply down over the trees that surrounded the airfield, Porter suddenly saw a gaping hole in the ground right on his touchdown point – no doubt caused by recently stolen PSP sections. With a controlled reaction that came from ten years of flying Spitfires, he dabbed the throttle for a burst of speed then landed heavily on the short runway just after the hole. His speed was in danger of carrying him to the far end of the runway and into the trees. Porter applied careful but assertive braking that stopped the machine with fifty yards to spare.

Porter radioed to the rest of the squadron to warn them of the dangers, ordering them to "avoid the runway threshold – land late and brake hard." All aircraft followed this instruction and landed safely, although some pilots were shaken by the experience. They refuelled quickly from supplies cached at the airfield, then the airmen carried out their own checks of their aircraft. The airfield's paradise setting was not appreciated by the pilots, who couldn't spare the mental energy required to think about anything other than the job in hand: starting the next section of the journey, the northerly leg to Manila.

All the pilots relished the opportunity to land at Nichols Field, the main airport in Manila. Famous for a hard-fought battle near the end of the Second World War, when US troops had taken control from the Japanese, the airfield became the Philippines' central hub for commercial and military flights. Arrival and landing were easy compared to the strips they had used en route, and the pilots were welcomed into the terminal, as it was grandly referred to, but in reality it was no more than a series of single-storey buildings. The exhausted pilots attended an impromptu reception held by the station commander before gathering in the briefing room. They didn't stand on ceremony: having no fresh clothes to change into, the pilots wore their white flying overalls, which were splattered with oil and grease and stained with two days' sweat. They were numb from the concentration required to fly all day with the raucous sound of the Griffon engine pounding in their ears.

In the morning the Nichols Field weather service provided reports and forecasts for the local area and the wider region, including the route to Hong Kong. It did not look promising. The typhoon mentioned by Miss Charlton in Singapore had built more or less exactly as she had forecast and was tracking north, away from Hong Kong. The decision that Squadron Leader Porter had to make was whether to take a rest day or to press on. His orders were to get to Hong Kong with all haste. Porter took Flight Lieutenant Devon to one side. "Devon, what's your opinion on the likely weather we will see at Hong Kong?"

"Very challenging, sir, the reported wind strength and torrential rain at the moment at Kai Tak is more than the Spitfires could cope with. But as the typhoon is moving away, we can hope for an improvement. But there's a question over timing – we can't be sure of the conditions when we get there."

"What are our options?" asked Porter.

"If we can't get into Kai Tak, we're in serious trouble. We'll be low on fuel, of course, and will have little chance of diverting to another airfield. But my reading of the situation is that the typhoon will track north-west, opening up a window of half-decent weather for a couple of hours around the time we're expected to land. I would expect the wind direction to turn southerly, and that will give us a tailwind to help us along. It's a gamble, of course."

"Thank you, Devon. I agree with you. We stay with the plan to depart Manila this afternoon. Make sure you speak with the Met people for any updates. I will get the radio boys here to contact Kai Tak and have the Sunderlands airborne ahead of us to patrol the route. They should be able to handle the conditions."

Devon strolled to the Met Office, thinking about what had just happened. Had he really convinced the squadron leader to take a crazy risk? Had his desire to get the journey over with influenced his opinion and undermined his caution? He would take one more look at the weather forecast for the next six hours.

***

The seaplane commander at RAF Kai Tak, Squadron Leader Robert Condie, had a small office in the end section of a long Nissen hut. The seven-man crews of the two Sunderland flying boats stood around the chart showing the track of the Spitfires.

"Bloody tricky in this weather, sir," said Flight Lieutenant Andy Scott, who would be leading the mission, and carried the responsibility to rendezvous with the fighters. If any Spitfire had engine trouble and had to ditch, they would need to locate the downed aircraft, land in the sea and pick up the pilot. Conditions back at Hong Kong would be little better for the seaplanes on their return, but if necessary they could at least divert to a sheltered harbour to land.

"The aircraft are tied up at the moment and will be readied for the mission in a couple of hours," said Scott. "Our plan is to take off late morning before the Spits leave Manila, and link up mid-crossing. If one of the pilots goes into the sea early on, then we're going to have a hellish time finding him."

"Understood, Scott. I wish you good luck, and you, Clarke. Let's make a decent show of it, everyone. You all know of the threat from the Chinese across the border; these Spitfires will be vital."

***

"How's the weather looking, Devon?" Squadron Leader Porter had assembled all the pilots in the briefing room for final planning.

Devon was leaning over a map of the region, which had the weather information pencilled on it. "The typhoon has tracked more to the west, sir, which will help us. Although the centre will be a couple of hundred miles away, there will be strong winds and heavy rain, but it's scheduled to improve all the time. For the last hundred miles or so, the wind direction should be right behind us." Devon's dry mouth and raised heart rate reflected his nerves about committing the squadron to such a hazardous flight. It was Porter's decision to go or to delay. He looked thoughtful, and a silence fell over the group.

"Right, let's get to it," Porter said confidently. "We will depart at 2 p.m. Go and make your final preparations. Fitzjohn and Devon, stay here."

Many of the pilots were smiling and nudging each other as they hurried up to the dispersal hut, buoyed by the prospect of some serious flying to complete the final leg.

"Gentlemen, we need to maintain a good formation. I don't want any aircraft wandering off and out of sight. We have the two Sunderlands to look out for as soon as we depart Manila. If the weather deteriorates en route, I will decide before the halfway point whether we turn back or go on. Any questions?"

"No, sir," Fitzjohn and Devon chimed together.

***

The climb out of Manila was smooth and smartly executed. The fifteen aircraft took up their well-practised positions in groups of five, with Porter leading the formation. They took great care to keep the correct heading to Hong Kong; any deviation from the planned track would add extra miles to the journey. Strong crosswinds were expected, and they made frequent revisions to their heading. After an hour of flying in good conditions, the sky ahead darkened and heavy clouds loomed up.

"Descend to 2,000 feet." Porter's instruction would ensure they flew below the cloud base, keeping the sea in sight and maintaining visual contact with each other. Flying into cloud was inherently dangerous, as the risk of a mid-air collision was very real.

Suddenly the radios crackled into life. "Sir, Taylor here. I've got a problem. Glycol coolant level is down and steadily reducing. Engine temperature increasing."

"Hell, and we still haven't seen the Sunderlands," Porter whispered. He called over the radio. "Taylor, ease back power, try and let the engine cool. Everyone, reduce speed, stay in formation."

Taylor was a member of Devon's flight and a very experienced pilot. He could nurse the aircraft along and, if necessary, should be able to ditch without crashing the aircraft into the sea. A successful sea landing would give him time to climb out and wait for rescue – if any rescuers were out there.

"But sir, that will endanger the whole squadron!" interjected Fitzjohn. "Taylor will be ditching soon and there's nothing we can do."

"Sir, Devon here. I suggest that all aircraft press on but I will stay with Taylor to circle over the sea until the Sunderlands make contact. I will be able to direct them." Devon's voice was calm but authoritative. Porter had little choice but to agree with him. His actions could result in the loss of two aircraft and pilots, but why put the whole squadron at risk?

"Right, Devon, stay with Taylor. Come on to Hong Kong as best you can."

Before Devon could reply a message sang out over the radio. "Spitfires, Spitfires, this is Sunderland One, are you receiving me? Over." The flight lieutenant's voice over the radio was hugely reassuring to the fighter pilots.

"Affirm Sunderland One, Spitfire leader receiving you. Our position is approximately 370 miles from Hong Kong, heading 330 degrees, 2,000 feet. We have one aircraft in trouble, about to ditch. Looking out for you. Over," said Porter.

"Roger, Spitfire leader, we believe we are in your area, maintaining 1,000 feet," said the Sunderland pilot.

No more than three minutes had passed when Bryant spoke up.

"Sir, Bryant here. I think I have the Sunderlands in sight." Bryant occupied the far right-hand position in the squadron and had kept a good lookout. "About two miles, 030 degrees." The huge white fuselage of the leading Sunderland stood out from the cloudy grey sky.

"Good man, Bryant," said Porter. "Sunderland One, Spitfire leader. We have you visually. Look to your right."

"Contact, Spitfires! We will pass on your right then follow up from the rear. Keep this radio channel open."

As the seaplanes took up position behind the squadron, Taylor's oil temperature shot into the red and he entered a controlled descent. "Taylor to leader, preparing to ditch."

"Spitfire leader, Sunderland Two here. We have sight of the aircraft and will land in the sea to pick him up. We will see you in Hong Kong tonight. Line up the beers for us!"

"Excellent. Devon, rejoin the squadron," instructed Porter.

As the flight continued, the wind came round to a south-westerly crosswind, forcing the aircraft to head 20 degrees off the magnetic track to Hong Kong. An hour after the rendezvous with the Sunderlands the wind changed to a more southerly, and helpful, tailwind. Much to Devon's relief, although the conditions remained dangerous, with heavy squalls and poor visibility, at last they reached the eastern coast of China and spotted the Pearl River estuary. To their right were Victoria Harbour and Hong Kong Island. The aircraft approached cautiously. The Peak on the island rose to over 2,000 feet, and with the cloud base at around 2,400 feet there was little room for error. There were still strong buffeting winds in the area, making flying a battle to keep the aircraft straight and at the right altitude. Devon's assessment of the weather on arrival was spot-on, but it would still test the capabilities of the pilots. The gusting typhoon winds shook the Spitfires and the pilots had to maintain control without overreacting and risk stalling.

Kai Tak Airfield had two runways, giving them a choice of the best landing direction. "All pilots, squadron leader here. Looks like the runway to use is 25, best option into the wind. We will fly around the south of the island, turn right and right again to approach up the harbour. Space out – one aircraft to land at a time. Follow me."

The squadron leader led his flight down the approach route, followed by Fitzjohn's section then Devon's. All aircraft made good landings and taxied to the hard standing. Porter was on the tarmac, supervising the ground crew as they tied the aircraft down. After landing and securing his own aircraft and checking those in his flight, Devon walked over to the squadron leader.

"Ah, Adam, well done!"

The boss using his Christian name was a good sign.

"Excellent judgement on the weather – everything worked as you forecast. Bloody decent piece of work."

"Thank you, sir. Any news on Taylor?"

"No, not yet. Let's go into the ops room and see what we can find out. Here comes Fitzjohn. Go easy on him, Adam; he was only thinking of the safety of the whole squadron."

"Of course, sir. Fitzjohn made a very sensible and logical proposal that we should abandon one of our colleagues without even trying to save him." Devon's cynical smile indicated his true thoughts.

TEN

The Spitfire pilots, filthy, exhausted and stressed after the harrowing journey, were herded into the dispersal room for tea and sandwiches. As they settled down, a group of reporters came in with the station's intelligence officer, Captain Rodney Blake.

"Gentlemen, your attention, please. A few minutes of your time to meet members of the Hong Kong press corps. Go ahead, James."

"Thank you, Captain Blake. My name is James Roberts. I'm the East Asia correspondent for the London *Evening Standard*. I'd like to ask you a few questions. Who is Squadron Leader Porter, please?"

Porter raised his hand.

"Squadron Leader, what can you tell me about the flight from Manila and the loss of one of your pilots?"

"There was no loss of a pilot. We have just heard that he was successfully picked up by the Sunderland and will be landing in the harbour shortly. The weather conditions were challenging, as you can see. Otherwise the flight was uneventful." Porter avoided detailed discussions on the operation. They had arrived safely, and that's all that counted.

"Can I ask, how do you see your role against the Chinese forces, Squadron Leader? Matthew Chant, *The Times*."

"That's confidential, Matthew." It was the intelligence officer. "Let's stay with discussing the flight here."

"Understood. Squadron Leader Porter, you arrived in awful weather. Wouldn't it have been wiser to delay by a day or two, or were you concerned about potential actions by the Chinese?"

Porter saw the trap. "We made the judgement that the typhoon in the area would move north and the weather would improve, so we continued. Successfully, as you see."

"Derek Ramsden, *Manchester Evening News*. I understand that Flight Lieutenant Devon is in the group." People turned to look at Devon. "What message would you like to give to your home town on life in the RAF and the dangers you face, Flight Lieutenant?"

"The RAF offers a great career to people from all walks of life and from all areas. We have a job to do, we're well trained, and we have great aircraft."

"Spitfires are being phased out, aren't they, in favour of the new jets? Does this mean you are now largely redundant and will return to civilian life?" Ramsden's question was meant to provoke.

"Some pilots will wish to apply for retraining. How successful they will be is an open question. In the meantime, we have an important operation to carry out here, and that's what we are concentrating on."

"Thank you. Now could we take a group photograph, please?" Chant from *The Times* stepped forward, his photographer beside him.

"Really?" said Porter. "What's all the fuss about, Chant?"

"The eyes of the world are on you, Squadron Leader. If the Chinese should try to invade Hong Kong, you will be on the front line. Your arrival today is a key deterrent factor, of course, and people at home will be concerned about the situation here. And I'm sure you see that publicity would be a better deterrent?"

"Very well. Men, line up, please."

After the meeting with the press had broken up, the station commander's adjutant stepped into the dispersal room. "Gentlemen, facilities are now ready for you to wash and brush up and change into clean clothes. Your accommodation is a short walk to the Victoria Harbour side of the field. The CO will be hosting drinks at seven thirty, to which you are all cordially invited. You will also have the opportunity of meeting the rest of the officers and senior aircraftmen stationed here, together with the crews from the Sunderlands."

"Very kind. We will see you then," said Porter. "I'm certain the men would welcome a couple of beers and time to relax."

As well as the RAF, Kai Tak Airfield shared the complex with the Royal Navy, colonial armed forces personnel and staff from the growing civil aviation companies. The base was situated on the southern tip of the mainland and looked out towards Hong Kong Island. Being part of Kowloon meant that the restaurants, bars, hotels and clubs were easily accessible. The Star Ferry service provided frequent shuttles from the clock tower terminus on Kowloon to Central on the island. These quaint shuttle boats operated every few minutes, making the trip to the island and back cheap and easy. They were a favourite with the servicemen, who preferred Hong Kong Island's attractions to those of Kowloon. Squadron Leader Porter's next job would be to ensure that 28 Squadron's pilots and ground crew did not enjoy the distractions too much.

***

The officer with strategic responsibility for flying operations at Kai Tak, Wing Commander Mike Martin, was an experienced fighter pilot who knew that sustained and testing operational exercises were vital to keep a squadron in the best shape to fight a war. His orders for the first full day after arrival were for all Spitfires to be serviced, refuelled and armed. The Mark XVIII version was able to be fitted with rockets, bombs for attacks from height, and cannons with explosive shells and machine guns for low-level strafing.

The colony of Hong Kong comprised the island itself, the mainland areas of Kowloon, and the land mass to the north known as the New Territories. This region was the food-growing area for Hong Kong and acted as a buffer for any Chinese advances down to Kowloon and Hong Kong Island. It was vital that it was adequately defended. The small garrison of British ground forces maintained observation stations along the border, but had relatively little war-fighting capability should they face a massive attack by the Chinese.

Over the first few days of operations, as the weather steadily improved, the squadron's pilots would become more familiar with the terrain of the New Territories and Hong Kong Island. The high ground surrounding Kai Tak and on many of the islands was a constant concern. The wing commander issued an order that no aircraft should enter Chinese airspace unless instructed to do so or there was a real and present threat to the safety of any aircraft. Most of the patrols would be along the border with China and along the Pearl River estuary to ensure that no seaborne activities could threaten Hong Kong.

Martin suggested to Porter that Fitzjohn should take his flight of five aircraft and patrol the Sham Chun River – the border between China and the northern areas of the New Territories. Should the Chinese army cross the border, the squadron would attack the invaders to hold them up and delay progress. This would give the British forces time to defend the New Territories as best they could and prevent incursions into Kowloon and Hong Kong Island. And so the squadron's routines were established. They were a clear warning to any Chinese commander who wanted to take them on.

ELEVEN

After the first week of operations, when all the aircraft had been serviced, the full team of engineering and maintenance staff and all required ammunition had arrived and was in place, Wing Commander Martin allowed the men regular periods of leave. They quickly became familiar with the bars and restaurants near Kai Tak and gradually explored new venues in Kowloon and on Hong Kong Island.

Flight Lieutenant Devon had showered after his late afternoon run around the airfield perimeter track.

Young was waiting in his room. "Good afternoon, sir. Will you be going with the boys over to Happy Valley tonight? It promises to be an excellent evening out. A bit of betting on the horses, some drinks and food. Wednesday is the big night out for Hong Kong people."

Devon rarely got enthusiastic about nights out. He preferred to listen to his classical records. "I'm not sure. It's a busy day tomorrow." He knew that was a lame excuse; there was nothing special going on in the morning, and he wasn't surprised when Young came back with a little more persuasion.

"We needn't be too late, sir, and it would be good for morale in the squadron if you came along."

"What can we expect there?"

"Well, sir, it seems that everyone in Hong Kong is mad for gambling. There will be a large crowd like a football match back home and the atmosphere is electric, apparently. There will be food stands where you can get chicken chop suey, chow mein and sweet and sour pork. All good stuff when you've had a few beers! Plenty of Brits, Yanks and Aussies go there, and a night at the races is very popular with the expat ladies, sir."

"OK, Young, what time do we depart, and how do we get there?"

"We have a couple of trucks to take us to the Star Ferry terminal, then we'll pick up some taxis on Hong Kong side. We're leaving at seven o'clock."

Happy Valley Racecourse was built on just about the only flat area on the island and run by the Hong Kong Jockey Club. The Chinese residents of Hong Kong were wildly enthusiastic about gambling – on horses in particular. The RAF men were almost as keen, and quickly found the bookies to place their bets. Some were reckless, getting carried away and gambling more than they could afford.

The races generated a good deal of excitement in the crowd. There were some close finishes and only a couple of favourites won, meaning good winnings for those who had the nerve to back the outsiders. Devon admitted to himself that he was enjoying the evening. He had a couple of drinks with the aircraftmen, who were as intent on getting to know the ladies as they were on picking out the winning horses.

"Having much success, Devon?" Fitzjohn's broad smile and the glass of beer he held indicated he was enjoying the evening to the full.

"I've had one winner, but I'm down a few dollars. How about you?" Devon wasn't at all interested in Fitzjohn's luck but felt he had to make the effort to ask.

"A grand evening, old boy. You need to know your horses – which to back and which to avoid like the plague. And be bold with your stakes. No good playing for peanuts!"

The rest of the group approached the pair.

"Sir, we're heading back in about twenty minutes if that suits you?" Young said.

"Yes, that's fine, thank you. I'm sure Flight Lieutenant Fitzjohn will be coming with us."

"Just time for the last race, chaps." Fitzjohn hurried off to place his bet.

"Had a successful evening?" asked Devon.

"Not too bad, sir – a little bit of luck here and there. Some of the other chaps were not so fortunate. And it seems that Mr Fitzjohn has lost a packet!"

"Really, Young? That's tough. I thought he was doing well," said Devon.

"He doesn't hold back with the amount he bets, sir. But he's had some bad luck tonight, I gather. Mackie, his orderly, told me he's been chasing his losses."

As the men waited on the Star Ferry pier, the water in Victoria Harbour glistened with the reflected lights of Wan Chai and Central. The men were boisterous and happy, even if some had lost a little money. Plenty of beers and the sense of being on leave, albeit for only one night, had lightened their mood. They had recovered from their move from Singapore and the long flight to Hong Kong. The Chinese army were not showing any signs of building for an invasion so the role of the squadron was to 'put on an air show', as some of the men described their daily routine. Life wasn't bad at Kai Tak, even though their mission might not last long and the future of the squadron was uncertain.

TWELVE

The Peninsula Hotel on Salisbury Road, Kowloon, occupied the most enviable position in the colony, looking out across Victoria Harbour towards Hong Kong Island. Built in the 1920s as a flamboyant colonial-style baroque structure, the hotel was elegant and stylish, and it also had a history of hosting the most illustrious guests, including royalty, film stars and US presidents.

The hotel's imposing entrance left visitors with no doubt they were in a very grand establishment. All who entered were in awe of its magnificent white marble and gold columns and high ceiling. The wicker furniture and potted palms brought a sense of coolness and calm to the bustling lobby. The hotel was the most popular venue for social gatherings in Hong Kong.

After the end of the war and Japanese occupation, the hotel quickly re-established its reputation as *the* place to see and be seen. It held regular dances and special gala evenings. Afternoon tea was a highlight of life at the Peninsula, which offered a traditional English menu and fine teas, all to the accompaniment of a harpist playing light melodies.

The backbone of British Empire colonial administration was the cooperation between government officials, senior businessmen and the military. In Hong Kong this included expat British, American and Australian residents, the Chinese Hong Kong community and other enterprising nationals from India and South East Asia. The elite gathered at places where deals could be done, relationships built and enduring friendships made. Hong Kong was essential to British commercial and colonial interests.

Some of 28 Squadron's officers and other ranks formed a small social and entertainment committee soon after they arrived at Kai Tak. They put on plays and musicals – more hilarious farces than serious theatre – and everyone joined in. Dressing up was *de rigueur*: all the shows were put on by the men, and some were more naturally disposed to play female parts than others. The more outrageous the show, the better. But attending gatherings off the station was a different matter. Officers particularly were expected to exhibit social graces and represent the service in the best light: no heavy drinking, no inappropriate humour, and to show respect to the government and commercial people.

Shrewdly, the Peninsula's management organised a gala dinner at their own expense to welcome the squadron to the colony, and invited people from all aspects of Hong Kong society. Wing Commander Martin and Squadron Leader Porter were naturally top of the guest list, and were asked to extend the invitation to all officers and senior men. Delighted to oblige, Porter passed on a handful of invitations, on the back of which was printed the name and address of a gentlemen's outfitter in Kowloon where men could hire appropriate evening wear – this was to be a formal black tie event. The general manager at the Peninsula, Jonny Chan, knew that a recently arrived operational unit would not have their service dress uniforms.

On the Saturday of the gala, the officers' orderlies ensured that their officers' shirts, suits and shoes were immaculately pressed and polished.

The senior NCOs prepared their own outfits to no lesser degree of precision. A poorly turned out officer would reflect badly on the service.

Looking well dressed enough to be admired by all guests, the airmen were taken to the hotel in staff cars and assembled in the hotel forecourt, as instructed by Squadron Leader Porter. The men were clearly excited and a touch apprehensive when they saw the grandeur of the hotel. Wing Commander Martin briefed his team on the importance of circulating, being careful not to mention sensitive operational matters, and to enjoy themselves. He looked to Porter for any further comments, but he simply nodded and smiled.

The group strolled into the salon for the drinks reception and collected glasses of champagne from waiters dressed in immaculate white uniforms and holding heavily loaded silver trays. There were already over a hundred guests, and the buzz of their conversation created a welcoming atmosphere.

Adam Devon, with Bryant and Taylor, walked across to a small group to introduce themselves.

"Good evening. My name's Flight Lieutenant Adam Devon, recently arrived at the RAF station at Kai Tak. My colleagues here are Flight Sergeant Alec Bryant and Pilot Officer James Taylor."

"Good evening – it's a pleasure indeed to meet members of the new squadron. My name is Tim Chadwick. I'm with Universal Commodities Company. We import and export metals and manufactured products in Hong Kong. Terribly mundane to you flying chaps, no doubt!"

"Not at all, Tim. And how is business?" Devon instinctively warmed to Chadwick's jovial nature.

"Excellent, actually. Things are moving forward at a pace – Hong Kong is such a key asset to Britain in developing its influence in the Far East. Now, can I introduce my good friend Isaac Golding, general manager of the London and Hong Kong Bank? We must be nice to Isaac – he funds most of our business!"

Devon gave a gentle nod and shook hands with the banker.

"Nice to meet you, Flight Lieutenant, welcome to Hong Kong," said Golding. "I hope you enjoy your stay, and that your presence has the desired effect on the Chinese."

Straight to the point, this man, thought Devon. "Thank you. We all hope that we won't need to take action, but we're here to do the job if necessary. I presume you have banking interests on both sides of the border?"

"We have a well-established branch in Shanghai, but there's little prospect of development while the Chinese revolution is under way. We prefer to bank for the businessmen of the future here in Hong Kong."

Tim Chadwick cut in. "Now, chaps, let's not talk shop all evening. Tell me, Adam, did you get to attend the Olympics in London?"

Changing the subject to sport set Devon at ease. "Unfortunately not; I was in training at Cranwell. But I followed all the action in the newspapers and the newsreels. The Empire Stadium looked terrific. I would have loved to have been there."

"What is your sport, Adam?" Golding seemed genuinely interested.

"Apart from cricket and football, I'm a track and field man. I particularly enjoy the mile. Not much opportunity for serious events here in Hong Kong, but I keep fit running the perimeter track at the airfield."

"How else do you amuse yourself when you're not flying?"

"I have my record collection with me and a portable gramophone. Beethoven is probably my favourite composer – I enjoy his *Pastoral Symphony* in particular. I also have some Vaughan Williams, William Walton and Holst – *The Planets* suite is one I enjoy hugely."

"You have good taste. You may not know it, but the bank sponsors music evenings here in Hong Kong. You would be welcome any time."

"That's very kind, thank you. Are you a sportsman yourself, Isaac?"

"Not really – I never have the time. The bank keeps me busy, of course."

Just then a gong sounded, and discussion across the room reduced to murmurs. The Peninsula's impressive Rose Room was ready to receive guests for dinner.

Devon was struck by the opulence of the room, by its beautifully laid tables with crystal glasses and Royal Doulton china. He found his place name and was pleased to see that Tim Chadwick was one of the eight guests on his table. As others arrived, they introduced themselves. There were three women from the governor's office, all very attractive in the latest ball gowns; a maritime engineer, short and breathless and with a damp handshake; and the owner of a food import business. One of the three women sat next to Devon. The seat on Devon's right was empty as the group sat down, but as the waiter went round the table serving white wine there was a late arrival. The man made his apologies and said a quick hello to his fellow guests.

He turned to Devon. "Good evening. My name is Hind, Captain Derek Hind. I'm with the Australian Military Attaché's office. Sorry I'm late – I had some ruddy paperwork to finish." He had a strong Australian accent.

Devon shook hands with him. "Nice to meet you, Derek. I'm Adam Devon with 28 Squadron."

"Of course – all this is in your honour, I believe."

"Well, perhaps. Tell me, what do you do exactly at the attaché's office?

"Boring desk work mostly, mate! Running around for the attaché himself, that sort of thing." Devon realised that he probably shouldn't enquire too closely into the work of the military attaché's office – it was often where strategies were developed for future operations and intelligence was gathered.

Devon glanced at the menu card on the table. A cold roast Peking duck salad to start, crab soup, grilled tournedos 'Peninsula' and Asian vegetables, followed by peach melba. White and red wines would be served, with a sweet Sauternes to accompany the dessert.

"How the hell can they get all these foods when rationing is still in force in England?" Devon mumbled.

"Yes, wonderful, isn't it?" one of the women from Government House sitting to Devon's left said to him in a conspiratorial voice. The two exchanged smiles. "Let me introduce myself properly. I'm Valerie Hetherington-Brown. People call me Val."

"Good to meet you, Val." Devon was perfectly comfortable in the presence of good-looking women and those from a monied background, as Val obviously was. A tall woman with green eyes, she had poise and class. Her primrose ball gown looked expensive and fitted her slim figure perfectly. She looked to be in her mid-thirties. Devon noticed her beautiful hands, her long fingers and perfect nails. The benefits of working in an office, rather than a factory, he thought.

"What is your role at the governor's office? How long have you been here?" he asked.

"I've been here a couple of years. My job is to help develop business interests in the region. I read economics at university and worked at the Ministry of Food during the war. I couldn't resist the opportunity to come out here. I guess it was the same for you?" Val gave a knowing smile.

Devon shrugged. A serving pilot had to go wherever he was sent; he had little choice in the matter. "Tell me, who are all these people? Why should the Peninsula put on such a show?"

"The Peninsula's management want the place to be seen as *the* place to go. As well as you military types, there are diplomats, government administrators, managers of import and export firms, land and property owners, and insurance and banking people here tonight. That table over there has a couple of ladies from the London and Hong Kong Bank, which is one of the largest in the region. I can see the Lloyd's of London representative too."

Devon glanced to his right and noticed that the RAF guest at that table was Fitzjohn. Looking entirely at home in the expensive restaurant, Fitzjohn seemed to be holding court. Sitting next to him, gazing up at him adoringly, was a pretty dark-haired woman in a midnight-blue satin dress. Fitzjohn was giving her the benefit of his charms. Val noticed Devon looking. "That's Hannah Shaw, recently arrived in Hong Kong. She's with the LHK."

"Right – I met the general manager at the drinks reception. Isaac Goldman?"

"Golding," said Val. "Yes, he's the big noise in banking here, has all the right political and commercial connections."

"Political?"

"Oh yes, nothing gets done here without the agreement of Government House. He's a firm favourite with the governor's circle of friends. Some say he has wider political ambitions outside Hong Kong, connected to his Jewish heritage, but that's all speculation. He is re-establishing the Jewish presence in banking in this part of the world after lying low during the war. It was tough here for Jews, apparently, but not as bad as the horrors of Europe. He's also linked to funding the building of the home for the new Knesset in Jerusalem."

Devon looked puzzled.

"In a few years' time the Knesset will be the permanent home for the Israeli government. Their own Houses of Parliament in Jerusalem. As I said, Golding has lots of connections."

"Is the London and Hong Kong Bank a Jewish bank?"

"No, not exactly. They specialise in the Far East, of course. And it seems they have recruited several Jewish members of staff to help develop the business. But enough of the Hong Kong commercial world. Tell me, Adam, when your tour of duty is finished here, what does the future hold for you?"

"I'm not sure. A new posting for the squadron, perhaps. Could be back to Singapore, maybe somewhere else in the region. We're unlikely to return to the UK as a unit, given the introduction of jet fighters to home defence."

"And you personally?"

"That's a big question. I'm engaged, and my fiancée wants me to go home and get a safe factory job – with Avro, actually. I would prefer to stay in a flying role, either here or back in the UK. Our squadron leader, David Porter, has lined up a plum job with BOAC. Something like that would appeal if I left the RAF."

The waiting staff filed in to clear away the many plates, cutlery and glasses. The maître d' announced that coffee and drinks would be served in the ballroom, and the guests took this as their cue to depart the Rose Room. Music was floating from an adjoining suite – the ever-popular big band sound and the upbeat lyrics of 'Let's Dance Again Tonight'.

Devon stepped outside for a few minutes for some fresh air and to absorb the entrancing view across Victoria Harbour. A multitude of lights glistened on the hundreds of boats that bobbed in the harbour, reflecting in the water. As he turned to go back in he noticed a couple in conversation in the gardens below. It was Fitzjohn and the dark-haired girl from his table. They were clearly getting on very well. Fitzjohn held the girl's hand in both of his, his head forward, no doubt romancing her in his smooth style. The sight irritated Devon, although he was not sure why. He felt the need for a nightcap.

As he ordered a Scotch at the bar, a familiar voice called out from behind him. "And set one up for me too, barman. Don't mind if I join you, Adam?" It was Captain Hind.

"Please do," said Devon. "Have you enjoyed the evening so far?"

"Yes indeed. You know, mate, these functions can be a pain in the neck, but this has been a good do. And yourself?"

"An excellent meal, and it's been very nice meeting some of the Hong Kong dignitaries."

"You mean Val Hetherington-Brown. Not a bad Sheila, that's for sure! But a tough cookie too, I would say."

Bryant and Taylor came up to join the two officers, saving Devon from making any response, although he agreed whole-heartedly with Hind. "Derek, can I introduce two pilots from my flight – Alec Bryant and James Taylor."

"Good to meet you, boys. Captain Derek Hind, Australian Military Attaché's office." Hind shook hands with the airmen.

Taylor led the conversation. "Have you been out here long?"

"A couple of months or so. Before that I was in Malaya."

"Really? We had a spell in Penang," said Bryant. "A group of your countrymen provided some sport for us – a little jolly into the hills to shoot up the commies. What was it, James? Hill 33, or something like that?"

"No shit, mate! I was there myself with a recon team. Things got a bit awkward and some of your Spitfires lent a hand."

"That was us!" Bryant beamed. "It's nice to meet a real live customer. Let's get another drink to celebrate."

"Yes, let's do that. We really owed it to the last man in – he did a fine piece of flying and some nice shooting that gave us a chance to scarper. Man, that sure was tight."

Taylor smiled. "Captain Hind, let me introduce that pilot to you. It was none other than our flight lieutenant here, Mr Adam Devon."

"Ah, mate, then it's an even greater pleasure to meet you. Thank you for getting us out of that mess."

"All part of the job, Derek. I did wonder what a group of Aussies was doing in that part of the country."

"It was all hush-hush at the time but I can tell you now. We were a special reconnaissance team, looking at how the Communist Terrorists' supply chains worked and how to disrupt them. We were not supposed to engage with the enemy, but we got trapped in that valley. The operation was a success otherwise – we got some useful intel to pass to the British and Australian army commanders."

"And now what are you up to?" Bryant asked.

"Nothing too exciting, mate. Apart from attending functions like these, military attaché work is about doing deals, assessing the local politics and sounding out potential allies. Can be a bit boring."

"I'm sure it's intriguing work, Captain," said Devon, then changed the subject. The group had a final drink before getting ready to leave.

"Adam, thanks again for what you did back there in Malaya. It saved a bunch of Aussie lives."

"Thanks, Derek. I hope you enjoy your new work and can get out from behind your desk occasionally."

The RAF personnel met up on the front drive of the hotel to be taken back to the airbase, but Porter and Fitzjohn were missing. Devon stepped back into the lobby to see if he could see them. There was no sign of Fitzjohn. Devon saw that Porter was talking to Val Hetherington-Brown. They ended their discussion with a handshake, and Porter came over to join the group.

Back at the base, the airmen dispersed to their quarters. Devon and Porter strolled into the Nissen hut that made up the officers' quarters.

"A very good evening, I think. It's worth getting to know the people we're serving here," said Porter

"Yes, sir. And to learn about some of the matters that concern them, politically and commercially." Devon heard himself echo Val Hetherington-Brown's words. "Goodnight, sir."

Devon hadn't noticed that Fitzjohn had not returned from the Peninsula.

***

In the hotel gardens, Fitzjohn held the arm of the dark-haired woman from his table. "Hannah, it has been wonderful to meet you. Perhaps we could meet again soon. I can get a late pass on Monday – it would be great to meet for dinner. I can pick you up from the bank."

"I'm not sure. We've only just met. Don't you think it's somewhat hasty to think of having dinner together?"

Fitzjohn sensed that he was being brushed off. "Certainly not. I'd really like to get to know you better. Besides, isn't it your duty to promote the bank's relationships with the military?" He put on his best seductive smile.

"I'm not sure it is, but I tell you what, let's have a quick drink after work on Monday. Would that constitute me doing my job?" Hannah gave a small smile.

"It's a date. I'll see you at six o'clock at your offices."

"Very well. Now I must hurry along and get the ferry back to the island. Goodnight."

"Goodnight, Hannah." Fitzjohn took the liberty of wrapping his arm around Hannah's waist to draw her close, and planting an unexpected kiss on her cheek. Instinctively Hannah pulled away and walked quickly back into the hotel to meet her bank colleagues.

THIRTEEN

Devon knew his mother worried about him and his sister, but he felt she worried too much, stifling them and doing little to help them achieve their ambitions and dreams. It was just who she was. In 1944 Devon's sister, Joan, had volunteered as an ambulance driver with the civil defence. Joan's job was to get the ambulance as near as possible to bombing casualties. Many members of the civil defence were killed or injured during the war, and every night Joan's mum waited up for her to return home safely. Eventually she reluctantly seemed to accept Joan's job: the country was at war and everyone had to do their bit. She was patriotic, but she wished that the dangerous work could be done by others. Devon's father, Arthur, worked at the Avro factory as an electrician fitting out Lancaster bombers. His mother even fretted that the Germans might target the factory, but this fear proved to be unfounded.

After the war, Devon had to deal with his mother's greatest concern – his decision to join the RAF. He had always been crazy about aircraft and joined the Air Training Corps as a teenager while at the local tech. A technical college education was designed to give young people skills and knowledge in sciences and manufacturing, which served as a foundation for anyone wanting to learn about the theory of flight.

When Devon was hoping to be selected for pilot training, he was shocked when he was told that his mother had phoned the ATC commander and asked him to turn Adam down on the grounds that he had a sensitive nature and wouldn't be suitable for an aggressive front-line role. She said he'd be better off becoming an electrician like his father – it was a safe occupation. The commander ignored her request, but mentioned the call to Devon. Adam went on to qualify as a pilot and then, after further assessment, to fly fighters. However, his mother took every opportunity to try to persuade Adam to quit flying.

***

After the squadron arrived in Hong Kong, Devon wrote to his mother and fiancée Amy. He usually found time to write every week to his parents and twice a week to Amy. They had met when they were both sixteen at a youth club dance in central Manchester and they had been attracted to each other immediately. Two years later, when the war ended, they got engaged, and had planned to marry as soon as Devon's military service was over. Amy had said she hoped that this would be no more than the National Service minimum of eighteen months, but in 1944, aged eighteen, Adam had signed papers for five years.

Amy was very unhappy at having to wait for Devon to be free from the RAF, and encouraged him to come home as soon as he could.

***

A few days after his arrival in Hong Kong, Devon was in his room preparing his papers for the squadron's daily briefing. His orderly, Young, knocked on the door and entered, carrying a tray.

"Good morning, Young," said Devon. "Thanks for the coffee."

"And there is some post for you, sir."

Adam's mother's letter had arrived at the same time as Amy's latest. He opened his mother's first.

> *Dear Adam,*
>
> *Thank you, darling, for your lovely letter to your affectionate parents. We were so pleased to read in the Manchester Evening News about the squadron arriving safely in Hong Kong, and thrilled to see you mentioned – very proud indeed. I do hope those Chinese don't cause any trouble. We have spoken to Amy and she is also proud, but very sad because she wants you to come home now and settle down with her. I'm sure that's what you would like too, now that you have nearly reached your five years' service.*
>
> *You can resign from the RAF any time you wish, you know, Adam. Dad has spoken to the personnel manager at Avro and they would be very pleased to have you at the factory. Dad said they could give you a job working on the new radar and navigation equipment. Dad also said he will lend you a little money to help you and Amy put down a deposit on a small house. There's a new development being built nearby on a cleared bombsite that would be lovely for you both.*
>
> *Sidney Higginbotham is the new secretary at the cricket club. He has told Dad that you would be very welcome to join the club. That would be nice, wouldn't it? Some of your old school friends are members and you would easily become friends again, wouldn't you?*
>
> *Dad was able to buy some pre-war 78s for your record collection, Mozart and Schubert included. We will keep them here for when you return – if we post them, they might get broken.*
>
> *Please take care, my darling. I do worry so much about your flying. Don't you think you have done your bit and it's time to*

come home? Joan sends her love, and she says you should come home too.

Take care, my dear, and lots of love,
Mum and Dad

Devon sat quietly, thinking about the image the letter conjured up. A steady job, lovely wife, good friends and the chance to build a new career. It had its attractions, but it wasn't the life he had wanted. Devon knew that Squadron Leader Porter was planning to join BOAC, and that would mean a lot of flying. Could he apply for a similar job?

Devon opened Amy's letter, which was written on pink Basildon Bond envelope and paper and smelled faintly of the Chanel No. 5 he had given her for Christmas 1946.

My darling Adam,

I was so excited to get your letter from Hong Kong. Being in the newspaper – you're such a famous person now! My friends all think I'm so lucky to be engaged to a hero. I tell them you have always been such a brave chap. When you come home you can tell me all about your adventures!

I have some exciting news! I am to be trained for a new job in paediatric nursing (that's children's care, but I'm sure you knew that). I'm overjoyed. I have worked hard on the women's medical ward but I'm really looking forward to starting a new career. You see, it is possible to go into something new in life, if you want to.

For the last few Saturdays I have gone to the hospital social club dances with my friends. They have a band playing the latest swing and jive dance music – it's jolly good fun and a chance to meet new people. I know you don't really like that kind of music, but you can't dance to Beethoven, can you? The people are all so

THE PEARL RIVER | 87

nice. I think you'll really enjoy going to the dances when you're back home.

Your mum has said that you have a job offer from Avro. That would be wonderful, as you can keep working with aeroplanes yet have a steady job, which we will need if we're going to buy a house. Your mum also said you could join the cricket club. That's nice of her, but of course you know I find cricket to be such a long and boring game. You will think of my feelings, won't you, Adam?

I'm so looking forward to seeing you soon, my love. Please let me know when you expect to be home. Just think – we can go into Manchester to look at furniture for the house and plan our wedding. It will be wonderful!

Please take care.

Sending you all my love,

Amy xxx

Devon's heart sank. The prospect of a nice little house, a job in a factory and regular dance nights felt so tedious. It wasn't only the flying that he loved; the daily challenges and dangers made him feel alive and passionate about the life he was living. He was quite sure he loved Amy, and many of his friends back in the UK were settling down, but he knew it wasn't for him – not now, at any rate. His letters back home that week would be short and to the point, he decided. Glad to hear everyone is well; congratulations Amy on your new job; say hello to Joan for me. No comments on resigning from the RAF.

Devon jumped up from his bed and grabbed his flying helmet, notepads and pencils. Ten minutes later he was at the briefing with the other pilots, and he had forgotten all about home.

FOURTEEN

As the East Asian summer progressed, one warm, misty morning Devon took his breakfast – a fine spread of egg, bacon and English sausages followed by white toast and Robertson's marmalade and a large mug of strong tea – in the Officers' Mess. The British forces always feed their people well, he thought, and for a few minutes he felt as if he was back in Cranwell. After breakfast there was a briefing on the latest intelligence from the Chinese side of the border. Despite the poor weather conditions, the squadron carried out an uneventful sortie to the south of Stanley, practising in-line strafing attacks on the target ships. After landing, as all was quiet, Devon returned to his quarters. On his desk was a pink envelope from England. He lay on his bunk and opened it.

> *Dear Adam,*
> *I hope you are well. It was so nice to receive your last letter, but I was sorry to see that you didn't mention whether you had resigned. This has helped me to come to a decision about us.*

I wanted to be faithful to you, Adam, but you're so far away and not coming back any time soon... I started going to the dances at the hospital to keep myself busy and meet new people. I met one person there who has become very special to me. His name is Edward and he is training to be a doctor! Such a wonderful profession, don't you think?

I'm very sorry to tell you that I have decided to break off our engagement. Please try not to be too upset; I'm sure you will find someone else if you ever come back to England. I'm so proud of you, and I know you love me, but I hope you can see that this is for the best.

I have returned your engagement ring to your mother. She wasn't at all surprised or upset and very kindly wished me luck. She also said that I should tell you that you'd better hurry up and accept the job at Avro or they won't have you.

With best wishes,

Amy

Devon lay back on his bed and stared at the ceiling. A wave of regret swept over him. Had his reluctance to return to the UK cost him Amy? He closed his eyes to think. He concluded that it might not be too late to win Amy back, and decided to write to her immediately. He sprang up from his bed. "Young, are you there?"

Within ten seconds, Young entered Devon's room. "Yes, sir?"

"Find out when the next post collection is, would you? I need to send an urgent letter home."

"I know the answer to that one, sir: in about an hour from now the Air Mail flight will be leaving."

"Excellent. Come back in half an hour, would you?"

"Yes, sir. Not bad news from home, I hope? Everything fine sir, with the little lady?"

"Well, I don't generally like to share my personal life with the Mess but no, not bad news."

Young's question stopped him in his tracks and sharpened Devon's mind. She can go to blazes, he thought. I'll get by very well without her. He set to writing his letter back. He knew it wouldn't take long. At last he could clearly see what he wanted from life, and it didn't include Amy.

> *Dear Amy,*
>
> *Thank you for your letter. I am, naturally, surprised and upset to hear your news. I had hoped that you would be happy to wait for me, even if it was for a year or two more.*
>
> *I know how much you want to settle down. That is not something I'm looking for at the moment, so if you wish to break off our engagement then that's fine with me.*
>
> *I hope you will be happy with your new admirer.*
>
> *Yours sincerely,*
>
> *Adam*

Young returned promptly after thirty minutes and took the letter to the postal hut next to the Officers' Mess.

"Make sure this gets on the next flight out, would you, Arnold?" said Young. His good friend Arnold Ridgewell was one of the longest-serving members of the squadron. He had joined the RAF in 1930, before many of the younger men were born. He showed profound respect for the officer class, even though he came from a working-class family. The RAF had given him a good life. In recent years he had been assigned to post and communications, and he had an ambition to join the General Post Office after retiring from the service in a year.

"What's the rush?" said Ridgewell.

"Affairs of the heart – please get it out, would you?"

"Ah, I see, important RAF business. I think I can help you there, Steven." He added the letter to the dispatch bag the instant before the Chinese boy working in the office ran out to drop the bag in the aircraft.

FIFTEEN

At the western end of Wan Chai on Hong Kong Island, close to Central, the hotels and bars were upmarket, designed to appeal to a broad international clientele with money to spend. Only a short walk away, business executives or wealthy tourists could enjoy Wan Chai's seedier forms of entertainment: girls, gambling and opium. Many trading companies had smart offices along the northern shore of the island, looking out to the harbour that was the colony's lifeblood and *raison d'être*.

Causeway Construction's premises were at 120 Gloucester Road. The exterior of the building was modern and eye-catching, in a post-war style of concrete and glass that could have been designed by Le Corbusier. It showcased new concepts in architecture that reflected the direction the world was moving in. At six storeys the building stood higher than most of its neighbours. The top floor was recessed at the front, with a small balcony that looked out over the harbour. There was one large room across the front of the building with floor-to-ceiling windows.

In that room, two men quietly conversed. At the head of a large oval boardroom table sat Isaac Golding, the general manager of the London and Hong Kong Bank, in a dark grey suit, white shirt and a blue and red striped tie. To his left was a tall, suntanned, fit-looking man of around thirty five. He had a large scar across his right temple, leading into his hairline. It glared pink in the light streaming in from the window. He was wearing a dark sand-coloured suit and an open-necked white shirt.

"Thank you again, Isaac. It's very helpful to have you working with us."

"We must all do what we can to help, Peter, but please, as soon as your mission is completed let me know. It's vital that the British authorities remain entirely unaware of our connection. For now I will leave you in peace."

The two stood up and shook hands. Golding took a side door out to a private office and shut the door behind him, then a hidden door to the lift lobby to leave the building. Peter Kahn pressed the intercom button and said, "Show our guest in please, Miss Walker."

A much younger man in casual brown slacks and a white short-sleeved shirt entered through the main door to the room. He placed a pile of papers on the table and picked up the top sheet, which had a photograph clipped to it.

"Good morning, David, what do you have for me?" Kahn sat forward.

"This is Flight Lieutenant Henry Fitzjohn. He's been flying for about five years and is highly regarded. Our sources tell us he has applied to retrain on jets but his application was turned down – we don't know why at this stage. We believe he will be interested in continuing to fly. He comes from a wealthy family, but it would appear he has a strong liking for gambling and the high life. Our feeders tell us he doesn't have much luck, so I think the money we are offering could be an incentive."

Kahn picked up the paper and picture. "Not exactly the character we're looking for, but his flying skills are undoubtedly what we need. What does Hannah think?"

"She has only met him for a drink so far, but she believes he is very likely to be willing. She has not yet asked him directly; we're waiting for your approval to do so, sir."

"Then go ahead. Time is of the essence, David. Remind Hannah that she *must* ensure that Fitzjohn maintains absolute secrecy."

"Yes, sir, understood."

"Before you go, do we have any other options?"

"The squadron has many good pilots, sir, but we don't have the same detailed intelligence on any of them that we do for Fitzjohn. He is our only possibility at the moment. We will keep looking." Then David Hartman left the building, feeling at last that he was involved with something that had real purpose, something that would bring him some solace after the death of his parents in the war. Hartman also wanted to do well for personal reasons. This was his first assignment overseas and he had struck lucky. The other agents envied the opportunity he had been given to work for Peter Kahn, perhaps the most successful intelligence officer in the service. At the beginning of the Second World War he had been living in Paris with his English mother and French father, who was Jewish. They escaped to England and Peter quickly signed up for the British Army. Serving in the Parachute Regiment, he rose to the rank of captain and took part in Operation Varsity in March 1945: the crossing of the Rhine and the final push to Berlin. He was badly wounded when a bullet grazed his head and was discharged from the army in 1946. He immediately travelled to Israel, sought to join the army, and was assigned to the intelligence service. Ironically, his role was to monitor the British peacekeeping forces in Palestine. His intelligence and strength of character soon marked him out and within a year he was commanding a team working undercover assessing the threat from Arab countries opposed to the establishment of the State of Israel.

The newly formed Israeli Air Force needed pilots experienced in flying Spitfires. Israel had acquired from Czechoslovakia over twenty Avia S-199s, a modified Messerschmitt Bf-109, which had performed so well for the Germans during the Second World War. However, the modifications made the S-199s difficult to fly and unreliable. Fortunately, they also acquired nearly sixty Spitfires from Czechoslovakia. The Israelis needed to get the Spitfires fully operational to counter the threat from Egypt and other Arab states. Israel absolutely had to achieve air superiority, and that could only be done by engaging foreign pilots. They had already managed to recruit Hugh Gregson, the Canadian, to fly for them.

These pilots would certainly be paid as mercenaries, but if they were also motivated to fight for the cause – the establishment of the independent Israeli state – then so much the better. The Israeli preference was for Jewish pilots from around the world to come forward, as so many others had done to join the Israeli army, but in the meantime the Israeli Secret Service had a mission to seek out and recruit pilots, Jewish or not. Peter Kahn had been sent to Hong Kong to identify any potential recruits – perhaps American, Canadian, Australian or British pilots of fighter squadrons that had been disbanded after the war.

After his training and minor operational roles in Tel Aviv, Hartman was sent to the Causeway Construction offices to link up with Kahn, ostensibly as a trainee surveyor. His real role was to support Hannah Shaw, his fellow secret agent, to identify and recruit pilots.

***

In a small Chinese restaurant in Central, Hannah sat waiting for her contact. It was ten minutes after their agreed time when Hartman dashed in. A warm embrace and smiles all round fulfilled their agreed cover as a young couple in the early stages of romance. It was unlikely that any agency would be watching them, but one moment's relaxation could jeopardise their mission.

After the waiter had departed with their order, Hartman leant forward and spoke in low, clear tones. "Mars wants you to proceed." Hartman used Peter Kahn's codename in public places. "As soon as you can, approach Fitzjohn and make the proposition. You can offer $1,000 immediately, $5,000 on arrival at the office."

Hannah knew he meant the airfield in Israel.

"And $5,000 per month. US dollars, of course. Take this book – the first $1,000 is in the back." Hartman pushed a bound volume on Asian flowers across to Hannah. She picked it up and after admiring the first few pages, placed it in the document case she regularly carried to and from the bank.

"I'm meeting Fitzjohn on Friday evening," said Hannah. "He has asked me out for dinner. If the circumstances are right, with your permission I shall make an offer. You and I can meet for coffee on Saturday morning to debrief at the Star Ferry terminus in Central, if that's OK with you?"

"Yes, on both counts. I'll see you at ten o'clock on Saturday. I will brief Mars in the afternoon. Remember that secrecy is vital. If Fitzjohn can't be trusted, then don't bring him in."

SIXTEEN

Hannah had arrived in Hong Kong on her twenty-second birthday to take up the role of marketing officer in the London and Hong Kong Bank. She kept her deep brown hair a touch longer than shoulder length, and straight and natural. Hannah was not one for following popular trends, and disliked curls and high shapes. She looked more experienced and sophisticated than her real age; she could have been mistaken for being in her late twenties. She was slim and well-shaped and above average height for a woman.

When she smiled, the right side of her mouth curled, and a matching line appeared on her cheek. Her laughter was short and restrained. Her full lips usually had a light touch of pink lipstick; she avoided the current fashion for ruby red, knowing that her natural beauty needed no such enhancements. Her dress sense was refined and flattering to her figure. As clothing restrictions after the war were easing, she wore a good-quality cotton suit and often a silk blouse to the office. Out of work, her leisure clothes would not look out of place on a luxury cruise liner. Today she had changed at the office into a demure scarlet dress for dinner.

Hannah loved music and ballroom dancing. Her favourite ballroom dances were quickstep and foxtrot, but she was also adept at Latin dances like the rumba and polka. Her dance style was fluid but not showy or extravagant. She danced with elegance and a natural poise.

At 6 p.m. sharp Hannah took the lift to the ground floor of the bank's offices in Central. She had half-expected Fitzjohn to be waiting for her, since the date had been his idea, but he wasn't there. She waited patiently. After twenty minutes he strolled into the lobby and smiled at Hannah.

"Good evening, Hannah. I hope all is well with you, my dear?" There was no apology for being late.

"I'm fine, thank you. How are you?" Hannah held out her hand but Fitzjohn leant forward and kissed her on the neck, just below her right ear. Hannah suppressed a shudder. He was not an unattractive man, but she did not feel any desire to get close to him.

"I'm in good shape, thank you. I have a taxi waiting for us outside, and I have booked the Peak Vista restaurant," Fitzjohn said with a flourish. Hannah was clearly supposed to be delighted with his choice of venue – and indeed, she had to admit that she was excited to be going to one of the best restaurants on the island. The view across the harbour from the Peak tonight would be wonderful: the air was clear and warm with the gentlest of breezes. The Peak Vista restaurant served Chinese food with a British or Continental twist. The restaurant owners knew that the subdued lighting, candles on the tables and a good wine list would attract people who wanted to impress or visit somewhere upmarket for a special occasion.

Hannah chose a chicken fricassee with steamed rice and bok choy. Fitzjohn showed off his knowledge of good food and ordered a bluefin tuna steak, cooked rare, with roasted lemon potatoes and shimeji mushrooms.

"Would you like a G&T?" Fitzjohn asked.

"That would be nice, thank you."

"And a bottle of Moselle to follow." Fitzjohn did not pose this as a question. Hannah smiled politely but knew she had to be careful; she wasn't used to excessive alcohol.

Hannah started off with a question she felt would give Fitzjohn plenty to talk about – himself. "Tell me, Henry, where are your family in England? Where did you grow up?"

She was right. Fitzjohn took Hannah through his school years, life on the family estate, his sporting achievements and his selection for the RAF.

"I have never felt that my role in life is to take over the running of the estate; my brothers are more than capable. I look for a little more adventure. I love flying, of course, and hope to make a career out of it when I return to England, either continuing in the RAF or commercially. But perhaps after that I'll do something in the City. I've heard it's quite fun to be a Lloyd's underwriter, or perhaps I'll work for a bank. Maybe even the London and Hong Kong! Trouble is, these options sound so dull – you know, office life. Ha! No disrespect to you, of course."

"Well, it's not so bad." Hannah steered the conversation back to flying. "What made you want to join the RAF?"

"A friend of my father was the CO at the RAF base at Duxford during the war, not far from home. They had Hurricanes and Spitfires and Douglas Bader's famous Big Wing. I was allowed to visit the airfield, and got hooked. It was quite a sight to see over sixty fighters forming up to give the German bombers hell.

"When I was nineteen, in 1945, Father's pal took me up in an Anson that was used for flying senior officers around. I was given a go at the controls. The CO recommended that I join up – saw that I had the right attributes. After pilot training I asked to join a Spitfire squadron, and via Penang and Singapore that's how 28 Squadron came to be here."

Hannah smiled. "What sort of flying would you be interested in after the RAF?"

"I applied for a jet conversion course." Fitzjohn did not add that he had been rejected. "Some of the commercial work could be interesting – you know, flying doctor in Australia, transatlantic stuff perhaps."

"Can't you stay with 28 Squadron?"

"Not in the long term. In a year, possibly less, the squadron will be disbanded. Or it might join with another; no one can be sure at this stage. Peacetime armed forces are kept to the minimum and many service personnel are being sent home to face a new life in merry England. Of course, it's not so merry nowadays with all the industrial turmoil and no one wanting to be part of the working class anymore."

"What do you mean?" said Hannah.

"Back on the estate at home it's nigh on impossible to get labourers, pigmen and tractor drivers. We need a new land army, and that's likely to made up of displaced Europeans who will work for a sack of potatoes a week and a tied cottage."

"There will always be a need for RAF pilots, won't there?"

"Yes, my dear, naturally, but the question is how much longer Spitfires will be in use."

"There are other countries with Spitfires in their air forces." Hannah was about to get to her point when the restaurant door opened and a group of six young women bustled in, smiling and laughing – they had probably had a drink or two before arriving. The owner greeted the guests and escorted them to their table. The first woman was clearly the organiser and instructed the others where to sit. When they had done so, she glanced across at Hannah and Fitzjohn. A look of recognition swept across her face, and she walked over to the couple. "Why, Hannah, how nice to see you, and with a friend…"

"Oh, hello, Agnes, nice to see you. This is Flight Lieutenant Henry Fitzjohn. Henry, Agnes and the others work at the bank."

"Pleased to meet you, Henry." Agnes gave her best smile and fluttered her eyelashes. "The girls and I are treating ourselves to a special meal. It's Pamela's twenty-first today! Now, I had better leave you happy couple in peace. Enjoy your evening."

"Nice lady," said Fitzjohn, not moving his gaze away from Agnes's rear view as she walked away.

This is unfortunate, Hannah thought. There's no chance of making the contract proposal to Fitzjohn with the office girls within earshot. I'll have to shelve the plan for the time being. She directed the conversation to harmless subjects.

The meal was delicious. As they looked at the dessert menu, Fitzjohn said, "You live on Hong Kong Island, presumably? Where exactly?"

"Mid-Levels. In fact, we passed my house on the way up here. The bank provides accommodation for expat staff. It's a small villa but very comfortable, in one of the nicest districts on the island."

"Splendid! We can finish off here then go and have a nightcap at your place."

Hannah was shaken. She hadn't been inviting Fitzjohn to her house; he had hijacked the discussion and invited himself. Given the mission she was on, she bit her lip and said nothing. Perhaps after dessert and coffee he would realise that he had been too forward in suggesting the visit on their first date. She convinced herself that he was simply being friendly and she should go along with the idea of a last drink before the end of the evening. Of course, she might be able to offer him a flying role in Israel in the privacy of her home...

Fitzjohn paid the bill and asked the waiter to arrange a taxi for them. As they stepped outside, the sounds of birds and insects chirping filled the air. They could see the security lights around Kai Tak Airfield across in Kowloon.

"What time does your evening pass expire?" Hannah asked.

"I have a two-day pass, so no rush. Might just stay on the island tonight."

The ride down the hill to Mid-Levels took less than ten minutes. The house was one of a group of four small single-storey villas on the hill above Government House. It was convenient for the office and a short walk to the Hong Kong Botanical Gardens, which had become one of Hannah's favourite places to relax. Hannah opened the door and switched on the hall lights, then went through to the living room to switch all the lights on. She did not want to create any feeling of warmth or intimacy.

"Very nice, Hannah. Why don't you show me around?"

Hannah duly led Fitzjohn from the living room through to the kitchen and dining area and back into the hall. She waved her hand to two closed doors. "Those are the bedrooms."

Fitzjohn stepped past her and opened the first bedroom door, to Hanna's bedroom. As he returned to the living room he said, "Very cosy indeed. So, what's in the drinks cabinet? Do you have any Scotch?"

"No, just gin and tonic."

"That would be splendid."

Hannah carried the bottles into the kitchen and took down glasses from a high shelf. Suddenly Fitzjohn came up behind her and wrapped his arms around her waist. She froze. "Hey, enough of that! I'm not that sort of girl. Go back into the living room and wait for your drink."

"Ha, ha, yes indeed. Be a good boy, Henry!" Fitzjohn sounded mocking. Hannah knew he had every intention of not being a good boy.

Hannah poured the drinks – gin for Fitzjohn and just a tonic water for herself. Fitzjohn stood at the window that faced the sea, swaying a little. Hannah joined him.

"This is a beautiful spot, my dear," he said. After a long pull on his drink, he placed the glass on the windowsill and turned to face Hannah. Smoothly he took her arms and kissed her briefly on the lips, then again, more passionately. His hands moved up her back to pull her closer to him. Hannah resisted, leaning away from him.

"Henry, sit down. There's something I want to talk to you about." Hannah took her normal seat, at the end of the settee nearest the window.

"Come on now, little lady, there's nothing wrong with getting to know each other and having a bit of fun." Fitzjohn sat next to her and placed an arm around her shoulder. He pulled her roughly towards him and kissed her again, then put one hand on her knee and pulled her skirt upwards. Hannah jumped up in shock. "Henry, no! I didn't invite you here for this. In fact, *you* invited yourself here. Leave me alone and listen."

"Not so fast. We can talk later."

Hannah backed away, but Fitzjohn advanced towards her. She stepped into the hall, with the aim of getting out of the front door, but Fitzjohn grabbed her wrist and pulled her into the bedroom. He pushed her onto the bed then threw off his jacket and gave her a lewd grin. "Don't be so shy, Hannah, let's enjoy ourselves." He climbed onto the bed and ran his hand up Hannah's inside thigh. She sat up and slapped his face, making him jump back. Panting, Fitzjohn sat astride her. He grabbed both her arms in one hand and with the other pulled at the shoulder of her dress, snapping off three of the buttons. Hannah struggled wildly and finally managed to tip him off her. She rolled off the bed onto the floor and, sitting up, grabbed the alarm clock from the bedside cabinet. She knew the heavy old clock would make a useful weapon. She scrambled to her feet and threw it at Fitzjohn. His reactions were quick. He ducked, and the clock crashed against the wall behind him. The noise seemed to snap Fitzjohn out of his crazed behaviour. "Bloody hell, girl, you could have killed me!"

"Don't be stupid, Henry. Get out of my house."

"Now don't be hasty…"

"Get out now! Pick up your clothes and get out."

Fitzjohn slammed the front door behind him in a final show of petulance. Hannah sat on the edge of the bed, shaking. Tears welled in her eyes. She was glad that her secret service training had included elementary unarmed combat; it had helped her to keep her head and manage the situation. She told herself the incident was the price she paid for the work she had to do. How was she to know that Fitzjohn would be such an animal?

***

Hannah slept badly, fearing that Fitzjohn would return. Knowing that was not logical or likely did not assuage her concerns. The next day, after rising she showered quickly and left the house. She took the paths through the botanical gardens, allowing the beautiful flowers, plants and birds to calm her, then she walked down the quiet road to Central and the café at the Star Ferry terminal. She had an hour to wait for David Hartman. She picked up a copy of the *Hong Kong Telegraph* conveniently provided by the café for customers. Barely able to concentrate, she flicked through the pages, noticing references to further British troops arriving to reinforce the garrison and an article highlighting the Dior influence on fashion trends this year. She looked at the cinema listing for the Alhambra – anything to distract her from the discussion she had to have with Hartman.

Hartman arrived promptly at ten, bought his coffee at the counter and joined Hannah. "You look awful. What's wrong?"

Hannah choked and couldn't speak for a moment.

"It was awful, David. Fitzjohn tried to force himself on me. He took me to the Peak Vista restaurant for dinner, but it was too busy for me to talk there – there were girls from the office. We went to my house, he was drunk, and he pushed me into the bedroom."

Hartman sat up straighter. "And … and … did he…?"

"No, no. I fought him off and ordered him out of the house. I'm glad to say he went, but it was awful. I was so frightened and sickened. He might have thought I was willing, as I had allowed him to come back to the house. And I failed miserably in the assignment. I'm so sorry."

"Don't apologise, Hannah. You – we – couldn't have known he was such a shit. I will report back to Mars. In the meantime, if Fitzjohn contacts you, have nothing to do with him. I will come to your house this evening to check you're OK. Now, I'll get you another coffee and stay with you for a while."

SEVENTEEN

The commanding officer at Kai Tak Airfield was concerned about 28 Squadron's ability to halt a sudden and massive attack by the Chinese, should they advance simultaneously across the land and down the Pearl River estuary. The squadron's deterrent factor depended on keeping their presence and capabilities very clearly in the minds of the Chinese, with regular patrols within their sight and sound and regularly practising bombing and strafing techniques. The Royal Navy's small contingent in Hong Kong worked wonders in commandeering old and worthless shipping from around the harbour, which they towed out to sea to be used for target practice.

There was some form of patrol most days – sometimes a low-level sweep up the border of the New Territories and China, at other times providing close support to British ground troops, coordinating with their exercises. At least once a week the whole squadron exercised together in a show of strength and firepower. This week would see three days of continuous operations, starting on Monday, when three sections of aircraft would have different tasks: patrolling Victoria Harbour, low-level flying over the Pearl River, and simulated ground attacks in the New Territories. On Tuesday there would be live firing target practice south of Stanley Harbour, creating what Squadron Leader Porter called a 'loud show'. Wednesday would see the squadron of twelve aircraft operating together as a single fighting unit.

Planning and briefing took place in the pilots' operations room. The CO gave the orders for those flying that day, and a political update on the situation on the mainland. Most of the pilots cared little for the politics, but relished the flying. Conditions were often difficult, with a thick sea fog rolling in from the South China Sea and a general haze due to the humid conditions across the whole region. And as the pilots knew, severe storms and typhoons were always a possibility. It was vital that every pilot knew the area like the back of his hand to avoid becoming disorientated.

On Wednesday morning, Porter gave the briefing. He pointed at the large-scale map of the area. "Today's mission will involve the whole squadron in three flights of four aircraft, each in a V of three with one following astern. I will lead Red Section, Flight Lieutenant Devon Blue Section and Flight Lieutenant Fitzjohn Green Section. And I want to see first-rate formation flying. As usual, we can expect to be observed by Chinese agents throughout the exercise – so let's not display any sloppiness. We will be fully armed, of course, with full machine-gun and cannon canisters and four under-wing bombs." He picked up a piece of paper from the desk. "The Met forecast is not good – heavy low cloud, high humidity and ground mist. Difficult flying conditions, that much is certain, but nothing we haven't trained for." He turned back to the chart. "We will form up out at sea, here, about a mile west of Stanley on the southern tip of Hong Kong Island. The Met people say we will climb out of the clag at about 2,500 feet. From there we will turn right, pass over Lamma Island and continue to Lantau. We will avoid the Po Lin

Monastery by passing half a mile south of it, and then comes the interesting bit. We turn north here…" He pointed to the western end of the colony. "Then we follow the Pearl River along the border, staying on our side. At the eastern end of the New Territories we will turn 180 degrees and reverse our route back to Kai Tak. This is an exercise, but defence of the river will be key should there be an invasion, so let's make sure we're well acquainted with the area. If we get separated, do not, I repeat, *do not* cross the border into China. You know your orders: no attacks on any perceived or actual enemy unless I specifically say so. Is that clear?"

All pilots responded with a quiet but clear, "Yes, sir."

"Right. We take off in forty minutes. Prepare your equipment, chaps, and remember that we will be carrying personal sidearms on this exercise – Browning 9mm. If we need to make an emergency landing in Chinese territory, we have to be able to defend ourselves if required until we are extracted by the ground forces. The armourers will hand you your weapons as you emplane."

Each pilot wore their white overalls at the briefing. Before they climbed into the aircraft they all put on their Mae West lifejackets and buckled the pistol holster at the right of their waist. Their mission kneepads containing the key flight information for the exercise were ready to be fastened to their right thigh when in the aircraft. A leather helmet incorporated the headphones and microphone for the radio. The pilots stepped into their cockpits. The aircraftmen standing on the wing helped them strap into their parachutes, which formed part of the seat. Then they fastened the harness that secured them in the aircraft. Each pilot kept their Spitfire's canopy open as long as possible so they would not overheat in the intense sun. They went through their start-up checklist, ensuring that their aircraft was airworthy prior to starting the engine. Flight Lieutenant Devon was a stickler for complying with the correct procedures – he knew it was better to identify a problem on the ground than in the air. He insisted that all pilots in his flight diligently carried out the checks before every flight and confirmed that they were good to go.

"Blue Section leader here, confirm start-up checks."

Matt Black was the first to respond. "Checks completed and ready to go, sir."

Then the two other pilots in Devon's flight confirmed that their checks had been completed. Excellent, thought Devon. At least we don't have any unserviceable aircraft. Then he heard over the radio that Fitzjohn's Green Section was likewise ready to depart.

"28 leader in good shape and ready to roll. Blue Section, lead the way after start," Squadron Leader Porter said over the radio.

A red light was switched on at the dispersal hut signalling the instruction to start up.

Calls of "Clear prop!" sounded across the tarmac as the pilots warned the ground crews that they were about to start. The Spitfires' Griffon engines fired into life. A burst of flame and blue smoke snaked back from the exhaust outlets as the mechanics took away the wheel chocks and the pilots held the aircraft in position on the brakes. They ran through after-start checks then powered up the engines to operating temperature and checked all flight surfaces – the ailerons, tailplane and rudder – for free movement. Devon taxied his flight out to the runway threshold and the aircraft took off in pairs, initially climbing straight ahead before flying over Hong Kong Island.

The haze was worse than they had expected. The pilots used their flight instruments to keep the aircraft straight and in a steady climb. When they passed 2,000 feet, visibility improved. The section leaders could clearly see an aircraft on each wing and the fourth aircraft behind, in the mirror fixed to the outside of the windscreen at head height.

Porter looked round to see the whole squadron in a tight formation, cruising south over Stanley Harbour. "Standby for starboard turn. Turning now."

All the aircraft made the right turn simultaneously, maintaining the shape of the formation, and headed for Lamma Island. Porter led the aircraft over the island and with Lantau Island in sight ahead held the direction until the distinctive shape of Po Lin Monastery was 45 degrees to their right. The monastery, a shrine to Buddhism, with its beautiful terracotta roof tiles, made an excellent visual reference point. Out of respect, and to avoid disturbing the monks with the noise of the twelve Griffon engines, the squadron flew south of the monastery. In poor visibility conditions the high ground surrounding the monastery was an ever-present danger to the pilots.

As the squadron approached the western end of the island, Porter gave an order: "Descend to 1,000 feet, maintaining a heading of 330 degrees." This brought the aircraft down into the sea mist, again reducing visibility to less than half a mile. Good formation flying was just about possible with each pilot keeping a close eye on those around him. The risk of a collision was very real. Porter ordered a further descent to 500 feet and a turn to the right for a flight along the Pearl River estuary and up to the Chinese border. In a few minutes they had reached the end point of the exercise.

"On my order, turn to starboard, 180 degrees. Stand by." A few moments passed. "Turning," said Porter.

Again, in good formation, the twelve Spitfires banked to the right. As they turned, the sea mist became a sheet of white cotton wool draped across the cockpit. The morning sun was now directly in their eyes, making forward visibility through the illuminated fog almost impossible. But with reference to their compass direction and known height, the route back through the islands should be straightforward.

As they approached the western tip of the colony, they met with low cumulus clouds.

"Steady 170 degrees, climb to 2,000 feet." Porter's instructions were aimed at keeping the formation in shape and climbing over Lantau Island.

Porter's flight was in the centre of the group, with Devon's to the left and Fitzjohn's to the right. There was barely enough lateral visibility to see each other in the formation. The greatest difficulty was for the pilot flying astern of each group, who carried the risk of running into the aircraft in front. At the north coast of Lantau Island the rising ground pushed up the wind off the mainland, helping further, denser clouds to form. Porter looked in his mirror for Pilot Jameson, who should have been behind him.

"Jameson, where are you? Do you have eyes on me?"

Silence, then: "No, sir, uncertain of position, looking out."

"Do you have land in sight?"

"I … I'm … I'm not sure, sir."

This was dangerous. Jameson could run into anyone in the formation. Porter decided to break up the group into three units to provide some protection.

"Blue Section, break to port and take up an orbit one mile west. Green Section, break to starboard for one mile. Jameson, position report." Porter kept calm: he knew the pilot would be stressed and did not want to add further tension.

"North coast of Lantau, sir. I'm not sure … I'm in cloud."

"Height?"

"Eight hundred feet, heading 170 degrees."

Jameson had clearly descended to try to get sight of land so he could fix his position. What the hell is he doing? thought Porter. "Climb, Jameson, climb, to at least 2,000 feet. High ground ahead." Then he shouted into the radio. "Climb, man! Look out for the hills straight ahead!"

Losing the squadron, afraid of crashing into the hillside, Jameson froze in panic. He could barely think straight and fly the aircraft. Desperately he tried to snap out of his trance. "Climb, climb," he repeated out loud. Before he could pull back the control column, the forested peak of Lantau Island filled his windscreen. Jameson's eyes widened in horror and he automatically wrenched the column back, but he was too late. The Spitfire slammed into the dense jungle at 300 mph. Its wings were ripped off and its nose dug hard into the ground, pushing the massive engine backwards into the fuselage. Jameson was killed instantly.

***

"Kai Tak operations, this is Squadron Leader Porter. Come in, over."

"Go ahead, sir." The ground radio operator sounded calm.

"Aircraft down, Lantau Island, north side. Likely fatality. Get the emergency team there as quickly as possible. Squadron returning to base. Out."

"Yes, sir! Message received." The radio operator immediately pressed the red airfield alarm button to summon the crash recovery team. They were quickly apprised of the situation and called for the waterborne rescue craft to make all speed to the island and to start the journey into the hills to recover the pilot and the remains of the aircraft.

The rest of the squadron heard the radio transmissions. They were shocked at Jameson's fate. Porter kept calm. "Blue and Green Sections, proceed direct to Kai Tak and land. Red Section, follow me."

To give the two sections time and space to approach and land, Porter took his own group in a wide arc out to the Pearl River before curving round towards Stanley and across Hong Kong Island. As he landed, he could see that all the aircraft were back safely and parked in their usual positions. He instructed the men to get their flying kit off and complete their logbook entries.

An hour later the pilots filed into the ops room. Porter stood on the low platform. The mood was sombre; there was no banter or jokes among the men. After ten years service as a fighter pilot, including the war, Porter had seen the effect that the death of a fellow pilot had on the others: it was impossible to predict who would shake off the mental impact and who would break down. But an accident such as the one they had witnessed would rattle all the pilots.

"Men, take a seat, please. Clearly, this is a very unfortunate business."

Pilot Tom Forrester put his hand up. Without waiting to be given permission to speak, he asked, "What happened, sir?"

Porter knew that Forrester was a close friend of Jameson and would be feeling the shock more than most.

"It would seem that Jameson lost positional awareness in the cloud and crashed into the hill at Lantau. There will be a formal investigation, as you know. For now, we will assume it was a pilot navigation error." Porter had his own suspicions. He felt it likely that Jameson had frozen under the stress of not having visual contact with the ground. His mistake – commonly made by pilots – had been to descend to identify his position, forgetting about the high ground ahead. Sometimes the ability to think and react effectively disappear when a pilot is experiencing severe anxiety. No amount of training can prepare a pilot for the mental impact of a deadly situation.

"What we do know is that there was no enemy action. We don't want any suggestion that Jameson's aircraft was damaged in any way or brought down by ground fire. We can expect the Chinese to try to gain capital from the incident, and they may even claim to have shot the aircraft down. Nonsense, of course, but that's propaganda. Be prepared to be interviewed by the station intelligence team, but do not, I repeat *do not*, discuss the incident with other ranks, services or of course the newspaper men. All leave is cancelled for the next forty-eight hours. Do not leave the station; you are all in lockdown. Any questions?"

"Will we be continuing operations, sir, while the investigation is under way?" asked Devon.

"Certainly. In fact, I want you and Flight Lieutenant Fitzjohn to plan two sorties for tomorrow – you along the Pearl River estuary, Devon, and you to the northern border of the New Territories, Fitzjohn. Flights of three aircraft. Fully armed again – let's show those who have an interest that the loss of one Spitfire doesn't change our capabilities. No more? Then that will be all."

The pilots walked slowly out onto the tarmac. Devon went to his room and took down his writing paper. He would need to write to his mother urgently. Devon was in no doubt that the incident would be reported in the press in the UK, and he wanted to calm his mother's concerns. An operational fighter squadron must take calculated risks, and sometimes the worst happens. There was no time for the pilots to have a long-lasting emotional response to the crash; they just had to get a grip and crack on.

EIGHTEEN

During the Japanese occupation in the war, the freedom of the Hong Kong people was severely curtailed. One of their primary occupations was gambling, which continued behind closed doors – in houses, flats, gambling dens and in the workrooms of the factories. When Hong Kong was liberated, the gambling cartel bosses moved in and took over many of the gambling houses. The man in the street could easily be attracted into dice and card games that required little skill and very small bets. But the aim of the dens was to make the game addictive: over time, gamblers would place bigger and more bets as they tried to recover their inevitable losses.

Back home, most of the British military personnel had indulged in gambling to some extent, from a flutter on the Grand National to doing the weekly football pools. In Hong Kong the servicemen's evenings out often consisted of some street food and beers, and a bit of fun with the dice.

The gambling houses vied for the business of the armed forces, who often had money to spare and looked for the more salubrious clubs.

Establishments with good-looking hostesses dressed in form-fitting silk dresses were the most popular.

The men of 28 Squadron liked to meet the other servicemen from the navy, army and colonial forces. While during the day the squadron personnel were commanded by their senior officers, the other ranks led the social activities, unrestrained by the formality of military hierarchy.

Squadron Leader Porter and Flight Lieutenants Devon and Fitzjohn occasionally accompanied the men on nights out, knowing that morale is enhanced in units where the senior officers are seen as human. They were, of course, expected to show restraint and not to get drunk or mesmerised by the dice and make fools of themselves. Fitzjohn was always the first to accept an invitation to go for an evening's gambling, whereas Porter and Devon were more reticent. A busy week of flying then the lockdown had built up the men's thirst for drinks and socialising.

"What's it to be tonight, Watkins? The Green Lotus?" Leading Aircraftman Joe Cootes called across the tarmac to Aircraftman Mike Watkins.

"Yeah, maybe, Cootesy. Let's start with a couple of drinks at the Kowloon Hotel bar. We might meet up with the Aussies – they're always a laugh. Then we can go from there. Fitzjohn is joining us at the airfield gates."

"Good show, mate!" Cootes' poor Australian accent made Watkins smile.

The night proved to be one of the best outings the men had enjoyed. The Green Lotus was a smart drinking club, with gambling in a room through a discreet side door. Three of the men had made good winnings at the blackjack tables and treated everyone to rounds of whisky. As midnight approached, the group knew it was time to get back to the airfield before the guardhouse clock struck twelve, and started to drift back in threes and fours. To be late would mean breaching their evening pass conditions, and that would lead to being grounded on the station for a week, or worse, or being charged with being absent without leave.

Devon had spent the early part of the evening in the Officers' Mess. The topics discussed were the same as every evening – what the Chinese forces might be up to and what the future held for the squadron. There was little expectation that the Chinese would attack Hong Kong now, and each man had his own thoughts on his future air force career. Devon took his leave early, wanting to spend an hour or two with his gramophone records before turning in.

In the silence of the middle of the night, Devon was jolted into consciousness by a strong hand vigorously shaking his shoulder. "What the hell is it, Young?"

"Sir, there's trouble. Flight Lieutenant Fitzjohn has gone missing. He didn't return with the chaps last night and there's talk he may have gone AWOL."

"Nonsense, Young – not very likely, is it? Who told you this?"

"Flight Fitzjohn's orderly, sir. Mackie." Young spoke quickly.

Devon climbed out of bed and dressed fast. "Get Mackie here and a couple of the other men who were with you last night. We're going to look for him. I'll speak to the night security officer, get passes for us and borrow a truck."

The group were soon cruising the streets of central Kowloon, looking into side alleys and doorways. Then Devon had a thought. "Young, where did you end up last night?"

"At the Green Lotus, sir."

"Right, let's go there."

Charlie Zhang, the owner, feigned surprise when the RAF contingent knocked hard on the door of the now closed club. Without waiting to be invited, the men strode in. Devon immediately saw Fitzjohn, passed out on a red velvet banquette, an empty whisky glass on the table in front of him.

"Mr Fiss very nice man – we look after him!" Zhang was clearly frightened and keen to make his peace with the airmen. "He have good time, play dice, plenty drinks, now sleep."

Three other Chinese Hong Kong men stood to one side of Fitzjohn. Devon thought they looked like a father and two sons. They said nothing and were obviously ready for a fight.

Devon shook his head, then gestured at two airmen. "You two, help him up and out to the truck. Heave him into the back." His tone indicated his anger at having to rescue a drunk officer – and from a gambling outfit to boot. He turned to Zhang. "What is he doing here, and who are these people?"

The man froze and glanced at the central figure in the group of three.

"Mr Fiss have good time, he like drinks and dice," he stuttered.

Devon looked at the three men and knew that something was wrong. Had Fitzjohn been enjoying a late drink with gambling friends, or had he been held here by these people? They were probably carrying knives, and Devon wasn't there for a brawl.

"Right, Young, let's go."

As the truck approached the airfield gates Devon leant out of the window. "Flight Lieutenant Devon and party returning."

The guards made no effort to open the barrier. An RAF Regiment sergeant emerged from the guardhouse – not the same man who had given the group passes an hour ago. "You're very late, sir. Mind if I ask where you have been?"

"Into Kowloon. One of our squadron members was taken ill. We have been to the hospital to collect him." Devon knew the story was far-fetched, but had to stick to it. "Turned out to be something dodgy he had eaten. He's OK now, they cleaned him out." Devon added a look of disgust to emphasise the point.

"Rather unfortunate, sir." The sergeant didn't sound at all

convinced. He walked round to the back of the truck and peered in. Fitzjohn was slumped on a bench seat, snoring gently.

There was little the guard could do; he couldn't argue with Devon. After a moment he called to the private on the barrier, "Right, open the gates, let them in."

"Thank you, Sergeant."

***

Devon woke in the morning with a feeling of dread. He called Young for his coffee.

"Where's Fitzjohn?"

"Still in his bed, sir, safe and sound," replied Young.

"Good. Keep last night's episode to yourself and tell Mackie and the other men to do the same. We may be able to keep a lid on this, otherwise Fitzjohn's for the high jump."

"Yes, sir."

As Young hurried out of the room, Devon reflected on the night's events and the sinister group at the gambling house. He would have a chat with Fitzjohn as soon as he returned to the land of the living. At around 10 a.m. Fitzjohn surfaced, pale and with a pounding headache, and called his orderly. "Mackie, what the hell happened last night? How did I get back?"

"A few of the lads and I came back to the Green Lotus to pick you up. It was about three o'clock, sir. You were a bit far gone, and we thought you could be up for an AWOL charge." Mackie went to leave.

Fitzjohn barked at him, his hangover giving him a worse temper than usual. "You just strolled out of the station and picked me up – is that what happened?"

"Well, sir, Flight Lieutenant Devon organised everything. He got us the passes and talked our way back into the station."

"Oh, great. Devon was in on it, was he? No doubt he will have informed the squadron leader."

"No, sir, we've all been told to keep mum."

"Then keep it that way, Mackie. Where is Devon?"

"In his quarters, I believe, sir."

An hour later Fitzjohn knocked on Devon's door and entered before he could respond.

"Ah, Fitzjohn, good to see you up and about. Feeling well?"

"No, I am not," Fitzjohn snapped. "But a word, please. Mackie tells me you're keeping a wrap on last night's episode. Well, good show."

Devon knew that a straight thank you from Fitzjohn was unlikely, but he didn't care.

"Tell me, Fitzjohn, what happened? Who were the unfriendlies in the club? A bunch of bandits looking to make trouble, it seemed to me. What was going on?"

"It's no concern of yours, Devon, but there was a misunderstanding over a couple of wagers. They seemed to believe I was unable to honour my line of credit. Nonsense, of course, but they insisted I continued to enjoy the club's hospitality until I gave them the cash they were looking for. I explained I had exhausted my immediate monetary resources and they thought they could hold an RAF officer to ransom, silly sods."

"You'd better get back there and clear this up. If you owe them money, then pay up – those heavies will want this matter settled or they'll come after you."

"There's nothing to settle; it was all a mistake. I would be obliged if you would not interfere with something that does not concern you." Fitzjohn spun on his heel and marched out of Devon's room.

But Fitzjohn knew he had to clear the debt, and the only way was to go back and hope for a change in his luck. Simple, really. He'd had a losing streak. That would soon change and everyone would be happy.

***

Squadron Leader Porter was sitting at his desk when Captain Robson knocked on the door.

"Good morning, sir. Mind if I disturb you for a moment?" said Robson.

"No, not at all, Captain, come in. How can I help the military police?"

"Unfortunately, one of your men overstayed his late pass last night and had to be brought back in the early hours by Flight Lieutenant Devon and a small group of helpers. The party in question was Flight Lieutenant Fitzjohn. Devon gave the gatehouse a cock-and-bull story about Fitzjohn being unwell and being treated at the hospital. But we know that he didn't attend the hospital – we checked. The sergeant on the gate was convinced that Fitzjohn was drunk and incapable. We do not plan to take any action, sir, we will leave that to you, but I would ask you to keep better order among the men. Being absent without leave is a serious business."

Porter stood up, frowning at the news. "Yes, indeed. Thank you for advising me, Captain. I will ensure that the matter is noted."

"Thank you, sir. As I said, Flight Lieutenant Devon was one of the men who brought Fitzjohn back. Very disappointing behaviour from an officer on such an important matter." Robson saluted and marched himself out of the office. Porter knew Fitzjohn's behaviour was serious but decided to take no action other than adding a note to his staff file. Inwardly he smiled and admired Devon's initiative; he had been a good officer and colleague who had saved Fitzjohn from a sticky situation.

NINETEEN

Fitzjohn decided against the usual Wednesday night trip to Happy Valley, slipped quietly out of camp and took a taxi into Kowloon. After a couple of whiskies in the Peninsula Hotel bar, he ambled nonchalantly, hands in pockets, up Nathan Road. A few minutes later he took a left turn, then turned right and stopped twenty yards from the Green Lotus door. The lights were on and Hong Kong Chinese and western clients were filing in to be greeted by Zhang. After some hesitation, wondering if it was a good idea, he stepped up to the door.

"Mr Fiss, so nice to see you! Welcome, drinks on house. Come in! Bobby, take Mr Fiss to best seats."

A uniformed teenager scampered ahead of Fitzjohn and directed him to a secluded table. The waiter came with a whisky, a bottle of spring water and ice cubes. Bowls of Chinese delicacies were laid on the table. Fitzjohn pushed them away, local food was not his style. But he liked the VIP treatment. He felt he deserved some respect from these people, given his status in society back home. His concerns about the gambling debt soon disappeared. He was confident the Green Lotus would extend his credit, which would allow him to win his money back.

The dice can't keep working against me – stands to reason. It was all a silly misunderstanding, he said to himself.

Zhang came over to his table. "Mr Fiss, you want some fun tonight, game of dice maybe? Good omens for you tonight!"

"Very well, Zhang, it would be my pleasure to attend your tables. Get me another drink and I'll be with you."

Fitzjohn was escorted into the rear room and as before was charmed by the quality of the fittings, the lovely girls and the wealthy and sophisticated clientele – mostly Chinese but with a few westerners, some of the banking and commercial types he had seen at the Peninsula. The atmosphere was heady and enticing.

Initially, luck was with him. As the drinks flowed, however, his thought processes floated away and he lost track of the amount he thought he had won. But he had slipped into losing again, and continued to sign credit cheques. As time passed, he had just enough sense to stand up and bid goodnight to his fellow guests and head for the door. As he stepped back into the bar, the three Chinese men from the previous evening took his arms, marched him into the manager's office and unceremoniously dumped him in a chair.

"What the hell?" Fitzjohn gazed in astonishment at the three men.

Zhang followed them in. His pretence of gushing friendliness had disappeared. "Mr Fiss, you owe my friends five hundred dollars, US. They want payment now. They no like people who not pay debt. You not that kind of guy, are you? Believe me, you must pay now or they—"

"Or they what? You're talking rubbish – now let me out of here. I'm not having this, it's outrageous. You can't hold a member of the British forces. Five hundred dollars? You must be crazy!" Fitzjohn made to stand up, but the older of the thugs stood over him aggressively.

Fitzjohn sat down again. "Look here, I can get the money. It will just take a little time."

The youngest of the three men crossed his hands in front of him, wordlessly showing Fitzjohn the six-inch blade he held.

"Mr Fiss, they don't want to hurt you, but you must pay now!" The manager pulled a sorry face. "Or they cut you bad."

"I don't have the bloody money with me, you fools, otherwise why would I want a credit line? Give me a few days. I will find it somehow." Fitzjohn knew this was an empty promise; he had no money at the airbase and couldn't ask his parents to cable a bank order. Well off though they were, his father was a stickler for good behaviour and would not lift a finger to help his son repay a gambling debt.

"You no have the money," Zhang said. "But we can help you. You do small job for us, we forget the money you owe."

Fitzjohn was astounded. "What the hell could I do for you?"

"Small favour. You have keys to gun store at Kai Tak. You give me the keys – only for few days."

"You're crazy. Do you really think I would do that? And how the hell do you know who holds the keys? What are you, bloody commie infiltrators?"

"No, we businessmen. We have people work on the base, so we know who has keys. We need to protect ourselves against bad Chinese people who want to steal our business. We take only two Brownings. And a little ammunition. No one notice. Help us sleep at night."

So that's it, thought Fitzjohn. Local rivalry among the Chinese gambling bosses. He knew there was constant conflict between gangs that fought over the ownership of gambling territories, prostitution and the distribution of narcotics. His indignation at the idea of being set up as a traitor, helping the Chinese forces, dissipated, and he considered his new position.

"You would write off all my debts? How will I know you will limit your thievery to two guns?"

"We honourable people, Mr Fiss. You must trust us."

Slowly Fitzjohn stood up. Two pistols would make no difference to the RAF and would get him out of trouble. It's not treasonable; I'm not associating with the enemy, he thought feverishly. "Very well, gentlemen, you have a deal. Wait for a few days. I will return on Saturday evening with the keys. Now, if you will excuse me."

Outside, Fitzjohn hailed a rickshaw and wasted no time in getting back to the airfield. His self-assurance soon returned, and he laughed to himself. *This is easy money. The bloody Chinese can do what they like to each other with the guns; I'm the one who will sleep well tonight.*

TWENTY

Kai Tak was in a high state of readiness, prepared to move to a war footing at a moment's notice. It was sensible to expect that any incursion by the Chinese forces would be preceded by attempts to damage or destroy the aircraft on the ground and to blow up the ammunition supply. Twenty-four hours a day, the airfield was guarded against an attack by Chinese saboteurs.

The munitions and armaments for the squadron were housed in a solid brick and steel-walled armoury on the eastern side of the airfield, a good distance from where the aircraft were parked and near the waterside boundary. The building had one main entrance where vehicles and bomb carriages could gain entry, and there was a side door for personnel. Protecting the arms dump was a top priority, and it fell to the RAF Regiment, the 'army' unit within the air force, and the military police, to secure the area and ensure no intruders could get near. Since there was regular live firing of the Spitfires' machine guns, bombs and rockets, there was a daily movement of munitions to the aircraft parking area. This was also the store for the base's small arms –

rifles, pistols and machine guns. There were hand grenades, flares and smoke bombs.

All personnel with authorisation to gain entry to the armoury were listed and known to the guards. No one not on the list was allowed access without specific permission from the station commander. The armourers and fitters charged with managing the supplies and arming the aircraft had open authorisation, as did the squadron leader and the two flight lieutenants. Each night, the guards secured and locked the access doors and posted armed sentries. The lights around the perimeter of the airfield included coverage for the arms store and the open ground surrounding the building. It was very difficult for anyone to approach without being seen.

It could be said that the people of Hong Kong, and Kowloon in particular, never slept. There was always activity in the streets and on the water. At night, a gentle buzz of background noise pervaded Kai Tak, with occasional shouts and laughter and the chime of bells from boats that rocked gently on the water. The airfield security teams could not rely on obscure noises alerting them to an incursion; their job was to keep patrolling and watching.

Sentries changed shifts at two-hour intervals. This was always the riskiest time, as the team going off duty were tired and the new men had not acclimatised. Three days after getting the keys, at the 2 a.m. change of guard, a figure dressed in black, his hands and face camouflaged, walked quickly from the perimeter fence and into a small triangle of shadow at the rear of the armoury. The strong security lights created dark shadows where a clever intruder could hide. Moving into the light needed to be timed carefully to avoid the patrols. After a few seconds he moved to the side access door and quietly unlocked it. Once in, the intruder silently closed the door behind him.

A couple of hours later, at the final change of guard before dawn, the man clicked open the door and peered out. He saw a two-man patrol walking away. He stepped out and locked the door behind him. He dashed silently to the perimeter fence, outside which two more men crouched. They had scraped a shallow depression under the fence and the intruder slid under. The men then replaced the soil and smoothed it flat, leaving little sign of their presence. Crouching low, the team soundlessly melted away into the dark night.

***

The night-time RAF Regiment guards savoured the prospect of being first in line for breakfast when service started at 6 a.m. Sergeant James McAllister took his group of eight men direct to the canteen and ordered a full English for each of them. His only nod to Asian food was the mixed fruit bowl he chose, with lychees, pineapple, bananas and dragon fruit. After being on duty all night, the men were ready to eat then get some sleep before their free time in the afternoon.

McAllister had been asleep for around an hour when the door to his dorm opened with a crash and three military policemen thundered in.

"McAllister, get up." The officer leading the MPs spoke with authority, without shouting. As McAllister stirred, the other men on the dorm also started to wake.

"McAllister, get yourself dressed and outside. You have five minutes."

An experienced sergeant, McAllister knew there was trouble. He snapped into life and quickly dressed in his light tan Far East uniform.

"What's the problem, Captain Robson?" he asked when he had left the dorm and was facing the MPs.

"Come with us, Sergeant. You will know soon enough."

The group marched to the armoury, where Wing Commander Martin stood with half a dozen more military policemen and Lieutenant Haslen from the RAF Regiment.

"Ah, McAllister. You were on duty last night, were you not?" said Haslen.

"Yes, sir. From midnight to 6 a.m. Is there a problem, sir?"

"The morning inventory check has discovered two missing Browning pistols and some boxes of 9mm ammunition. There is no evidence of a break-in. Did you see or hear anything?" asked Robson.

"No, sir, the night was quiet, nothing out of the ordinary. How could anybody get into the armoury without a key?"

"Were all members of your squad present, alert and carrying out their tasks as required?" the wing commander asked, tension in his voice, he disliked mysteries and would have felt some relief if a scapegoat could be found in the security team.

McAllister pulled his shoulders back. "Yes, sir, everything was in good order," he said with conviction.

"Right, Lieutenant Haslen, let me have your written report in an hour. And add an extra patrol to security tonight!"

***

The mysterious loss of two pistols and ammunition plagued Sergeant McAllister all that day. Feeling that his reputation was on the line, he was determined that, if there had been an intruder, he would not have the good luck to evade the guards and break in a second time. But Robson had said there was no evidence of a forced entry, so how the hell had they done it? The inventory system was watertight; there was no chance of a miscount. It must have been done using a key to the side door – but McAllister would never believe that the officers who held keys would be complicit in a robbery. He vowed to watch the door constantly tonight, and every night. McAllister grabbed a couple of hours sleep before taking on the guard duty at midnight.

The guardroom was a hundred yards from the armoury. From

there, the sentries had a short walk to their patrol area. Following the standard pattern, guards worked in pairs and ensured they covered all sides of the building. McAllister was confident they had a foolproof rotation system that would foil any further attempt to approach the building. To satisfy himself, he found the energy to stay awake all night to patrol the perimeter fence and keep a careful watch on the area.

The first streaks of sun had appeared low on the horizon when Sergeant McAllister decided to take a final tour of the site with the benefit of daylight before handing over to the morning guard. He didn't notice the day-old disturbed earth under the fence on the far side of the armoury.

TWENTY-ONE

After scurrying away from the airfield, the men in black climbed aboard a junk moored in the harbour a few minutes' walk from the airfield boundary. A small oil lamp gave off a faint glow, and they hurriedly disappeared below decks. As the first light appeared on the horizon, the crew of the junk worked on their nets and lines, like the men on all the other boats on the waterfront. As the sun peered over the horizon one man quietly untied the junk, hoisted her battened red sails, and the junk took a heading to the west and out to sea.

Four hours later the junk returned. As she pulled alongside the quay the crew brought up boxes of fish ready to stack on the landing. They had not achieved much of a haul, but the dealer was satisfied. He paid the boat master and loaded the boxes onto his small open-backed truck. With work finished for the day, the five crew made their way to the food stalls at the rear of the docks. Only two of the men returned to the junk.

The truck headed along Salisbury Road before the driver turned north up Nathan Road. A couple of turns more, and he stopped at the rear entrance to the Green Lotus. The kitchen boy emerged to carry the fish boxes in. One included a package wrapped in waxed cotton. No words were spoken. Then the truck made its way back down to the docks.

Daytime at the Green Lotus was spent cleaning and preparing food for the evening. The restaurant opened at 6 p.m., and early diners could enjoy a full menu including favourite dishes of fish Chinese-style, prawn and pork wontons, duck, chicken and slow-cooked brisket of beef with oyster sauce. The mid-evening clientele changed subtly as the early diners departed and the night hawks sought amusement other than gourmet food, with drinking and gambling at the forefront of their minds.

***

"Ah, Mr Fiss, good to see you, we have your table for you." Zhang bowed and his sickly, sycophantic welcoming smile had returned. Fitzjohn was not impressed. He was there simply to get his keys back.

"You too early. My friends are out of club at the moment, back soon. You have drink on the house."

Fitzjohn did not decline. He knew that giving the thugs the keys had been a stupid thing to do; he had heard about the missing pistols and naturally joined in the debate in the Officers' Mess as to how they came to be missing, but of course he knew exactly what had happened. He would get the keys back, and the whole thing would blow over.

"Where the hell are your boys?" He was losing patience. "I haven't got all night, and I want my property returned."

"Please come through, have some fun with the dice, sir."

Fitzjohn looked at his watch. Ten o'clock. He had a couple of hours; he might as well use it profitably. He strolled through the door to the very familiar room, filled with gamblers and a haze of smoke –

the usual gathering, including some smart-looking office types from the island, no doubt enjoying the expat life. After an hour of dice, Fitzjohn noticed a further door open momentarily. The kitchen boy peered in then closed the door. Something's happening, he thought. A few minutes later Zhang came in. "Please, Mr Fiss, come to office."

Fitzjohn groaned and got up and went to the office. The rear door then opened and the three thugs came in, crossed the room and joined Fitzjohn.

"Well, let's have the keys," he said.

The older thug spoke. "Not so fast, mister. We have new special deal for you. We need more goods from airfield. We give you keys back when we have more pistols. Then no one at RAF will know you gave us keys."

Fitzjohn lost his temper. "You filthy dogs, give me the keys now or I'll get a pistol myself and blow your brains out! Bloody blackmail me, will you? And in any event the doors are now permanently watched, you wouldn't get away with it."

The older man nodded to his youngest companion. The knife appeared from his sleeve and he moved towards Fitzjohn, who stepped back in shock and ran to the door into the main bar. As he placed his hand on the door handle, the boy stabbed his arm. Fitzjohn screamed. "You bastards – want a fight, do you?" He launched himself at the leader of the thugs and grabbed him by the neck.

One of the others pulled Fitzjohn back. The man with the knife stood up tall and pointed the knife at Fitzjohn's throat. As he drew his arm back, the door from the bar was kicked open and three men in army fatigues dived into the room, guns in hand.

"Drop that! Stand still! Get your hands where we can see them!" shouted the leader, aiming his pistol at the young thug's head. He dropped the knife immediately. The older thug plunged a hand into the back of his belt and pulled out a pistol. He levelled it at the leading soldier and pulled the trigger, but he was too late. A split second sooner, one of the supporting troops had fired a burst from a Sten gun into the man's chest. A line of four bullet holes ran from his stomach to his collar bone. He lurched backwards, his own shot going high. As he fell, streaks of his blood splattered and smeared down the wall behind him. Screams could be heard from the bar, and another gunshot came from the gambling room. The two other Chinese men held up their hands, the young one shouting, "No shoot, no shoot!"

"Sergeant Daines, find out what's happened in the other room and get a couple of men in here to cuff these drongos," called the officer leading the group.

"And get a medic for me!" Fitzjohn shouted. "The bastard stabbed me in the arm."

Daines dashed out of the room. In the bar, a group of four soldiers had all the diners frozen at their tables. The gamblers were standing, looking shocked, facing a glamorous, immaculately dressed woman with a Walther PPK in her hand.

"No one move! Get away from the door!" she shouted.

"We heard a shot, ma'am."

"It's OK, Daines. I put one through the ceiling to let these guys know I meant business. Some of them were minded to make a run for it out the back door. Get the MP team in here."

The sergeant called out to the soldiers to send in the military police. They would get the now very unhappy gamblers lined up for questioning. All but one person, that is – the woman's companion at the dice table, a British man of around fifty.

"Raleigh, thanks for your help tonight. I'll see you back in the office tomorrow," she said.

"Sit down, Mr Fitzjohn." The medic with the raid team opened a battle dressing and applied it to Fitzjohn's arm. "We will have you dressed and out to the ambulance shortly. Too late for the other guy."

"Who the hell are you, and what's this all about?" Fitzjohn addressed his question to the officer who led the operation. He felt the man looked vaguely familiar.

"Captain Hind, Australian Army Intelligence. You're under arrest, Fitzjohn."

"What nonsense! There's no harm in taking some R&R with the odd game of cards or dice."

"Forget it. We've had these people under observation for the last three months. Our main interest is counter-insurgency – looking for Chinese communists building subversion or planning sabotage. We're working with the British MI6 and MPs. These jokers here are cheap crooks, but we're still not going to ignore them. You're not the first serviceman to run up debts and then be blackmailed. You will not be surprised to hear that the dice are loaded. That's not really our first concern, but giving them the keys to the armoury? That does concern us. After medical treatment you will be taken to the Kai Tak glasshouse."

The smartly dressed woman came into the office.

"Good work, Val," said Hind.

"You ... you're part of this?" Fitzjohn recognised the lady as one of the expats from the dice game.

"Meet Val Hetherington-Brown, British Secret Service, MI6," said Hind.

"Ah yes, now I remember, you were at the Peninsula. But you said you worked at the government office or something. What about the man with you tonight?"

"Fitzjohn, I'm sure you will not be surprised that we have to cover up our intelligence operations with at least a veneer of diplomatic service. The gentleman you saw with me this evening is part of the team. You've been hoodwinked, Fitzjohn. These crooks are always on the lookout for an easy mark, and you fell nicely into their trap. The guns they stole with your help have been recovered, and you'll get the chance to explain your story at the court martial."

"B-b-but how did you find out?"

"We have agents working for us, of course. You don't need to know who and where."

Fitzjohn's face was pale and drained – partly due to blood loss but mainly to the sickening realisation that he would be thrown out of the RAF and given a long prison sentence back in England. Pain suddenly surged in his arm and he gasped, before fainting and falling to the floor.

The soldiers and military police processed the guests, and finding no villains among them, soon let them go. The staff at the club started to clear up as soon as Val Hetherington-Brown had walked through the kitchen and out to the rear yard. The kitchen boy looked up at Hetherington-Brown, who passed him a bulging envelope.

"Thank you," she said.

TWENTY-TWO

David Hartman was frustrated and despondent. The mission to recruit pilots to fly for the Israeli Air Force was not going well – the crash and the subsequent lockdown had made it impossible for Hannah to set up a meeting with Fitzjohn, and he had not contacted her. As Hartman entered the lobby of the Causeway Construction offices, he realised he had bad news for his boss. The other option, it seemed to him, was to get Hannah to approach another pilot. But who?

"Come in, David, sit down. First, tell me what progress you have made, then I have some news for you." Peter Kahn sat at his usual place at the head of the table. Hartman realised that the sun always shone through the windows behind Kahn, silhouetting him and making him difficult to see clearly.

"Well, sir, you're aware of the Spitfire that crashed a week ago and that the airfield was locked down for two days. Fitzjohn has not made a date with Hannah – we're still waiting for him to contact her. He may not be interested in what we want him for, and we might find it difficult to get close to him now to make a proposal. I think we should widen our search."

"This is unfortunate. Hannah has clearly put him off. Tell her she must contact him again, show some enthusiasm."

"But, sir, given what he tried to do to her – he tried to rape her – how can we ask her to meet him again?"

"The lives of millions of people and even the existence of Israel are at stake here, David. We all have to play our part. Make her cooperate and get close to Fitzjohn."

Hartman was silent for a moment, then he said, "I shall endeavour to do that. But she is very reluctant. She feels she's inviting trouble if she appears to be chasing him."

"Well, David, that's just a risk she has to take. Let me brief you on the other issue. The intelligence service in Israel has picked up news of Egyptian agents here in Hong Kong – we believe they are also looking for pilots. We are now in a race to get the right people. So, all the more reason for Hannah not to delay."

"I see, sir. This is worrying news. I will go and see Hannah this evening."

"At the same time, we must all look at other potential targets, widen our search. As you know, the future of the squadron is uncertain and many of the pilots might well be discharged. Some might resign."

"We need to get closer to them, sir," Hartman said quickly. "A number of pilots were at the Peninsula Hotel where Hannah met Fitzjohn. The squadron leader, another flight lieutenant, several other pilots. I wonder if the bank's people have made any contacts."

Mars' hands rested on the table and he slowly clenched his fists. "I have already asked Golding. He believes there could be others who could be approached. In particular, the other flight lieutenant in the squadron. Devon is his name. On Friday the bank are holding one of their cultural evenings – part of the post-war rebuilding. Golding has sent invitations to the military. You will attend and you must instruct Hannah to be there as well. She must find out what she can about the pilots. It will soon be October and the pressure is mounting to secure pilots before the Egyptians gain air superiority."

"Right, sir, I understand."

"And David, take care to ensure the British don't get to hear of our work. The situation in Israel at the moment is very sensitive. We must assume their intelligence services are monitoring us. We know the British are not actively against the establishment of the State of Israel, but they will obstruct any attempts by us to recruit their pilots or any other servicemen, even if they have resigned from the forces. Same for any attempts by the Egyptians, fortunately."

***

Hannah peered through the side window to see who had knocked on the door. She was confident it would not be Fitzjohn, but her nerves had been shaken by their last date, and she was being very cautious. She hoped it was one of the other expat girls from the office calling in for a chat, and she felt both relief and trepidation when she saw it was Hartman. The whole mission had weighed on her mind. Doubts about her ability to play the role had crept into her mind. Was she really cut out for secret service work? Or would she be happier working on a kibbutz? She tried to convince herself that that would help the establishment of the Jewish State just as much as recruiting pilots, but she knew that was a lie. She had to carry out the work that had been assigned to her; no one said it would be a piece of cake.

Hannah unlocked both bolts on the door. "Come in, David."

"Thanks, Hannah. Everything OK with you?"

"Yes, thank you. Still no contact from Fitzjohn, I'm glad to say."

"Look, Mars wants you to try again. Say how pleased you are to hear that he's safe and well, etc., etc. Charm him a bit, that sort of thing. Say you want to meet as soon as he can get leave. Could you send a cable this evening?"

"Yes… if you wish, but won't this risk Fitzjohn thinking I'm willing to—"

"There's a chance of that, for sure, but you can handle him. Once he knows why you're interested in him, he will forget his aim to get you into the bedroom."

"Alright, I'll make one more effort to arrange a meeting. We can walk down to the Post Office now. They do urgent deliveries to the air station."

"Let's do that. I have something else to discuss with you."

They took the winding road down to Central. Fifteen minutes later they were in the main Post Office and Hannah wrote out a saccharine invitation to meet. "If he ignores this, he really has gone off the idea of getting close to me," she said to Hartman.

During the slower walk back up the hill afterwards, Hartman raised the question of other potential recruits. "Mars wants us to think about other targets. Of course, you will know about the reception and concert being held on Friday at Government House, sponsored by the bank."

"Yes, indeed. It's for the business community, bank clients and government officials. There won't be any forces personnel there."

"Mars fixed it for invitations to be sent from Golding to the wing commander at the air station. Invitations have also been sent to the army and Royal Navy so people don't think the RAF are getting special attention. You and I will be there. I'll be using my cover working for Causeway Construction. We must hope that Fitzjohn and at least some of the pilots attend, and we can size them up."

"OK. Perhaps Fitzjohn will get back to me before the concert. I hope to hell he doesn't!"

"I know how you must be feeling, Hannah, but if he does make contact, you will play your part, won't you?"

"Don't worry, David. I know what I have to do." She had thought that Hartman supported her and felt sympathy for the risks she was taking, but this had quickly vaporised. She knew she was dispensable; a pawn in a bigger game of chess.

TWENTY-THREE

The main entrance to Government House on Hong Kong Island faces south, looking uphill towards the Peak. Well-groomed lawns and flowerbeds created more than a touch of the English country garden and the sweeping carriage drive completed the stately home look. The governor's office had allowed the London and Hong Kong Bank to use the ballroom for the concert and provided drinks and canapés for the guests on arrival. The limited space allowed for about a hundred guests. Included in these were four representatives from the RAF.

"Good to see you again, Adam." Isaac Golding stood at the doorway to welcome guests.

"And you too, Mr Golding. May I introduce my colleagues, Pilot Tom Forrester, Flight Sergeant Alec Bryant and Leading Aircraftman Joe Cootes."

"You are all very welcome – please come in. Refreshments are being served to your left."

As the group walked into the lobby, Devon noticed some people he recognised from the Peninsula evening. The lady from the government offices – Val was her name, he recalled. And the dark-haired girl from the bank, who was assisting with welcoming the guests. There were numerous business types – the Lloyd's of London man and others. He could see a chief petty officer from the Royal Navy, but no other military people.

Devon was a touch surprised that more RAF men had not accepted the invitation, but he guessed that chamber orchestra music didn't appeal to many of the younger members of the station. Since Fitzjohn's trouble, the CO had been cautious about giving passes for social events, but he had clearly seen this as a harmless cultural evening.

The room was filled with the murmur of conversation. Devon noticed a smartly dressed young man who he assumed worked for the bank talking to his RAF colleagues. The young man broke away and came over to Devon.

"Good evening. My name's David Hartman. I work for Causeway Construction."

"Good to meet you. I'm Flight Lieutenant Adam Devon."

The men shook hands.

"What do you do at Causeway, David?"

"I'm a surveyor. Well, a trainee, actually. Causeway are expanding their business here and need more people. There are lots of opportunities in construction – not just war damage but also new projects."

"Yes, the development of Hong Kong is remarkable with all the new buildings and land reclamation – maybe an expansion of the airport at some point?" said Devon, smiling.

"That would indeed be a great project to be involved in. Tell me, do you fly the Spitfires over at Kai Tak? We can see them sometimes from our office flying along the harbour."

"Yes, that's us."

"Must be fun." Hartman deftly changed the subject. "Are you an admirer of Beethoven? I notice from the programme that we will be hearing extracts from the 5th Symphony."

"Oh yes – that was one of the reasons I accepted the invitation. There is also a Benjamin Britten piece I'm looking forward to."

Then a bell rang, and the waiters returned to collect glasses from the guests.

"Enjoy your evening." Hartman said genially. As he entered the ballroom he saw Hannah and gave her a furtive look, then switched his gaze to Devon. She seemed to get the message. He guessed that Hannah was inwardly very happy that Fitzjohn was not included in the RAF group, and hoped she would make an effort to speak to Devon.

The music was of a high standard, even though Devon knew the orchestra was made up of keen amateurs. The relaxing atmosphere gave Devon the warming, positive feelings he associated with classical music. He glanced around the room as the music played and noticed the dark-haired young woman again. Perhaps she sensed his gaze, because she turned to look at him. Devon looked away, puzzled by the sudden strong attraction he felt towards her. He had no desire to get to know her; she had spent time with Fitzjohn at the Peninsula in a way that suggested they were involved.

After an hour or so the orchestra stood, to keen applause, signalling the interval and more drinks in the lobby.

As Devon took his glass, the woman came up to him. "Hello – have you enjoyed the music so far?"

He had to be polite, at least. "Yes indeed, and yourself?"

"Yes, thank you. I liked the Mozart piece especially."

"Me too," replied Devon.

"My name's Hannah, by the way."

"Ah, yes." Devon now recalled Val Hetherington-Brown had mentioned her name at the Peninsula. "Adam Devon. Very nice to meet you." They shook hands. "You're with the bank, aren't you?"

"Yes, in marketing and promotional work. It's not hugely exciting, but it's great to be here in Hong Kong. I arrived three months ago."

"Yes, it's a buzzing kind of place. Where are you from in England?"

"Before coming out here I lived in Clapham in South London. Previous to that Cambridge. Do I detect a touch of a northern accent in you?"

"Ha, yes, guilty as charged. I'm from the Manchester area."

They smiled, and for a moment just looked at each other. Devon immediately forgot his reservations. "Have you seen much of the island since you have been here?" he asked.

"Not really; work keeps me busy. I've been to the tourist places, such as they are – Stanley market, Happy Valley races, that sort of thing. How about you?"

"Same as you, really. We only have limited leave and we're always on call, of course. I did have an evening at Happy Valley with the boys and attended the Peninsula dinner. You were there, I noticed."

Hannah felt a blush rise from her neck to her cheeks. She thought it was nice that he had remembered her. "I was indeed. An excellent evening, wasn't it?"

The bell rang again.

"The second half includes a piece from *Peer Gynt*. Let's meet at the end – you can tell me what you thought of it," Devon said quickly.

"I'd love to. See you then."

Devon could hardly concentrate on the music for thinking about Hannah. But it felt natural – he wasn't shooting a line, he really did want to ask her views on the music.

At the end of the concert, there was warm applause that lasted for several minutes. Devon glanced across at Hannah, who was rising to leave. They met at the doorway to the lobby.

"Great, wasn't it? 'In the Hall of the Mountain King' is one of my favourite pieces of music," said Devon.

"Yes, excellent. They played very well."

"Hannah, I need to return to the airfield with my colleagues. If you're free tomorrow, perhaps we could meet? I've never been to Repulse Bay but I hear it's a great place. Would you like to go there? I can grab a taxi from the Star Ferry terminal and pick you up."

"Um, yes, that would be nice, thank you. What time did you have in mind?"

"Say half past ten?"

"That's fine. I live at 21 Ford Villas, Old Peak Road, a little way past the botanical gardens."

"I'm sure the taxi driver will find it, 21 Ford Villas. I'll see you then. Goodnight, Hannah."

"Goodnight."

As Devon and the other RAF men left the building, Hartman emerged from the crowd in the lobby. "Success?"

"Yes – we have agreed to meet tomorrow morning, to go to Repulse Bay," said Hannah.

"Excellent. I will call round for a report first thing Monday morning, before you go to work. Look out for me."

"Wilco."

Hartman smiled at Hannah's use of RAF radio-speak.

TWENTY-FOUR

"Young, come over here, mate." Aircraftman Barry Johnson had the kind of character that demands – and gains – the attention of all those who knew him, regardless of rank or role. "Give us the latest on the squadron's disbandment – you must be in the know."

The Mess was busy so Young placed his food tray on the end of the long table and sat with Johnson and the half dozen men enjoying their lunch.

"Don't be a berk, Johnson! No one is talking about disbandment at the moment. Once this China business has been sorted out, we could be posted anywhere. Or we might even stay in Hong Kong for a bit."

"Do me a favour, Young! The skipper will be off to BOAC in a couple of weeks and now that Fitzjohn has blotted his copybook it only leaves your guvnor as the new leader, and he isn't going to get an operational squadron straight off."

"Why not? Devon's the best pilot in the squadron and one of the leading Spitfire pilots in the air force. But I'm not going to guess what the top brass in England want to do with the squadron."

"It's alright for you, Young – you're on your way out soon. What have you done, seven years? You've seen the world. Some of the lads have only been in a year or two. And the National Service wallahs don't want to spend their time in some horrible location, like Yorkshire!"

The men at the table laughed. A trainee aircraft mechanic said, "I joined the RAF to learn a trade, to be a mechanic, so I hope they don't chuck us all out."

"Don't worry, Lyles. You'll be alright so long as you don't drop a spanner into a Spit's engine!" Senior Aircraftman Mike Welch was a career serviceman who had joined up before the war and had been at Hornchurch during the Battle of Britain. "And there will be plenty of work for Spitfire ground attack squadrons for a few years yet."

Perhaps the strongest attraction of life in the armed forces is companionship. Men and women who share profound experiences at a young age form strong bonds that last for many years, even a lifetime. Add the element of danger or the risk of death and the bond becomes all the tighter. Service personnel have to be good team players; their own or their colleagues' lives might depend on it. Trust in each other is the essential ingredient.

The work can be tough and demanding, physically and mentally. One of the main frustrations of service life is boredom, and not being kept informed. The maxim 'need to know' is ever in the minds of officers and senior personnel. If the men don't need to know something, then they won't be told. But often men would garner information by listening, observing and amalgamating snatches of conversations – putting two and two together and aiming for four. Being able to discern facts over speculation.

The aircraft mechanics, armourers, fuellers, officers' orderlies and RAF Regiment men enjoyed the banter and snippets of real information and news they shared in the Mess and when they took leave from the airbase.

Mike 'Streaky' Bacon, a self-confident young aircraftman from East London, a tall, gangling lad no more than nineteen years old, spoke up next. "My dad says there's no future in the armed forces as a career; you're better off in Civvy Street. When he left the army he got a job at Ford's factory in Dagenham on the production line. He loves it, and he's a shop steward in the union now."

"Is that what you want to do, Streaky?" asked Johnson.

"Well, no. I want to be an electrician. That's why I joined the air force, for the training, you know."

"Shut up then, tell your dad you're much better off in the services. And you won't turn into a zombie fitting the same bit to a car every day."

Welch came back in. "Don't forget, Streaky, you could be retrained on jet engines if 28 Squadron gets disbanded and there's no demand for mechanics on piston engines."

"Same as the pilots," said Young. "Lots of them have different aircraft types in their logbooks. It's just a matter of conversion training."

"There'll be a general election next year – the new Conservative government will make sure the armed forces are kept strong and fully operational." The men turned in unison to look at Peter Green, a fuel bowser driver and one of the older men in the service.

"These Labour types don't want to spend money on the services; they want to hand it all out to those that don't earn it. Mark my words, if they get in again it will be goodbye to a strong RAF and our jobs."

"But the Tories are for the rich, Greenie. They keep wages low, in and out of the services. If a full capability around the world is maintained, it will cost money and where's that going to come from? Taxes, that's where." Young Streaky recited his father's opinions on politics.

"Don't take socialism as the best for Britain, Streaky – we don't want to become a load of communists. Free enterprise and reward for hard work is the backbone of Britain. Always has been," said Welch.

"Talking of which, let's get back to work. Those aircraft won't service themselves."

TWENTY-FIVE

The taxi ride up to Mid-Levels reminded Devon of driving up an Alpine road, all climbs and hairpin bends. Vaguely, Devon wondered how Hannah could afford to live in this area. He arrived right on time, not wishing to appear overly keen or sloppy enough to be late. Hannah opened the door and welcomed him into the villa. She had no qualms about asking him into the house; he was very different to Fitzjohn.

"Good morning, Adam, come in. I'm just getting some things together." She leant forward and brushed his cheek with hers – warmly, he felt, but not too much, too soon.

The mist of the night had lifted to leave a clear, balmy morning. From here Adam could look down to Victoria Harbour and across to Kowloon. The early fishermen were at work in the Pearl River and junks plied the harbour from west to east. A Star Ferry had just left Central, its green and cream paintwork looking stately in the sun. Adam looked out of the villa's bay window to see tiny figures moving around at Kai Tak – the aircraftmen setting out the fuel and ammunition. He had two days' leave ahead, and it felt good to have the luxury of spending time with Hannah. He was glad he had suggested going to Repulse Bay with her. It was famous for its curve of deep yellow sand. Shark nets allowed safe swimming in the warm, blue-green sea.

"I've put together some lunch and drinks. If that's OK?" said Hannah.

"That's great. That will give us the whole day at the beach."

Before they left, a thought came to Adam. Did Hannah enjoy swimming? A bolt of pleasure ran through his mind as he realised he could learn something new about this beautiful woman. He had appreciated her physical beauty instantly, but getting to know her would take time, and this appealed to him. Devon dismissed any thoughts about her relationship, whatever it was, with Fitzjohn.

Ten minutes later, Hannah had finished packing their lunch.

"Excellent, thank you," Adam said, smiling at her. Silence hung in the air for a moment.

"Do you like to swim in the sea, Hannah? If so, we could have a dip."

She beamed. "Yes, that would be wonderful."

"Great, pack your swimming kit and some towels. Mine are in the taxi."

As Adam loaded the bags into the boot of the taxi, he heard the crackle and drumming of Griffon engines being started. A faint blue cloud of exhaust smoke drifted across the runway. It looked like three aircraft taxiing out. As he stood and gazed towards Kai Tak, Hannah put her hand on his shoulder.

"Don't think about it, you're off duty."

"Yes, I know. It's a routine patrol. Everything is quiet, we're told."

The drive south put the Peak behind them, blocking their view of the airfield, and Devon began to relax. As the road swept down towards the cove, the Repulse Bay Hotel came into view. Adam directed the taxi to the forecourt.

"Why are we stopping here?" Hannah asked, a touch of nervousness in her voice.

"I gather that for a few dollars we can use their facilities to change, then walk down to the beach. We can come back and have a drink here later."

Devon noticed that Hannah seemed to suppress a frown. "Er, yes, OK…" she said. He hoped she would not feel any anxiety with the idea, or concern that he had planned for them to take a room at the hotel.

Devon quickly engaged a Chinese man who found them a lovely spot on the beach and fetched loungers and a large straw sunshade. They relaxed into the warm morning.

"Tell me about yourself, Hannah."

"What can I say? As I mentioned, I grew up in Cambridge. It's a lovely place to live. There were always concerts and recitals going on, even during the war. That's how I came to be introduced to classical music. I'm not the biggest music buff, but I enjoy most of the classics. I was also a regular at dance classes. Anyway, I got a job with the bank in the City and initially commuted to Liverpool Street every day, which was very tiring, so I moved to London and shared a flat with a friend. I hadn't been at the bank long when I was offered the transfer to Hong Kong. I didn't think twice. I'm enjoying it here."

"Very different to England, isn't it? Particularly the weather! Perhaps we could cool off with a swim?"

"Yes, good idea."

Devon was a good swimmer, he took a dozen strokes out then turned to check on Hannah – she was to his right. He swam after her, and soon the two stopped and looked at each other. No words were needed. They turned and swam in parallel across the bay. Hannah turned onto her back and gently floated along. Instinctively, Devon reached out and took her hand. She squeezed his hand and gazed at the sky with a smile.

They swam on, staying in the safe area up to the shark nets. When they turned back, Devon called, "I'm ready for that lunch!"

"Me too," Hannah said.

They returned to the beach and dried off. The heat of the sun was oppressive, even with the shade of the umbrella. Hannah opened the picnic basket and they enjoyed some sandwiches, a green salad, sliced fruit and orange juice.

"I love it here, Adam, it's so relaxing. Thanks for arranging this."

"My pleasure. Yes, it's so different to Central and Kowloon. Less frantic. I can see why people come here at the weekend to get some space and unwind. And what with all the excitement going on at the airfield, it's great to get away from it all."

"Really? What's so exciting?"

"Ah, well, not really exciting, but there was an incident with Flight Lieutenant Fitzjohn. He's been arrested. It's not a secret, so I'm not telling you anything that's not in the public domain. Some business to do with gambling debts and breach of security at the airfield. I won't go into detail, but it came as a shock to us all."

Hannah was stunned. So that would explain why she hadn't heard from him, and why he hadn't been at the concert at Government House. She needed to tell Hartman as soon as possible. In the meantime, she had to be careful not to overreact to the news, but to carry on as normal.

"Goodness, that's awful. I hope it's not too serious." Hannah didn't want to linger on the matter. Staring out to sea, she said, "I rarely swam in the sea at home. It's always so cold. We had a holiday last year in Cornwall, in Constantine Bay, and I did go in there, but not for long. Have you ever been to Cornwall?"

"No – before the war we had holidays in Blackpool or Southport. You know, you can take pleasure flights from Southport beach now in a de Havilland Fox Moth. It's a biplane with a cabin below the pilot that takes four passengers. That could be something for me to do after the RAF: fly holidaymakers around Blackpool Tower!"

They laughed, but Hannah could see an opening for her to raise the subject of flying Spitfires in Israel.

"Do you think you might leave the RAF?" she asked.

"That depends on a number of things. I could be promoted to squadron leader, either of 28 Squadron or another one. Or I could convert to flying jets. Then there's the possibility of leaving the RAF and going into commercial aviation. That's what our skipper is going to do – fly for BOAC. I suppose it could be time to give up flying. I have the offer of a job at Avro working on new navigation equipment. It's a factory job, but it would lead to a career. There might even be opportunities to test-fly new radar and avionics like autopilot systems and bomb aiming, that sort of thing."

"It makes sense to think about your future. A steady job must be something you would want."

"Oh, definitely, but not today!" Devon jumped up and took Hannah's hand and pulled her up. "Come on, let's go for one more swim."

As they walked down to the water's edge, Hannah realised Devon had not let go of her hand. She was glad. She would try to talk to him about flying again but for now she was going to enjoy herself, relax in Adam's company and enjoy being with him.

**

After showering and changing back at the hotel, Devon suggested that they have a drink in the bar then stay for dinner. Hannah was delighted with the idea: it gave them more time together. She hadn't forgotten her mission, and was determined to go back to discussing flying.

A waiter took them through the restaurant to their table on the veranda. The sun was setting, and a chain of candles in little red Chinese lanterns hanging from the canopy over the seating area provided a pink-gold glow. They ordered their food and enjoyed the sounds of the night: insects chirping and the birds singing in the trees. The swoosh of waves lapping on the shore carried across the bay.

"Do you have a family?" Devon asked.

"A brother. And my parents, of course, still living in Cambridge."

"And … is there a special person in your life?"

Hannah hesitated. "No. I have had boyfriends, but at the moment I'm enjoying my independence. What about you?"

"Similar – parents, and a sister older than me. Dad works at the Avro factory that I mentioned. I was engaged to a local girl, but she called it off. She found someone new, someone who isn't thousands of miles away."

"I'm sorry to hear that."

"Mm, well, maybe it was for the best. We were very young when we met. You know how it is."

"I think so."

The pair fell silent. Devon looked up at the blue-black starlit sky. "Have you had a chance to go to the cinema here in Hong Kong as yet?"

"No. There is the Alhambra of course – maybe we could go some time?"

"Yes, I'd very much like that."

Devon finished his drink. "I'll get a late ferry back to Kai Tak after dropping you off, if that's OK with you?"

"Yes, sure." Hannah knew she should broach the subject of flying again, but decided against it. Today has been lovely; I'm not going to spoil it, she thought. When Devon glanced at his watch, Hannah got the message.

"We'd better be getting along. It has been a perfect day, Adam, thank you so much."

"I've really enjoyed it. Actually, I also have a day's leave tomorrow – well, almost, I will be on call. It would be great to meet for lunch if you're free?" He wondered if he was being too pushy. But he was never sure when he would be allowed leave, and he knew he had to take his chance when he could.

"That would be wonderful. Shall I come over to Kowloon to meet you?"

"Sure. Shall we say midday? Do you know the Victoria Restaurant? It's just before you get to the Peninsula."

"Yes, I've seen it." Hannah smiled as she pulled her jacket over her shoulders.

"I'll ask the waiter to get us a taxi. First stop your house, then I'll carry on down to the Star Ferry."

When the taxi arrived outside Hannah's house, Devon quickly got out and went round to open her door for her. "Wait for a couple of minutes, would you?" he said to the driver.

They strolled to the door of her villa.

"Thanks again, Adam. I really enjoyed myself today."

Neither of the two felt they should take the first step, but they found themselves naturally embracing. Devon gave Hannah the lightest kiss on the lips. She returned the kiss and held it for more than just a moment.

"Goodnight." Hannah walked into her house then closed the door behind her. "Oh hell," she cried. "How am I going to tell Adam it's all been a lie? What will he think of me?"

***

The next day Hannah dressed in her best clothes, in keeping with the expectations of a Sunday morning. She even used a touch of make-up and tied her hair neatly in a ponytail. Her head was light with anticipation of the day ahead. She had slept soundly and dreamlessly, and felt rested and happy. Sitting on the ferry boat, she thought it a good omen that she was on the *Northern Star*. Adam's a northern boy, she thought. At the Kowloon terminal she had some time to spare, so decided to walk to the restaurant. She could hear the sound of an approaching flight of three aircraft returning from the morning's patrol. This snapped her out of her musing as she remembered the purpose of her meeting with Devon. She felt such a strong liking, and desire, for Adam, and she hated the idea that she had to subdue her feelings. But she had no choice; her orders were to recruit pilots, not find herself a boyfriend.

Devon was already at the table, looking at the menu. He stood and touched Hannah's arm, then sat down before Hannah could offer a warmer embrace. Something was wrong, she felt. His demeanour had completely changed from last night. She wasn't to know that Devon had spent all night plagued by thoughts of Hannah's connection with Fitzjohn. He wanted to know about her relationship with him, and where he stood with her himself.

"Good to see you, Hannah, I hope you slept well," said Devon.

He's saying the right words but he's distant, annoyed about something, Hannah thought. "Yes, very well thanks. And you?"

"Fine, thanks. Here's the menu."

They discussed the options then Devon sat back, silent. After a while he said, "Hannah, were you on good terms with Henry Fitzjohn?"

So that's what's annoying him. "Not really. I met him at the Peninsula and saw him a couple of times after that. I had no idea about the trouble he was in. It was such a surprise when you told me yesterday." This was a lie. Knowing something of his character, she was not at all surprised to hear that he had been in trouble with the air force.

"Yes, I'm sure it was. But I can't help feeling that you and he, were … well, close. He's now out of circulation and it feels to me that I'm next on your list of possible paramours. Is that how it is? We had a lovely day yesterday, but I don't want a passing romance. I already know you're very special to me and I don't want to be led along."

"Oh, Adam, don't be so foolish. Henry was nothing to me, but I hoped I showed you last night how special I think you are." Hannah placed her hand on his.

"I'm glad to hear it. Sorry to be soft, but I needed to know how we stand, how you feel."

"Then don't give Henry another thought. He was a friendly chap, but there was nothing serious between us – not on my part," Hannah said, hoping that she would never have to talk about how she had been abused by Fitzjohn.

They ordered lunch with water and fruit juice. Devon was on call and therefore had to avoid alcohol. They talked about music and their day at Repulse Bay, becoming more relaxed and happy.

"It's only been a few days since we met, but I really enjoy being with you. Perhaps we can meet again next weekend?" Devon said.

Hannah hesitated. Nearly a week away seemed a long way ahead, but she couldn't bring herself to suggest a date during the week. "That would be nice. What do you have in mind?"

"Some of the chaps have rented a passenger junk for the day and taken a cruise along the Pearl River. Perhaps we could do the same?"

Before Hannah could answer, Devon suddenly stood up, looking concerned. At the front desk of the restaurant a man stood, speaking to the receptionist. She turned and pointed towards Devon and Hannah's table.

"Sorry, Hannah, but that's my orderly," Devon said. "I need to go and see what he wants." He walked across the room to speak to the man. "What is it, Young?"

"All pilots are to report for duty at 1500 hours, sir. There will be a special briefing by the station commander."

"About…?"

"Not known, sir, just the order to call all those on day passes and leave back to the airfield. You did leave a note of where you would be sir. I have a car outside waiting for us."

"Yes, of course. Thank you. I'll be there in two minutes." Devon returned to the table, where Hannah was already gathering her things. He sat down, apologised and explained he had to return urgently to the airfield.

"That's alright, Adam, I know how these things are. But if you have time during the week, perhaps we could have dinner one evening?" Hannah knew she was being forward, but this sudden ending to their lunch emboldened her to ask to meet sooner than the next weekend.

"Yes, I'd love to. I'll send you a cable when I know when I can make it." Devon said a hasty goodbye, kissed Hannah on the cheek, then dashed to the waiting car.

TWENTY-SIX

All the officers of the air station assembled in the ops room without the chat that usually precedes a briefing. Something was afoot, and they couldn't wait to hear the news. On the low platform Wing Commander Martin sat behind the briefing desk with Squadron Leader Porter and another officer not known to the men. They could see, however, from his uniform that he was also a squadron leader.

"Take your seats please, gentlemen, and we can make a start." Martin had stood up and moved to the side of the platform. "As you may know, we have been expecting some changes to the squadron, and I can now brief you on the rearrangements. Let me say first that no immediate change is planned for our role here. We will maintain our offensive capability and ensure we remain a deterrent to the Chinese. All patrolling, exercises and firing practice will continue as normal."

Martin turned to the two men sitting behind the table. "I will introduce our guest shortly, but first I'd like to confirm Squadron Leader Porter's retirement. The squadron leader has had a distinguished career of active flying service spanning more than ten years, including with 145 Squadron in the Battle of Britain, flying Hurricanes. Not a bad machine, but perhaps not quite up to the Spitfire!"

The assembled group laughed quietly, knowing the wing commander was himself a wartime Hurricane pilot.

"Squadron Leader Porter will be taking up a new role with British Overseas Airways Corporation and will be leaving Hong Kong at a date to be confirmed, around the middle of November. That gives us about five weeks to effect the transfer of leadership to our new commander. I know you will all want to congratulate David on such a splendid career, and wish him well for the future. We will, of course, be arranging a farewell bash. Now, gentlemen, I would like to introduce Squadron Leader Guy Wills, who will be taking over command of the squadron on David's retirement. After some time with 80 Squadron, largely flying Tempests, Squadron Leader Wills has spent the past two years at the Central Flying School. Squadron Leader Wills, would you like to say a few words?"

"Thank you, sir." Wills stood up and walked around to the front of the desk. "Good afternoon, everyone. I'd like to add my own congratulations to Squadron Leader Porter for such sterling service, both in active wartime operations and in the peacekeeping role we now have here. I can see from your faces that you might not see our work as keeping the peace when we are charged with being able to deliver overwhelming firepower if required. Well, it's not only having the aircraft and armaments that prevents any incursion into Hong Kong territory; it's the quality of the pilots. I'm very much looking forward to working with you all and will be joining the morning patrol this Wednesday. On Friday we will stage a full-squadron exercise under the command of Squadron Leader Porter. After that, I will take over."

Devon sat back in his chair, frustrated and more than a touch annoyed, and conscious of the sideways glances from the other pilots. Had he expected to be promoted and given the squadron? A lot of people probably thought so, but Devon himself had not set his heart on it. Taking leadership of a Spitfire squadron at this time would mean an end to any hopes he had of converting to jets and getting a home defence posting. But the news had come at a time when other career options were in his mind: some with flying involved, others more mundane desk or factory jobs. He hadn't made an application for selection for jet training, and this was something he would now consider carefully.

Wing Commander Martin came forward. "All ranks will be advised of the changes this afternoon at 1500 hours. No discussion, please, until after then. A news briefing will be held with the local media at 1700 hours. Flight Lieutenant Devon, would you attend this, please. Any questions, gentlemen?"

There were none, and the wing commander dismissed the men.

***

The frustration Devon felt at not being selected as the new squadron leader grew steadily in his mind, and his thoughts turned again to Hannah. He returned to his quarters and found a telegram pad. A minute later, he stepped into the hall and called his orderly. "Young! Young, are you there?"

"Yes, sir. Is there news about the squadron?" Young couldn't keep the excitement out of his voice.

"That's not why I called you. But don't worry, there will be a briefing later. Take this to the telegraph office, would you? Urgent delivery."

TWENTY-SEVEN

Devon took a last look in the mirror, straightened his shirt collar and smoothed his hair into a wave across his forehead. He felt a keen sense of anticipation blended with excitement that Hannah was happy to meet him again. His urgently written cable had simply said: *Let's meet. Victoria Restaurant 1830 Tuesday.*

There was a knock at the door.

"Sir, your taxi is at the main gate," said Young.

"Great. I'll be back before midnight and you will find me at the Victoria again if needed."

Two taxis coming in opposite directions stopped outside the restaurant. Hannah stepped out of the first, closely followed by Devon from his. Devon took Hannah's arm and gave her a brief kiss on the cheek. He was rewarded with a broad smile. The expression in her wide eyes made his heart race.

They entered the restaurant and the maître d' showed them to a table in an alcove at the back of the restaurant, perhaps correctly assuming that they would welcome some privacy.

"You look wonderful tonight. I'm sorry I had to dash off the other day."

"Don't apologise. I hope the emergency wasn't too concerning."

"No, no problem. Just some changes at the squadron, people coming and going," said Devon.

Hannah couldn't resist asking the question uppermost in her mind. "Will these changes affect you?"

"Only indirectly. Life goes on as normal, for the foreseeable anyway." Devon didn't mention his disappointment and frustration at the way he had been treated in regard to the promotion to squadron leader.

They glanced at the menu before placing their order, not wishing to waste time.

"Have you been busy at the bank?"

"Oh, yes. The bank is growing rapidly and looks for the best customers – those who borrow money but don't really need it!"

Devon smiled; her simple comment exactly matched his interpretation of banking. "Are there any more music events on the horizon?"

"Not for a couple for months, I understand. We're hoping that the London Philharmonic will visit Hong Kong later this year. That would be wonderful."

"Perhaps you will see them in London when you return?" Devon asked.

Hannah looked surprised. "I'm not likely to be in London for a while!"

"No, of course not, sorry. I guess I've been thinking about life back in the UK a lot in the past few days. Not that I'm likely to be there myself either; it's just that there are going to be some personnel changes at the squadron, what with Fitzjohn being incarcerated. I think I've mentioned the skipper's plans to retire from the RAF – well, that's happening next month. We met the new squadron leader on Sunday. Guy Wills is his name. Seems a good chap – plenty of fighter experience and has had time at the Central Flying School so he will keep a good watch over the younger pilots. It's likely to be his last posting before he retires too, if not from the air force then from front-line flying."

"And will this change your role?"

"Not really, at least in the short term. We still have a mission to fulfil here in Hong Kong. I'm expecting one of the up-and-coming pilots to be promoted to flight lieutenant to replace Fitzjohn."

"That's good news anyway."

"Would you still like to take the junk out on Saturday to the Pearl River?" Devon asked.

Hannah visibly relaxed. "Yes, of course, that would be wonderful. Will we have the whole day?"

"Why not? We can leave at around ten, stop at Lamma Island for lunch and return in the afternoon. And perhaps we could swim in the sea again?"

Hannah felt butterflies flutter in her stomach. She knew she couldn't wait any longer to bring up the question of flying for the Israelis. She hoped to heaven that breaking her cover wouldn't upset Adam and make him think less of her, or feel deceived. She so wanted to spend the day with him on Saturday. Surely it was possible to remain as close as they had become…

"Perfect. But first I have something to ask you," she said.

"Fire away."

"Well, I have certain … friends and acquaintances who can offer you a flying role – outside the RAF. This is a very delicate matter – secret, in fact, so I have to ask you to swear not to discuss what I'm about to say with anyone. It's really important, Adam."

"Fine, as you wish. Now come on, girl, spill the beans!"

Hannah took a slow, deep breath. "I have my job at the bank, of course, but I also work for the Israeli government." Hannah gave Devon time to absorb the news. He looked curious, so she continued. "We're recruiting pilots to join the Israeli Air Force in the new State of Israel. We need pilots experienced in flying Spitfires – you may be aware that we have acquired a couple of squadrons of Spitfires from Czechoslovakia. Israel is under threat from the Arab countries and we must build air superiority to deter the Arabs from attacking and seeking to destroy Israel before the country has really established itself."

Devon looked astounded. His face paled as he heard her words, but he could say nothing.

Hannah went on. "You will have read about the situation in Palestine, and even the news of the Spitfires, but the British government is not actively supporting the Israeli armed forces – possibly the opposite. Some foreign pilots have already been recruited – a Canadian and a South African. They have even had some success shooting down Egyptian aircraft. We're not just looking for Jewish pilots – we can take pilots of any religion or background. We will pay extremely well—"

"Wait a minute, Hannah!" Devon was agitated. "Let me get this straight. Have you been romancing me just so you could recruit me to the Israeli Air Force? I've been so stupid, thinking you felt something for me when all you wanted was to entice me into becoming a mercenary. I see now why you kept asking about the future of the squadron and my career. It was all a deception. Is that how it is? Is this why you were getting close to Henry Fitzjohn as well?"

"Adam, please, listen. That is not really how it is, believe me. My job is to meet potential recruits, give them details about the job, and if they're interested, introduce them to my colleagues in the Israeli Secret Service in Hong Kong. I couldn't have guessed that you and I would become, well, close. There is no deception there; my feelings for you are honest and true. As for Henry Fitzjohn – yes, we were interested in recruiting him, but we didn't get that far before his arrest."

"It's incredible, Hannah. I can hardly believe it."

"We know that the future for many pilots is uncertain, and you have said you wanted to keep flying. If I'm honest, I felt you would jump at the opportunity," said Hannah.

"Well, I do want to keep flying, but I would have to look carefully at any potential job." Devon caught the waiter's eye. "The bill, please."

"You wan' dessert and coffee, sir?"

"No, bring the damn bill!" Devon had lost his temper. "Apologies. The bill, please," he repeated more calmly. "I no longer wish to see you on Saturday, Hannah. Our relationship – if that's what it was – is over. I'm sorry that things have worked out this way. You know how I felt about you, but now I see what you were doing, and I can't get past that. It's all been a sham, and I don't feel I can trust you any longer." Devon stood up, dropped a handful of dollars on the table and strode out of the restaurant.

TWENTY-EIGHT

Hartman walked through Hannah's house to the living room. He sat down, a look of irritation on his face, holding the note she had sent as if it was incriminating evidence.

"So that was it – he simply got up and walked away? Couldn't you find a way of keeping him engaged, making sure you didn't lose contact? It will be bloody difficult to recruit pilots if you can't keep a simple friendship going." Hartman made no attempt to disguise his frustration. "It wouldn't surprise me if Mars had you sent straight back to the UK. You've not really impressed since you arrived here."

"That's not fair, David! It wasn't my fault that Fitzjohn behaved the way he did, and then got himself arrested. And we now know that Adam Devon is a principled individual who won't just grab the first flying opportunity that comes along. Promises of large sums of money hold very little sway with him. We must try new leads, look at the intelligence we have on other pilots. The new squadron leader, for example." Hannah had learned to hold her own with her superiors and to speak her mind.

Hartman looked thoughtful. "We must look at others, but let's talk about Devon first. Tell me, how were you getting on with him … personally, shall we say?"

"That's none of your business."

"But it is – men will follow any cause if there's a reason. *You* could be that reason. Meet him again. Make him committed to you."

"I hope you're not suggesting what I think you're suggesting, because you can forget it. I'm not going to prostitute myself for anyone or anything. Anyway, Adam is not that sort of person."

"Calm down. There is another way. Meet him again and we move to stage two – introduce me to him at the same time. I'll take over the flying discussions and you can bow out. Leave it to me to engage him."

"Alright, yes, we could do that. Let's hope he doesn't feel he's being shanghaied into joining us," said Hannah.

"Alright then, when do you think you could meet him?"

"I'll contact him in a couple of days. He needs that time to reflect, to think more about what I have offered. But my guess is he will still refuse to meet."

"Alright, let's do it your way. Try your best. I'll report back to Mars."

Hannah's message was plain: she asked Adam to meet for coffee as soon as possible, she wanted to tell him something important about herself. As she wrote the note, her anxiety grew. She wanted to see Adam again for who he was, for what he was beginning to mean to her. She couldn't turn off her personal feelings and stay in a cold-blooded, ruthless mode.

TWENTY-NINE

After his usual Saturday morning run, as he dressed in his freshly laundered Far East uniform, Devon sighed. He had suffered agonies since last seeing Hannah. He missed her terribly, and wondered if he had overreacted. He asked himself how wise it had been to accept her invitation to coffee – why stir up his emotions if there was no chance of carrying on the relationship? He just couldn't see himself trusting her again.

She had already arrived, and sat quietly in a comfortable chair in the lobby of the Peninsula Hotel, toying nervously with her pearl necklace. He walked up to her and paused. A waiter stood by.

"Coffee for two, please. Is that alright, Hannah?"

"Yes, thank you."

"We must keep this short. Nobody likes a long-drawn-out goodbye."

"Adam, I want to explain. There are things I should tell you."

"Really? What else are you going to spring on me?" Devon's cynicism was clear in his voice.

"You need to know more about me, listen to my story and find out how I came to be mixed up in this secret service business. Please, Adam, if there is anything between us you will at least give me the chance to explain."

"Alright. Go ahead."

"First, I'm not English by birth. I was born in Germany, and I'm Jewish. Shaw is not my real name – my family name was Steinberg. My natural father was a physics professor at the university in Berlin and worked closely with other academics in Cambridge. He visited Cambridge several times and once before the war, when I was about eight years old, my whole family came to England for a holiday and we stayed with my father's friend, Professor Austen, and his wife and daughter. The Austen family live in a lovely house on Trumpington Street." Hannah paused and steadied her breathing. "Eventually the Nazis took hold of universities and insisted on all lectures being anti-Jewish. My father opposed this, so he became a target for the Nazis. He was dismissed from his job in 1937 for being Jewish, and times became very hard for us. We could barely afford to buy food."

Devon was astounded by what he was hearing. "How did you come to live in England? Why did you change your name?" he asked gently.

"The pogrom went on around us; we could see the terrible way that Jews were being treated, but my father would not leave – he was too proud to believe he was not wanted in Germany. Then in 1939 one of my father's colleagues mentioned the Kindertransport to my parents. They were sending their two children to England and suggested that my parents should consider doing the same for me and my younger brother, Daniel. He was only five. I was twelve. Reluctantly they agreed. Our parents told us we were going for another holiday with the Austen family – they wouldn't say for how long, but seeing my mother cry was awful. I knew something was terribly wrong." Hannah's voice trailed off and she gazed into the distance as she relived the dreadful separation from her parents. "I held Daniel's hand. I was responsible for him and didn't want him to see me crying. I knew that I had to become my mother's replacement for him, and our mother had never cried. Until that day." Hannah closed her eyes for a few moments. "We were taken by train to Rotterdam, and then by sea to Harwich. Another train took us to London, to Liverpool Street Station. Professor Austen was our sponsor, and he met us there, and we took another train to Cambridge. It was so good to see a friendly face. The Austens were very kind – I knew we were lucky to have such a generous and caring host family. Many of the Kindertransport children were placed in hostels and with families that could barely afford to feed them. They suffered the trauma of separation more than we did, and ours was devastating. When war broke out and the German border closed, I realised that we wouldn't see our parents, uncles and aunts and cousins for some time. In fact, we never saw our families again. There were mass arrests and they all disappeared. They were taken to concentration camps and murdered by the Nazis."

"My God, Hannah, that's awful. I vaguely remember the Kindertransport but never thought about what happened to the children who came over," said Devon.

"It was so frightening. We had numbers around our neck to identify us, and were only allowed one small suitcase each. As I had been to England before, I knew what to expect. Most children did not – they might never have been outside their own town or city. Many were from orphanages, and were unloved, scared and vulnerable. The work of the charities and Jewish movements that brought us over to England was wonderful. Nearly 10,000 children were evacuated, but time ran out and all Kindertransports ended when the war began. I still feel so strongly for those left behind. Whatever happened to them? How could they have survived the Holocaust?"

"Slowly, Hannah, take your time." Devon took her hands in his.

His soft voice gave Hannah the strength to continue. She blinked back the tears welling in her eyes.

Then the waiter returned with the coffee tray and set down the coffee jug, cups, milk and sugar bowl. He asked if he should pour but Devon said he would do it; he wanted as little interruption as possible. Devon noticed that the lobby was getting busier, but they had the privacy they wanted in their quiet corner.

Hannah sipped her coffee and went on. "Life at the Austens' house was happy. Daniel and I quickly learned English and we started to go to a local school. Before we started, our name was changed to Shaw. Professor Austen was a caring, thoughtful man – he knew we would suffer if we had an obviously German surname. Sometimes the other children in the school were cruel about our German accents. I worked hard to have a good English accent and to blend in." Hannah kept her voice controlled and steady. "When the war ended we were adopted by the Austens, but kept the name of Shaw. I went to university in London – studied physics, of course, in memory of my father. As a student I shared a flat with another Kindertransport girl, Sophia. It was a good time for me – getting to know more people, understanding the world. After graduation I continued to share with Sophia in London. That's when I met some Jewish boys who were mad to get to Palestine, to build the new country. I became passionate about building the State of Israel, excited that the Jewish people would at last have a secure home and a strong future. We would never again be exposed to the treatment we received in Germany at the hands of the Nazis. It was time for me to do something about my convictions."

Hannah paused again. "During the war I waited for letters from my parents, but none came. I wrote letters myself – no doubt these were destroyed under German government orders. I have never forgotten my parents, or what happened to them. The hateful Nazis inflicted so much suffering, but they would never have expected the result of

their inhuman work to be the foundation of the Jewish State in Israel."
Hannah's voice took on a determined tone and she sat up straight, her
eyes intense. "We must build our own country. England has been my
home for the last ten years, but my real place is with my Jewish family."

Devon frowned.

"I don't mean my actual family, they are all gone. I'm talking about
my people – all Jewish people. We must build our own country," Hannah
repeated. "We now have the State of Israel, but we are being threatened.
You have seen newsreels about the war with the Arabs. We have to be
able to defeat the Arab forces before they set about destroying Israel.
We have few friends – even the British government will not throw their
weight behind the establishment of Israel."

Devon had seen reports in the newspapers – the British government
wanted to stay allied to the Arab nations, or at least not to make
enemies of them. The King David Hotel bombing in 1946 by Jewish
extremists had killed dozens of people, including British citizens, and
had turned many people against the Jews. Most of the British troops
departed Palestine in June 1948, prompting the Israelis and Arabs to
seek to dominate the region.

"In my last year at university, Sophia suggested that a job in a large
City bank would lead to a good career. I was referred to the London and
Hong Kong Bank – it seemed a very nice job to have."

"But Hannah, you lived in England, I presume happily and settled
– as much as anyone could be after the tragedy you suffered. How did
you come to be recruited into this secret service stuff?" asked Devon.

"I'm not supposed to discuss this, but I'll tell you, because of who you
are to me. The bank has connections with the Israeli Secret Service. They
recruited me soon after I joined the bank. I think now it was all planned
from my days at university and the Jewish friends I made in London. I
was then trained for this assignment in Hong Kong. As you know, I'm to
identify and recruit potential pilots who are leaving the RAF."

"It sounds so crazy. How can British pilots be of use?"

"You know that front-line flying is moving to jets – the days of the Spitfire will soon be over in the UK. But in Israel our air defence consists of two squadrons of Spitfires, and we need good people to fly them. We also need to ensure that the Egyptians don't get there first and recruit pilots. You know how important air superiority is. We must make sure that our pilots are better than the Egyptians, even if they and the other Arab nations outnumber us. So that's why I have been meeting the airmen from Kai Tak. Discussions about the future of Spitfire squadrons and the aircrew are going on all the time. It's very possible that disbandment would mean pilots becoming available, and I need to know who the best British pilots are, then try to recruit them for our air force. I have already said that we will pay well – very well. This is an opportunity for men who decide to leave the RAF but see a future for themselves in flying. Like you."

"So you thought I might be one of your recruits? And that's why you were getting close to Fitzjohn!" Adam said. "It seems that I mean nothing to you other than what I can do for Israel." He let go of her hands and sat back.

"No, no, please listen. I needed to get to know you, of course, to understand how you might respond to being recruited. But then other things got in the way…"

"Really? So now you're *not* going to offer me a job as a mercenary in the Israeli Air Force? I thought you and I felt something for each other. Please don't lie! You just saw me as a target."

"Adam, I do care for you – so much. But please try to understand my position. We must be able to protect the State of Israel. You have told me you plan to leave the RAF this year. Yes, I want to offer you a contract to fly with us. I have to set aside what I feel for you and put my country first, don't you see? And my job is to recruit pilots. You're one of the best Spitfire pilots around, you have said you're resigning from the RAF and that you want to fly. So how could I not ask you to come and join us?"

"Hannah, look, I'm not Jewish, so how could I fight for your cause? Sure, I know the history and I agree that the State of Israel should be formed and supported by Britain, but surely you want people who are from your own Jewish family, as you think of it?"

"We have Jewish people from all over the world coming to fight for the preservation of Israel, and we already have some international pilots flying with us. Like you, they are not Jewish; they're flying with us for the excitement, for the exhilaration of being on an operational squadron. Of course the money helps – they will be set up for life with what we're paying them. I believe they also understand and support the need for a free state for the Jewish people. They have seen stories of all the wartime atrocities, the Holocaust. How can anyone oppose the Jews' desire to build a safe place for themselves? Please think about it. We're desperate for pilots."

"Suddenly the thought of going home to the UK seems more attractive to me. I'm not against your cause, of course I'm not, but I don't see myself as a mercenary. My position is unchanged. Don't expect me to take up the offer!" Devon shouted. "I'm sorry, I shouldn't lose my temper. I have to get back to the station. I wish you well."

The two looked at each other; there were no words. Hannah finally broke the silence. "I'm sorry."

"Goodbye, Hannah."

***

In the Officers' Mess that evening Devon found solace in joining the men for a few drinks. All the talk was about the new skipper. In the two patrols Devon had flown with Squadron Leader Wills he had been impressed by his precision in formation and flying style, and felt confident that they would be able to work well together. Wills had made it clear that he wanted to see textbook flying, with pilots following the leader's instructions to the letter. On the radio Wills was precise and measured, and he pulled up a couple of pilots after patrols on sloppy approach and landing techniques. This was an operational squadron on a deployment of great importance, and with potential danger. If they were to see any live action he wanted it to be delivered with the utmost effectiveness.

Pilot Officer Taylor came over to Devon. "Can I get you a drink, sir?"

"That's very kind, James. I'll have a half of bitter."

Taylor placed the order with the barman and turned back to Devon. "How are you finding the new skipper, sir? Is he good enough for our squadron?" Taylor raised his eyebrows.

"Asking me to critique a fellow officer, James? We can't have that. But yes, off the record he is certainly an excellent pilot, very disciplined, knows how to handle a Spit. Maybe we need to knock off the training school shine and look for a bit more grit. If we do see action, then we're going to need all-out aggression."

"He has time on Tempests, so he should know all about ground attack. No doubt we'll get some training on that front – we can't just have regular patrolling and air-show jollies."

"They're all important in our role, James." Devon defended Wills but recognised that Taylor was right. "I'm sure that if the Chinese created a stir and we had to have a go at them, the squadron leader would lead from the front with all tenacity."

"Yes sir, I'm sure you're right."

A new group of officers came into the Mess, and Taylor drifted over to join them. Devon reflected on the decision of the CO and the higher-ranking officers to bring in a new squadron leader. He knew that his own promotion to the role would have come early in his career, but since his meeting with Green and Porter he had to admit that he had harboured the ambition to be given the squadron. Green and Porter had not discussed their decision with him; he had heard about Wills' arrival at the same time as all the other officers. He had been given no feedback from the interview, no feel for his chances of promotion at a future date or with another squadron.

That's always the way the RAF works, he thought. I'm not guaranteed a promotion in the future – and who needs it anyway? He wondered if he felt resentment at being passed over for a job he was keen to do. That was partly true, but Devon's aim was to enjoy his flying. He had plenty of years ahead on front-line squadrons, if that's what he wanted.

Devon had his mother's letter in his pocket. He took it out and glanced at it again. The opportunity she mentioned at Avro seemed so mundane, although it would be a stepping stone to building a career in avionics. Devon decided to think carefully about what he wanted to do, but his thoughts turned constantly to Hannah. It was no good. He wanted to see her again, he wanted to hold her and be close to her. But the only way that seemed possible was if he was willing to discuss flying for the Israeli Air Force. Now the idea didn't seem so crazy. On reflection, it would be very exciting flying, and well paid. Devon empathised with the Jewish people and believed in the formation of the State of Israel, but could he really say he was willing to fight, and kill if necessary, in the cause of a country that was not his own?

Devon slept fitfully, his dreams full of the irrational desire to avenge Hannah's loss of her family. He wanted her to think well of him, for her to see him as a partner in building a new Jewish society that would be safe from wars and persecutions.

Before dawn he finally drifted off to sleep for a couple of hours, then woke, exhausted. The desire to contact Hannah was overwhelming. He pushed away the thought that she had no feelings for him, that she had got close to him just so she could persuade him to join the Israelis.

Suddenly Devon jumped out of bed and strode over to his desk. He wrote a telegram to be sent immediately. He decided to throw on some clothes and go to the telegraph office himself.

The telegram contained one simple question: Hannah, *can we meet tonight at 7 at your house?*

THIRTY

The taxi from the Star Ferry terminal dropped Devon off a couple of minutes before seven o'clock. He didn't delay but pressed the doorbell, feeling anxious but certain that he was doing the right thing.

"Adam, it's lovely to see you. Come in," said Hannah. She looked beautiful in a simple cream cotton dress and white leather sandals. He recognised the pretty string of pearls she wore; they must be her favourite. Devon caught the aroma of jasmine and roses – could be Shalimar, he thought.

"Come through. I have some orange and mango juice."

"Great." They walked through to the kitchen. "Shall we take these drinks outside? It's a lovely warm evening."

The terrace had space for two rattan armchairs, close together, and a small table. They had been painted in a dusty pink, probably some years earlier. Two large glass lanterns in the corner of the terrace contained candles whose flames were motionless and gave off a cream-gold light. Devon sipped his fruit juice and Hannah sat patiently.

"This is nice. The sky is so clear." Devon looked up as the last glow of twilight turned to night. "The star to the right there is actually Saturn, not a star at all. We should be able to see Jupiter later." Devon knew he was hopeless at small talk.

Hannah smiled. "It's beautiful. I wonder if the stars are aligned for us," she said quietly.

Devon took a deep breath. "Thanks for seeing me at such short notice. I felt I had to come over to clear the air. We've only known each other for a short time, but I feel so much for you. I need to know if I'm being stupid, or do you feel something for me too?"

"Oh Adam, of course I do." She put her hand on his arm and pressed gently. "We haven't known each other long, but I know what I feel for you. I want to be with you. Don't go away again, please."

"I'm not planning to, but we should talk about us separately from your work. So, first, let's have that day out on the Pearl River. I have a full day's pass on Friday – would you be able to take the day off from the bank?"

"Yes, I'm due some leave," said Hannah. "Same plan – leave Kowloon at about ten?"

"Sure. I will book the junk and the crew will arrange somewhere for lunch. And bring your swimming kit again!"

They laughed at the shared memory, then Devon took Hannah's hands in his. They fell silent again.

"I know I reacted badly to your proposal to work for the Israeli Air Force, but I've had time to think about it. I have strong feelings about the way Jews were treated in the war, and part of Britain's role in the world is to stamp out tyranny and support rights for all people, something we have fought for many times. In other words, I'm not saying it's out of the question. I would like to know more. I want to know how it would work. And I would need to give a month's notice to the RAF."

"Are you sure, Adam? You must want to do the job for all your own reasons, not just to please me."

"Yes, my mind is clear. It's a cause I believe in. I want to keep flying, and the opportunities in the RAF are diminishing fast – this would be an excellent and testing operational role, something I would really savour. The question I have at the moment is whether you will be in Israel when I'm there. Will we be able to see each other?"

"I've thought about that. I could ask for a position at a bank in Tel Aviv. I'm sure LHK would help me find something. Israel is a small country, so we would never be far apart. After I've finished my assignment here, I'll be happy that I've done something worthwhile to help form the State of Israel. It will be time for me to build my own life."

"Then things are looking promising. Tell me what happens next." Devon felt a sense of excitement.

Hannah leant forward and spoke in a low voice. "You need to meet one of my colleagues from the secret service. His name is Hartman and he will be able to brief you on aircraft types, squadron strength, air defence tactics and that sort of thing. Not really my area. I'll try and fix a meeting for later this week, if that's OK with you?"

"I think I have met him. Was he at Government House for the music evening? A construction engineer or something."

"Yes, that's him, that's his cover. But please, never mention this to anyone. We do have enemies here in Hong Kong and security is vital."

"Understood. I could make an evening meeting on Wednesday, if that works?"

"Yes, that would be fine. There's a small Chinese restaurant in Wan Chai called the Sun Garden. I will not be there, but wait in the bar and Hartman will find you. And now, have you eaten this evening? Perhaps we can take a taxi down to Central for dinner."

"Lovely idea."

They stood up. Hannah reached up and linked her hands behind Devon's neck. He responded with a fervent and lingering kiss.

THIRTY-ONE

The pilots' operations room was a hive of activity. The day's missions included a three-aircraft patrol along the southern coastline of Hong Kong Island, two flights in close formation flying practice over Kowloon, and an individual Spitfire sent on a high-level photo reconnaissance near the Chinese border. Flight plans were filed and the final briefing given by Squadron Leader Wills. The weather was fine, with good visibility and a light wind. Wills read out the timings for each mission, the exact altitudes and compass headings to be flown, and the required landing time. He asked for questions, but his briefing was so specific and detailed, it was no surprise that there were none.

Devon's flight took the southern coast assignment. As stated clearly in the plan, the landing time for the first of his aircraft was 11.38 a.m., with the subsequent aircraft landing at one-minute intervals. Devon knew the geography well enough to time his crossing over the island and down to Victoria Harbour perfectly, and he landed at Kai Tak exactly at the appointed time. The other missions achieved their aims with similar precision.

After they had landed, the pilots waited outside the ops room in good spirits. Squadron Leader Wills talked to each flight leader and compared notes on their missions, asking them to describe how they achieved the precise movements and timings. It was almost midday and the heat was building when Wills called all the pilots into the ops room to write up their logbooks and reports. When they entered, they were surprised to see Group Captain Green standing at the dais.

"Squadron Leader Wills and Flight Lieutenant Devon, come with me, please," he said. "The rest of you, complete your paperwork as usual."

Green led the two officers out of the ops room and across to the Officers' Mess. The place was empty, as all the men were occupied in flying, maintenance or security, and it was not yet lunchtime. Green beckoned to a steward. "Coffee for four, please, Grayson."

"Yes, sir – for four, sir?"

"Yes. I'm expecting another officer shortly."

"Very good, sir."

"Gentlemen, I have some news for you that might come as a surprise. I don't wish to hear your opinions; you have to deal with the facts of the case and ensure that none of what you are about to see and hear affects the operation of the squadron. I'm sure I can rely on you both."

A car was heard pulling up outside, then a door slammed. A figure in RAF uniform swaggered into the Mess.

"Come and join us," Green called.

"Fitzjohn! What the hell is going on?" Devon asked. He and Wills looked astounded.

"How lovely to see you, Devon. Keeping well, I hope? And Squadron Leader Wills, I presume – very pleased to meet you, sir." Fitzjohn had not lost any of his bluster.

"Take a seat, Fitzjohn, then please be so kind as to explain recent goings-on," said Green. "We have seen the report by the military police and the charges brought against you. They are very serious indeed, but now you have been released and I have been advised by Wing Commander Martin that you are returning to normal duties. Tell us more."

"I'd be delighted to, sir. The fracas with the Chinese gambling house boys was a sorry mix-up. As my lawyers advised the military police chaps, I was in fact seeking to assist in the apprehension of a nasty little group intent on compromising British servicemen and blackmailing them. We really should not tolerate such behaviour against our people, so I took the initiative and did something about it. The officers involved in the arrests jumped the gun somewhat. I was on the verge of rounding up the scoundrels and putting an end to their racket. I didn't involve the security people earlier, as it was something I had very much under control." Fitzjohn ran his fingers through his hair, wearing a self-satisfied smile.

"But Fitzjohn, the report says that you gave them your keys to the armaments store," said Green.

"A ploy to gain their confidence, sir. I needed to infiltrate their little outfit and discover who was behind the organisation. As I explained to the officers, giving them access to the store and challenging them at the club worked perfectly to bring out the ringleader – now sadly deceased, of course, but perhaps he deserved his sticky end after taking a shot at the Australian."

"Come off it, Fitzjohn, you were up to your neck in debt and were trying to buy your way out!" Devon did not suppress his anger.

"Please mind what you say, Devon. I'm sure you're familiar with the law in regard to slander, and our two colleagues here will testify to anything you say, now or outside this room."

"There's no need to make threats, Fitzjohn," said Green firmly. "Devon, no personal opinions, please. The wing commander has been advised by the military police that all charges have been dropped, and you are to return to the squadron. I presume you are now fit and able to return to service?"

"Yes, sir. My arm is healing nicely. I feel little discomfort – it's a nasty wound but it has been nearly three weeks since the affair now," said Fitzjohn, in a tone that dismissed the wound as immaterial. "The medics have given me the OK."

"Squadron Leader Wills, you have ultimate command of flying operations. Are you happy to take Fitzjohn back?" said Green.

"Not quite, sir. I would like to take the flight lieutenant out tomorrow morning on a test flight, just the two of us, to put the Spits through their paces. I think every other pilot in the squadron is ready for any operational challenges the Chinese might throw at us. At the moment, I can't say that of Fitzjohn. He needs to prove to me that he is fully competent, both as a fighter pilot and a section leader."

"Fitzjohn, are you happy with that?"

"Of course, sir. I would be delighted to show the squadron leader how one can get the most from a Spitfire." Fitzjohn turned to Wills. "I understand you have spent some time at the training school of late, sir."

Wills looked riled by the inference that he might not be as sharp as he could be. "That's correct, Fitzjohn. Meet me in the ops room at 0830 for a briefing. Take-off will be at 0900."

"That concludes our meeting, gentlemen. Please ensure—"

Before Green could finish, Devon had risen from his chair and marched out of the room. He knew he had been insubordinate, but he couldn't care less. He was convinced that Fitzjohn was lying, and was angry at the air force for letting him off the hook. No doubt he had employed the best lawyers. Devon could do little but accept the news, but it further undermined his commitment to staying in the RAF.

***

Fitzjohn spent most of the evening in the bar in the Officers' Mess regaling the assembled company with his version of how he had dealt with armed assailants in the cause of airfield security. Having been deprived of alcohol during his time in the RAF jail, he took the opportunity to make up for lost drinking time. By 11 p.m. he was shuffled out of the bar by pilots in his flight – they knew he had a tough assignment in the morning and he needed his sleep.

They need not have worried. At 7 a.m. he was up, showered and alert, without a trace of a hangover. He called to his orderly. "Mackie, coffee when you're ready. And bring me over a good plate of breakfast from the Mess, will you? I've some swotting to do on the Spitfire handling manual."

Fitzjohn was already in the ops room when Squadron Leader Wills arrived, the regional airspace chart and his notepad spread across the desk.

"Good morning, sir. What do you have in mind for this morning's exercise?" Clearly Fitzjohn wanted to sound enthusiastic, even if he was offended by the suggestion that his flying might not be up to scratch.

"I have the flight plan here, Fitzjohn. Study it carefully, please." Wills placed the extensive list of objectives, waymarkers, altitudes and timings on the desk. Fitzjohn copied the details onto his notepad and looked up. "Will we be carrying out a simulated attack, sir?"

"Yes – we will be attacking the navy's target ship five miles south of Stanley. We will break at 3,000 feet, carry out a fast-powered dive to 250 feet, fire a three-second burst from the cannons then open fire with machine guns at 100 feet. Then we will climb away in a steep, turning climb at maximum rate and level out at 2,000 feet. Clear on that? I want to see all the gunfire strike home, Fitzjohn."

"Yes, sir." Fitzjohn's bluff was gone. This would be close to suicidal in a real combat mission, and not far from that as an exercise. He wondered what Wills was trying to do – kill them both?

As the aircraft taxied out, Wills' voice came over the radio. "You lead the way on the mission, Fitzjohn. I will follow your every move. Look out for me to your right in close formation."

"Roger, sir."

The climb away from Kai Tak to 3,000 feet was executed perfectly by both pilots and they cruised south before Fitzjohn made the first scheduled turn onto a heading of 225 degrees. Or approximately 225.

"Fitzjohn, get on magnetic heading now! I want absolute accuracy. Don't drift off."

"Copied, sir."

After two more heading changes that Fitzjohn executed with precision, the naval target ship came into view.

"Wait for my order, Fitzjohn."

No more than five seconds passed before the order came. "Attack!"

Fitzjohn simultaneously pushed the control column and the throttle lever forward and the Spitfire dived towards the target at maximum speed, approaching 400 mph. Fitzjohn kept the aircraft straight with steady pressure on the rudder and watched the altimeter unwind through 1,000 feet, then 500 feet. As he approached 250 feet he placed his left thumb over the cannon gun button, then pressed. Shells pumped out of the two cannons and crashed into the target ship. Fitzjohn switched to machine guns, keeping one eye on the altimeter. It passed 150 feet. He had left it late to fire, and his bullets sprayed into the sea beyond the ship. He pulled up into the near-vertical climbing turn that the flight plan required. The G-force drained the blood from his upper body and he held his muscles taut to resist blacking out. After a poor showing in the attack, he wanted to do well when handling the aircraft – clearly one of the key tests in the exercise. But before Fitzjohn reached anywhere near 2,000 feet he started to grey out, and he had no choice but to push the control column forward and start to ease off the climb.

"Fitzjohn, continue with the remainder of the mission. Go to the next turning point," said Wills.

Nearly an hour later the two aircraft made a curving fighter approach and landed at Kai Tak. Fitzjohn parked on the hard standing, slid the canopy open and wrenched off his helmet. He was sweating profusely and felt exhausted. He struggled out of the cockpit and walked to the ops room.

Soon after, Squadron Leader Wills entered. "Fitzjohn, write up your logbook and report to the station commander at 1500 hours." He sounded calm and clear.

"But sir, can we have a debrief on the exercise?" Fitzjohn was nervous. He knew he had not performed well: nearly blacking out, missing turning points, not holding the exact altitude, getting his timing out of schedule. All the things he should have got right in a flight test.

"No. As I say, report to the CO's office this afternoon."

***

Wing Commander Mike Martin sat behind his well-ordered desk and invited Wills and Fitzjohn to sit in the two seats opposite him. "Fitzjohn, I have received the squadron leader's report on the flight test and discussed it with him this morning. It does not make good reading. Your flying is not at the standard required for front-line operations. The exercises you undertook today have been successfully flown by all members of the squadron. What do you have to say for yourself?"

"Well, sir, I agree – I didn't get full marks. Perhaps there were a few minor points that might be improved. Nothing material." Fitzjohn waved a dismissive hand.

"Really? That's not the way Squadron Leader Wills and I see it. You have an injured arm and you have been through a stressful time recently. Your flying skills this morning left a lot to be desired – and I'm not convinced that your mental state would allow you to lead a flight. You're tired, of course. I think you need a break from flying. We have decided that you are immediately grounded for one month. You will undertake a programme of flight assessment and an independent flight examination before being readmitted to the squadron. Any questions?"

Fitzjohn exploded. "What! Grounded? That is entirely uncalled for, sir. There's nothing wrong with my flying!"

"I'm afraid there is, Fitzjohn, patently." Martin was firm and clear. "You will be assigned a role in the adjutant's office during your rest period."

"A bloody desk job! I want this taken up with the top brass, sir."

"That will not happen, Fitzjohn, and enough of your insolence, if you don't mind. The AOC Far East Air Force fully supports this action and indeed has expressed the view that it is the minimum requirement for a pilot in your situation. Now, unless there is anything else you wish to know, you are dismissed. Report to the adjutant at 0900 tomorrow."

***

"Come in, Devon, and take a seat." Wills remained standing and walked over to the window of his office. Gazing out at the parked aircraft, he briefed Devon on the outcome of the flight test. "Sadly, Flight Lieutenant Fitzjohn did not demonstrate the required skills this morning. He has been grounded for a month and will carry out administrative tasks in the adjutant's office during this time."

"Grounded, sir? He must be fuming!"

"We can't have someone in the squadron who isn't up to the mark, can we? Fitzjohn's escapade with the Chinese gang must have blunted his skills." Wills turned away from the window and faced Devon. A smile spread across his face and his left eye twitched in the slightest trace of a wink.

Devon smiled back. "Ah, I see. I understand, sir, thank you."

Walking back to his quarters, Devon laughed to himself. He felt that justice had prevailed on this occasion. Although the RAF had not treated him fairly in his desire to be squadron leader, his confidence in at least one of its commanders had returned.

THIRTY-TWO

Fitzjohn hit his first whisky of the evening hard, and immediately ordered another. As he sat at the bar in the Peninsula Hotel, he had time to reflect. He knew he'd been very lucky to get off the charge of assisting an intruder, but he couldn't shake off the unrest he felt over how the MPs had become aware of his involvement with the armoury keys. The woman – Hetherington-Brown – had said they were monitoring the Chinese for insurgent activity, but he didn't believe they were monitoring a small-time criminal gang, and that didn't seem to explain how they'd found out about his gambling debts and the rest of it.

There was only one explanation. It must have been a tip-off from inside the air station. Who the hell knew about his gambling activities? Fitzjohn gave some thought to having another drink and a small wager, perhaps at the Green Lotus, but decided against it. It would be foolish to return to that place.

A pair of businessmen approached the bar next to Fitzjohn and looked at the myriad of bottles arrayed on the mirrored glass shelves. The men wore pre-war mid-grey European style suits, double-breasted with wide lapels and turn-ups to the trousers, and garish silk ties. They had sallow Mediterranean complexions. One looked older than the other, probably in his fifties. The younger man carried a brown leather document case.

A smiling barman strolled up to them. "How can I help you, gentlemen?"

"Whisky, please. Let me see, what do you have?"

"Quite a range, sir. Do you have a preference? A single malt or perhaps a blended?"

"I'm not sure – there are so many to choose from. Perhaps this gentleman could make a recommendation?"

Fitzjohn looked over at them. "Certainly, old boy, you couldn't do better than to try this one, the 1936 Talisker. Isle of Skye, very pleasant, not at all peaty." Fitzjohn turned to the barman. "Bobby, set up a couple of large ones for these good people. My account."

"Oh no, no! Let me get these, and one for yourself. Three large Taliskers, please, barman."

"Most kind," Fitzjohn said.

"I see from your uniform that you are a British airman. Stationed here, I presume?"

"Yes, along the harbour here at Kai Tak. Are you chaps new to Hong Kong? Where are you staying?"

"Yes, sir, it's our first visit," said the younger man. "My name is Pierre Fazil and this is my manager, Mr Ahmad Kouri. We are staying here at the Peninsula. We are from Egypt. We are members of the trade delegation, specialising in high-quality cotton, cashmere and silk. We hope to find good products here in Hong Kong."

That explains the ties. Doesn't explain how they can afford the Peninsula's room rates, Fitzjohn thought. "Pierre? That's not very Egyptian," he said to the young man.

"My mother is from France."

"Ah, I see. I'm Flight Lieutenant Henry Fitzjohn. I thought you chaps avoided alcohol. My elder brother was in the 8th Army, spent some time in Alex and then Cairo. Very much enjoyed the place. Well, cheers, here's to successful bartering!" He chinked his glass with the other two and sipped his drink. "You will enjoy Hong Kong – there's plenty of nightlife, the food's quite acceptable, and of course there are some very friendly young ladies here!"

"We are here strictly for business," said Kouri, but with a smile. "Alcohol is not forbidden for us."

"And talking of which, it's my round." Fitzjohn clicked his fingers. "Bobby, the same again, please."

"Thank you, Henry. I can see you are a gentleman of quality and style who likes the best pleasures in life," said Kouri.

Fitzjohn knew they were foreign types who would flatter a donkey but nevertheless he was glad to receive compliments; they had been thin on the ground of late.

"You have excellent English, Ahmad. Spent some time there, have you?"

"Yes indeed," Kouri said with a smile. "My parents felt an English education would be good for me. I was a boarder at Millfields, if you know it?"

"Certainly – a very fine school."

"There are many British servicemen here in Hong Kong. It must be a very important place for you," said Fazil.

"Very much so. We came here to discourage the Chinese from thinking of invading. You have probably read all that in the newspapers. I'm glad to say that things have gone quiet with our friends across the border. Hong Kong is important for trade throughout the region so it's worth looking after. Without our stewardship, you chaps might not be able to do business here!" Fitzjohn said proudly.

"You fly the Spitfires, Henry?" Kouri asked casually.

"Yes. Lovely aircraft, packs a punch. Even in these days of jets, the Spitfire is pretty formidable. You have them in the Egyptian Air Force, don't you?"

"I believe so. I'm not an expert on these matters. I only know what I read in the newspapers."

"You prefer silk ties, eh? Can't say I blame you. More money to be made in that line of country than being a mere servant of His Majesty's armed forces!"

"But is it not the best job, Henry? Flying and being paid to do what you love?"

"There is that. But a chap has overheads, you know, and there is more to be made flying commercially these days, even if it is somewhat humdrum."

"Another whisky, gentlemen?" Bobby was an astute barman, quick to offer customers more drinks.

"My pleasure, I think." Pierre raised his hand.

"Tell me, Henry, do you like the horses? I hear they have a fine racecourse at Happy Valley. Have you been there?" Kouri asked.

"Indeed I have. A splendid track, very social too. You must have a night out there at some point."

"We are planning to go there next week for the regular Wednesday festival night. Would you care to join us?"

Fitzjohn gave it a moment's thought. He had vowed to stay clear of gambling and to keep a low profile. He had no wish to give the squadron leader a reason to delay his return to flying. But a social occasion wouldn't hurt, surely.

"You know, I think I would. Thank you, Ahmad."

"Excellent! I suggest we meet at the Star Ferry terminal in Central at 7 p.m. We can take a taxi to Happy Valley. If any difficulties arise, please call this number." Kouri looked at Fazil, who had already opened his document case and taken out a business card.

THIRTY-THREE

"Sir, message from the adjutant. You're asked to go to the governor's – sorry, sir – the wing commander's office at 2 p.m. The message mentioned that the squadron leader will also be in attendance."

"Thank you, Young. Message back that I will be there."

"Yes, sir. Nothing serious, I hope?"

"Ah, wait and see. I'm sure there will be something for you to say in the bar this evening, but nothing that will surprise anyone, I'm afraid."

"I think I understand, sir."

Devon knew that Young had a good idea about what his plans were. He appreciated his orderly's insight: it was part of his character and one of the benefits of long service in the forces.

***

"Come in, Devon, and sit down." Wing Commander Martin pointed to one of two chairs in front of his desk. Shortly after, Squadron Leader Wills came into the office and took the other one.

"Now, Devon, I must say I was very surprised to receive your letter of resignation," said Martin. "You have had an exemplary career in the RAF and there are plenty of opportunities for good people going forward. I realise that you wanted to lead 28 Squadron and the appointment of an outsider, so to speak, must have disappointed you. As I say, we still see a great future for you in the service. It is for that reason I have not processed your letter. I'm giving you the opportunity to reconsider and, if you wish, I will tear up the letter. What do you say?"

"Sir, thank you for your kind words. I have certainly enjoyed my time with the RAF. And I would really like to continue flying in my next role. At the moment I have not signed up for a new job; I'm considering my options. But I have no doubt in my mind that it is time to leave the RAF. This has not solely arisen from my regret at not being promoted, although that has influenced my decision. We all know the service is being reduced in size and Spitfire squadrons are being disbanded."

"There must be something you plan to do, Devon. What are those options you mentioned?" said Wills.

"Well, I'm open to commercial flying. Squadron Leader Porter has found an excellent role at BOAC." It was a diversion; Devon wasn't really that interested in passenger flying. "I'm also thinking about working in avionics – perhaps as a test pilot on new radar and navigation equipment. Then there are also aircraft manufacturing jobs – I've been offered something at Avro. It's not quite what I'm looking for, so I haven't responded yet." Clearly Devon was not going to mention the Israeli flying job; that was subject to secrecy. Also, he had no idea how the RAF would respond to a serving officer agreeing to fly for a foreign air force.

"There are certainly a number of routes a capable pilot could pursue," said Martin. "But back to my point, Devon. You will be leaving the service just as promotion is not far away and with many years of front-line service ahead of you. We can never be certain, but we have assurances from High Command that there are no plans for the squadron to be disbanded. And there are, of course, opportunities in other squadrons. I put it to you that you should reconsider. I can give you forty-eight hours to think it over."

Devon appreciated that this offer was a generous concession from the wing commander, but he had no doubts. He would be leaving. "Thank you, sir. It's kind of you to allow me the time but it's not necessary. I can say now that I have no reservations or doubts about my resignation."

"Very well, Devon, so be it. I wish you well for the future – you have been a great asset to the RAF. We will of course hold a suitable farewell for you when the time comes."

The three officers stood, then Devon saluted and left without any further ceremony. As he walked across the tarmac, he marvelled at how hot and humid the atmosphere was in the Far East. He'd never been able to become comfortable with it.

***

"How was the meeting, sir?" Young brought in a mug of tea, made strong, with condensed milk and two spoons of sugar. It was almost a meal in itself.

"Thank you, Young. Put it down there, would you?" Devon stood at his portable record player, placing one of his favourites on the turntable: *The Marriage of Figaro*. He wanted something uplifting.

"I can tell you now that I have resigned my commission."

"Goodness me, sir … although it doesn't come as a huge surprise. I thought – well, we all thought – you were destined for great things within the service, but there are many other opportunities out there for pilots. What will you do next?"

"I still have to decide that. My aim is to keep flying, but where exactly is still uncertain," said Devon.

"Sir, the men have been talking about the future of the squadron. We know there's a risk it could be disbanded soon. I have to decide whether I want to stay in the RAF or go into Civvy Street. And what with you leaving, sir, now might be the best time to move on. Trouble is, there's not a lot of exciting jobs in England right now. Having a job in the RAF makes a good career."

"No one can be sure of anything these days, but don't listen to gossip. I would be very surprised if 28 was disbanded in the next year or two. Tell me, what would you like to do after the RAF?"

Young shuffled his feet. Devon appreciated he was not used to discussing personal matters with his boss. "A friend of mine has a plum job at the Great Eastern Hotel in London, sir. He's a waiter in the Hamilton ballroom and restaurant, serving upper-class clientele and City gents. He says he could get me an interview for a job there."

"That would appeal to you?"

"Yes, sir, very much. Getting a job in a top London hotel would set me up nicely. And I could see my family regularly. They live not far away in Streatham."

"Then it certainly would be worth looking into, but don't rush anything, Steven. Leaving the service would be a big decision."

"No sir. And thank you, sir. Can I get you anything else?"

"Come back in half an hour, would you? I will have a telegram and letter for you to send. Keep all this to yourself for the time being."

"Yes, sir." Young gave a small bow as he left Devon's room, almost playing the part of the attentive waiter already.

Devon sat back and enjoyed the music. Reflecting on his discussion with Young, he knew he was making the right decision: it was time to move on. He took out a telegram pad.

Hello Mother STOP Resigned from the RAF STOP Hope to keep flying but will look at the job at Avro STOP Letter follows STOP Adam STOP

What else could he add? He couldn't tell anyone that he would be flying with the Israelis. He opened an airmail letter and started to write.

Dear Mother,

I hope this letter finds you well, and the same for Dad and Joan. We are keeping busy here with lots of flying but we also get a chance to explore the colony in the afternoons and evenings. There are some beautiful places to see – gardens, beaches, temples and of course touring the Chinese markets for nice things to send home.

I hope you received my telegram. As I said, I have now resigned my commission from the air force. I will be leaving in about a months' time, maybe longer. I know this is something you were keen on, but I have not yet decided what I want to do next. There are lots of commercial flying jobs around, and I would like to look carefully at what Avro might be able to offer. There are also other avionics firms, such as Decca in London or the Marconi Company in Essex, that are doing work I would be interested in – perhaps test-flying the new equipment. Anyway, I'm very excited about the next steps in my career and I will let you know what I have decided to do as soon as possible.

Your loving son,

Adam

Devon folded the aerogramme and sealed the gummed edges, ready for Young to take it and the telegram to the telegraph office.

THIRTY-FOUR

The patrol assigned to Devon's flight that morning featured one of his favourite exercises – low-flying and ground attack practice. His wingmen, Bryant and Taylor, kept a perfect V formation, a tribute to Squadron Leader Wills' insistence on accurate and disciplined flying. Debriefing in the intelligence officer's hut took a few minutes, then Devon was free for the rest of the day. He quickly changed into his running kit for a couple of circuits of the airfield. This always cleared his mind and helped him relax.

David Hartman sat at the bar in the Sun Garden restaurant, feeling that he had at last proved his worth to the senior officers in the Israeli Secret Service. Hannah had done well too, bringing Devon round to at least talk about flying for them. Informants from the airfield had briefed him on Fitzjohn's return and his grounding. Although they would keep a watch on him, he was no longer a priority; someone with his record was not likely to fit in to their air force.

Devon was a couple of minutes late, but when he entered the

restaurant he immediately walked over to Hartman. "Hello, David, good to see you."

Hartman stood and shook Devon's hand enthusiastically. "Good evening, Adam. Thanks for coming over to the island. What will you have to drink?"

"Just a beer, please."

"Sure. Why don't we go to our table? I have booked a private room for us."

As they sat in the small anteroom, the two men exchanged pleasantries: about the weather, Chinese food, the music at the Government House reception. Then Hartman turned to business matters.

"I believe Hannah has outlined our plan to recruit pilots," said Hartman. "I'm glad you're keen to join us. It is a matter of the utmost importance to the State of Israel that we build an air force capable of defending our territories from our enemies. I would like to discuss with you your reasons for wishing to join us, and then I will brief you on what you will be asked to do, the current aircraft we have, and of course the opposing military forces, in the air and on the ground."

"Thank you, David. My reasons are varied. Naturally, as a pilot I would like to keep flying, in particular in active service. The future for RAF pilots is uncertain and I want to control my own career. I know you are seeking Jewish pilots first and foremost, but I am aware that you have taken on non-Jewish people. The horrors of the Holocaust are known to us all and I'm not surprised that Jewish people wish to establish their own country. I feel very strongly that the British government should be lending assistance to the formation of Israel by ensuring peace in the region through supporting a strong air defence capability. Apparently that is something our politicians are struggling with, as they also wish to keep on the good side of the Arab nations. I just want to do a good job, as a deterrent, or if necessary, air fighting or ground attack. Probably all of those."

The Chinese waiters brought in their meals in a selection of small bowls and closed the door behind them. The two men ate quickly then returned to their discussions.

"It is indeed unfortunate that the British government has not lent the support we would expect, especially after last year, when Egyptian aircraft attacked RAF Ramat David Airbase and killed British servicemen."

"I read about that," said Devon. "It was a mistake on their part, I understand – they thought it was occupied by the Israeli Air Force. But the RAF responded well – they shot down most of the Egyptians, I gather."

Hartman leant forward. "Yes, but the Egyptian Air Force remains our main concern. They are equipped with Mark IX Spitfires and they might be getting some Mark 22s, supplied by the British – and jet fighters could follow in the future. You will be aware that we have already had numerous actions against the Egyptians. This is why we have acted quickly to build our own air force. Let me show you some further information." From his briefcase Hartman took a map showing Israel and the surrounding Arab countries and smoothed it out on the table. "Here are our airbases where we will operate our *tajesets* – sorry, squadrons – from Haganah, Ramat David, which is now in our possession, and Hatzor." Hartman pointed with a sharp pencil, very precisely. "On arrival at Ramat David, you will undertake training on type and join the other *machal* pilots in acclimatising to the area."

Devon looked quizzically at Hartman.

"Sorry again – *machal* is the name we give to foreign volunteers. You will get used to the language very quickly. The main role of the air force is interception, seeking out and destroying enemy aircraft in the air. We will also be attacking aircraft at their airfields and attacking army ground forces – something you are very experienced in. There are enemy bases in these areas." Hartman pointed at several Egyptian and

Syrian airfields and military sites across the borders. "The idea of course is to prevent the Arab nations from invading."

For the next hour Hartman provided an outline of the air force's structure and operational command. Devon seemed more and more committed to joining the Israelis – there would be some challenging flying, and real danger. Hartman felt Devon could handle both. He detailed the salary they would pay him – an astonishing sum of money to someone in Devon's position. Few people could deny that the financial rewards were a strong motivation.

"That's about all I can tell you for now, Adam, for security reasons."

"If I join, what are the next steps?" asked Devon.

"After you have completed your service with the RAF, you will travel on a commercial flight to Singapore. From there you will take a ship direct to the port of Haifa."

"Wouldn't I have the chance to go home first for a couple of weeks?"

"Sorry. We need to act quickly and get you operational as soon as we can." Hartman smiled sympathetically, but Devon knew he was being pressured. He was not surprised, given the situation in the region.

"Understood. David, I can say I will join you. Let me have all the contract papers and travel details when you can. I will not mention this to anyone in the RAF, or to my parents. They can find out in good time. I presume there is also absolute secrecy on your side?"

Hartman shook Devon's hand vigorously. "Adam, it's so good to have you join us. Secrecy is paramount; we don't wish to give our plans away to the enemy. Take this business card. It has the office address and my telephone number, but only call if absolutely necessary. Expect to hear from me in a few days."

***

Devon left the restaurant with a real sense of purpose. By thinking of the principles he lived by – fighting for what is right – he was able to subdue the inner concerns that always troubled him: the prospect of killing men to whom he felt no personal enmity. He was well practised in managing his emotions in operational flying. He could handle the dangers and stresses. He was excited and motivated about the prospect of the challenging new flying job. He knew he hadn't known Hannah very long, but his feelings for her were a very real part of the reason for his decision. He couldn't wait to see her again, to take positive action for their shared cause, to start a way of life that was absolutely central to her.

When he arrived back at the airfield he called in his orderly. "Young, could you arrange a junk for me to hire for the day on Saturday? Something decent for tourists, you know. Pick up at say, 10 a.m."

"Yes, sir. I understand that the Peninsula Hotel arranges trips for their guests and for RAF personnel – very nice boats, no smell of fish and diesel fuel!"

"Sounds good," said Devon.

"Will that be for two people, sir? Yourself and a certain young lady perhaps?"

"How the hell did you— ah yes, the Victoria Restaurant. Well, for your information, yes, please book it for two – myself and a certain young lady."

THIRTY-FIVE

"I wonder if you have a moment, sir?' Young stood hesitantly at Devon's door, a sheepish look on his face.

"Of course, Young. What is it?"

"Sir, it's about that possible job at the Great Eastern Hotel."

"Ah yes, a waiter in the ballroom and restaurant."

"Yes sir, the Hamilton ballroom. Well, my pal at the hotel has mentioned my name to the personnel manager and told her about my RAF service. She is very willing to give me an interview on the condition that I send her a satisfactory reference beforehand. So, sir, I was wondering if you could give me one? I know how busy you are, what with getting ready to go home, but after you've gone, I don't think there's anyone I could ask who knows me so well. And having a personal reference is so much better than the standard demob letter from the RAF."

"Of course. I would be very pleased to do that. In fact, I'll do it now and you can get it into today's dispatch bag. Should be in England in a few days' time. Would that suit? I'll need the name and address of the person to write to."

"That would suit very well indeed, sir. I'm much obliged. I have a note of it here: it's a Miss Lisa Ducal, Personnel Manager, Great Eastern Hotel, London EC2."

"But, Young, you would be resigning from the RAF without the certainty of a job to go to. A bit of a risk?"

"Yes, sir, but one I'm willing to take. I feel I have a sporting chance of the job at the Great Eastern, which is better than looking for work after you've been let go by the service and no prospect of even an interview. There has been a lot of talk in the Mess, sir, about new jobs on the production line in factories. Ford, for example, is expanding in Dagenham and they're looking for people. Then there are jobs at London Transport, driving the buses. None of these appeal to me, as you can imagine, but they could be a good fall-back."

"Yes – but as I have said before, it's important to carefully consider your decision to resign."

"I know, sir, but I think the time is right for a change – a bit like you, perhaps, sir?" said Young.

Devon smiled. His reasons for resigning were complicated and he wasn't sure he could express them, even if he was at liberty to explain to Young. "Possibly. Come back in about an hour, would you? I'll have the letter ready for you."

"Certainly, sir."

***

Devon had no difficulty in writing a glowing reference for Young. He had been an excellent orderly and Devon could easily see him as a competent, attentive liveried waiter in a top-class hotel. Who knew? He could go on to become the *maître d'* in time.

Devon lay back in his chair and gave some thought to the prospect that lay ahead for Young. After ten years of RAF discipline, he would have to adjust to a civilian life where austerity dominated and the competition for jobs was incessant. Would the hotel really have sufficient business to thrive in a bomb-scarred City of London? Devon realised that he was fortunate to have options himself – flying with the Israelis and a possible job in technical development in avionics.

THIRTY-SIX

"That was a bit of a shocker, Steven! Your guvnor handing in his cards – what's he going to do now?"

The Mess fell silent, as all those having lunch were keen to hear Young's response. A sudden resignation, especially after Fitzjohn's grounding, created an intrigue in the whole squadron. No one so far had had the nerve to ask the question that Aircraftman Barry Johnson put to Young.

"He's got lots of options, Johnny, but he hasn't chosen one as yet. Not that I know of."

"I reckon he's joining Porter at BOAC," said Johnson. "Plenty of money and think of all those gorgeous stewardesses in their lovely uniforms!"

The men at the table all laughed.

"Or maybe he's going to take that boring factory job his dad has set up for him at Avro."

"Never mind about that, Johnny, you're not supposed to know."

"Yeah, well, those boys in the telegraph office aren't dumb – they get to hear the real news. But it's a brave move from your boy, leaving the service without a job to go to."

"My dad says manufacturing is the future for Britain: cars, ships, aircraft. He'll earn good money if he gets a job at Avro. And the union will look after him." 'Streaky' Bacon was young and inexperienced, but he had the confidence to air his opinions – or those of his father – among the men.

"Do you really see Flight Lieutenant Devon standing on a production line day after day?" Young glared at Bacon. He knew he was getting riled by the banter.

Senior Aircraftman Mike Welch chipped in. "He's an excellent pilot – it would be a waste if he gave up flying completely. It's not as if he needs to get back to his fiancée now that she has called things off. He could fly anywhere – Australia or maybe the US. Lots of money to be made there."

Young had had enough, and gathered his cutlery and plates onto his tray. "Right, I'm off. Even if you lot haven't got anything to do apart from gossiping like washerwomen, I've got some paperwork to complete."

It was not just Devon's future that filled his thoughts; he had to consider his own plans. The position at the London hotel would really suit him, but he was more nervous than he cared to admit about resigning from the RAF before he had actually been offered the job.

THIRTY-SEVEN

Devon watched Hannah step off the *Rising Star* and walk through the Kowloon ferry terminal. She was carrying a canvas bag slung across her back and wearing a broad-brimmed woven straw hat. A long pale pink dress of layered cotton voile and her white sandals were the perfect choice for a hot day. When she saw Devon she ran the last few steps, impulsive and spontaneous, kissed him on the cheek and wrapped her arms around his shoulders.

"You look wonderful, Hannah."

"As do you, Adam. Quite the colonial!"

Devon was wearing smart cream trousers and a white shirt, its sleeves rolled up above his elbows. His white straw Panama had a blue and maroon RAF band.

As they stepped outside the terminal Devon said, "We can take a cycle rickshaw to the Peninsula. The junk will be waiting for us there. The plan is for us to cruise the Pearl River this morning, stop for a swim somewhere, then have lunch. I hope that's all acceptable!"

"Sounds delightful."

As they sat back in the rickshaw, little conversation was possible as the rider laboured to get a modicum of speed going. After a few minutes, Devon could see two uniformed Peninsula men waiting at the top of the stairs that led down to the water where the junk was tied up.

"Well, they're here on time, that's a good start. Immaculate service from the Peninsula as usual," said Devon.

The boat's crew helped the passengers onto the deck and took their bags into the cabin. "Good morning, sir, miss. Welcome aboard the *Happy Days*, the Peninsula's finest junk. I'm Mike Dau, your captain, and I hope you do have a very happy day!" A line he must have used a hundred times. "We will take the boat along Kowloon side and then out to the Pearl River, stop for swimming at Cheung Chau Island – a lovely little beach, the best place to see fish with our snorkelling kit. We will stop for lunch on Lamma Island. Happy day, yes!"

"That's great, thank you, Mike," said Devon.

An elderly lady brought out glasses of pineapple juice on a silver tray. She wore an emerald green dress with 'The Peninsula' embroidered in gold on her shoulder.

"Cheers," said Hannah. "I'm really looking forward to today. This is such a beautiful boat – it's a shame to call it a junk!"

"Cheers, I'm sure we will have a great day. The weather forecast is good – the morning mist will clear by 1100 hours and we'll have a light breeze, 8 to 10 knots, from the west."

Hannah smiled at his airman's overview of the day's weather.

Devon and Hannah sat on the silk cushions against the side bulwark where a cotton sunshade protected them and the motion of the boat was minimised. Devon looked around at the woodwork. Hannah was right: it was an impressive boat, burnished to a deep chestnut mahogany by the sun and regular polishing. He thought the junk was about fifty years old, but it was a long time since it had been used for fishing; there was not a trace of the sour aroma of fish. The two crewmen partially raised the three deep-red sails, but Devon could also hear the steady purr of an inboard engine that would ensure their trip would be completed smoothly and on time.

The captain held close to the south side of Kowloon as they progressed along Victoria Harbour, Hong Kong Island to their left.

"Look, there's the Peak, Adam. And I think I can see Mid-Levels. Difficult to actually see my house, hidden away behind the botanical gardens. I've never seen it from here before."

"And ahead and to the right is the Pearl River estuary, with mainland China beyond that," said Devon.

The cruise westward was serene and unhurried. Away from the mainland the air was fresh and clean, less humid. Devon and Hannah sat arm in arm.

"Adam, I know this is a special day for us, but we should talk about flying. David Hartman has briefed me and I'm so pleased you have agreed to join us. I'm sure you will have a great experience flying and living in Israel. Things have quietened down recently so there is no immediate danger from Arab forces. That shows why having the deterrent is so important."

"Yes, that's true," said Devon. "But I didn't really want to talk business today. Hartman has given me most of the details and everyone at the base knows I have resigned. Most people believe I'm taking the job at Avro or joining Squadron Leader Porter at BOAC. I have written to my parents but again, I haven't told them about the Israeli Air Force contract." Devon avoided asking if she would also be living in Israel when he got there; that could wait until later. "Now, let's put it all to one side, shall we, and enjoy the day?"

"Yes, of course. Look, is that Lantau Island ahead?"

The sea mist had indeed cleared, and the junk sailed steadily along in waters with no more than a gentle swell. The lady in green emerged from the galley with a fruit platter and tiny coconut buns. As they passed to the south of Lantau they could see the hill at Po Lin. A shudder ran down Devon's back as he recalled Jameson's crash, but he said nothing to Hannah.

Half an hour later the captain called from the wheelhouse. "We stop here – Pirate's Bay, Cheung Chau. Time to swim. You can use goggles and snorkel."

He anchored the boat in the centre of a small horseshoe-shaped bay with green hills on each side and a radiant white sand beach.

After changing in the guest cabin, Devon and Hannah slipped into the sea from the junk's rope ladder. They were instantly amazed at the array of tropical fish they could see: green, gold, blue and translucent, some only an inch long, in shoals of hundreds, others more than a foot long, feeding on the rocks in small groups. The pair swam ashore together and sat for a while on a bleached-white tree trunk that had been long ago washed up.

"No wonder pirates came here – it's such a secluded bay," said Devon.

"Perhaps there's buried treasure," Hannah said and kissed Devon. "It's such a nice place to be – a beautiful beach, lovely clear, warm water – maybe as good as Blackpool?"

"Ha! No of course not, there's no candy floss in sight!"

"Do you miss home, Adam? England?"

"Not really. Sure, it would be nice to see my family and close friends from school and the cricket club. But don't you think Britain has become so uninspiring? Entrenched in labour disputes and social troubles? We still have rationing, and who knows how we will be able to sustain the Empire. There are new and exciting opportunities in other parts of the world."

"Like Israel, you mean?" asked Hannah.

"Yes, in the short term, but I meant Australia, New Zealand, Canada. Maybe the USA. There are lots of people emigrating – these countries would offer great flying jobs. The only real hope in Britain is new technology: staying ahead of the world in engineering and science. That's the thing that appeals to me about home."

Devon noticed that Hannah looked concerned. He couldn't be sure if his interest in a new life in these far-off places tied in with what she saw herself doing: building a life in Israel or back in England.

"Are you OK, Hannah?" asked Devon.

"Isn't it time we swam back? We must be on our way soon." Hannah didn't wait for an answer but stood up and walked to the water's edge.

"Hey, hang on, what's the rush?"

"No rush. We have to watch the time, that's all."

After using the freshwater shower in the guest cabin, they relaxed on the deck with a cold glass of the Peninsula's own label white wine, served by the lady in green. Devon wondered how she could keep a bottle so perfectly chilled on a hot day out at sea. He glanced at Hannah. Her long dark hair was drying in the breeze and her cheeks had taken on a shade of pink from the sun. She was so beautiful, he could hardly bear to look at her. Conscious of his gaze, she turned to him and frowned. He knew something was wrong but did not dare ask; he might start a discussion he didn't want to have.

The captain sailed the junk right into the little port at Lamma Island and the crew hung a ladder over the side for Devon and Hannah to climb down to the quayside. The restaurant was a short walk away. Devon took Hannah's hand. She pulled away and Devon looked at her, puzzled. "What's wrong?"

"Oh, nothing, don't take any notice of me. It's just that so much has happened so quickly and I don't want to be separated from you. Silly, really." Hannah took back his hand. "Come on, let's eat."

Devon knew that Hannah had developed a liking for Chinese food. When they sat down, he asked if she would order for both of them.

"Of course." She smiled. Scanning the menu, she said, "Let's start with a cold ginger and pumpkin soup, then have Peking duck to share. And we should have fish for main course, as we have spent the day on the water. Would a sautéed pink grouper with crab sauce be acceptable?"

"Very good choice! What would the folks back home think of such luxury when the best they can get is cod and chips?"

They took their time over the meal and watched the junks bobbing in the harbour. At around four o'clock they saw their captain standing to attention on the quayside, not looking at the couple but gazing nonchalantly at the sky. Clearly it was a subtle sign it was time to go.

After they had cruised back, Devon asked for them to be dropped off at the harbour in Central so that they could take a taxi up to Hannah's house. The crew all lined up to say goodbye, and Devon left a generous tip with the captain. The old lady in green took both of Hannah's hands in hers, closed her eyes, smiling, and said something to her in Chinese. All the crew smiled and nodded in apparent agreement.

The sun had just set as they arrived at Mid-Levels, and the sky was a deep velvety blue.

"I'll ask the driver to wait a few minutes," said Devon, carrying Hannah's bags round the car to her front door.

"No, don't do that. Let him go, stay for a while."

"Sure, that would be nice."

"Come in, I will make some tea."

Devon followed her through to the kitchen. He was pleased to see her take a box of Fortnum's Piccadilly tea from the cupboard – he had had enough Chinese food and drink during the day.

"You like it nice and strong, don't you? And I even have some milk in the cool box that should be OK."

They sat outside on the rattan chairs, taking in the now familiar view down to the harbour.

"Oh, I have some news for you, Adam. I've acquired a small gramophone and a box of records. Someone from the bank was returning to England and didn't want to take them back. We can look at what's there and play a few, if you like?"

"What a good idea. Let's go in and have a look at the records."

"Here they are. They're a bit dusty, I'm afraid, rather unloved." Hannah took out three or four records. "Benny Goodman dance music. That's not bad if you like swing. Or Glenn Miller. Maybe not. Here, look, Brahms Violin Sonata No. 2, a lovely piece."

"Brahms, Hannah?" said Devon. "Aren't you averse to German composers? How do you feel about listening to German music when your family suffered so much at the hands of the Nazis? You would be forgiven if you wanted to cut off all connections and memories of Germany."

"I don't hate all things German – after all, I'm German myself. The fascism and nationalism that ran through Germany in the 1930s and 40s is not what the country is all about. I can't forgive anyone who was involved in the Holocaust – it was an obscene and disgusting episode, but there are so many good people in Germany."

"It's clear to see why Jewish people want to establish their own country – to have a safe place to live and bring up families. It's a shame that can't always be in your home country," said Devon.

"Many Jewish people are rebuilding their lives all around the world – in France, Germany, even in Russia. And in Britain, of course, and the USA. Not everyone wants to migrate, and I can understand why – they have centuries-old connections where they live, and why should they leave? But I believe in the independence of the State of Israel as the spiritual home for Jewish people, a place where we can live in peace with our Arab neighbours."

Devon felt the conversation was heading to a painful place for Hannah. That wasn't something he wanted to happen.

"OK, maybe not Brahms, but look we have some great American jazz here, if you like that?"

"Good choice. You can chose which to play," said Hannah.

They settled back into the settee, Devon with his arm around Hannah, she with her feet curled under her legs. When the music finished she knelt down on the floor and flicked through the box of records. "I've never heard of this one – 'Waves on the Water', Darius Delton. I think he's American."

"Let's give it a go. Sounds very appropriate," said Devon.

Hannah returned to the settee and they sat silently as the song started. A long slow piano introduction was followed by a soft baritone voice.

You want to know if I'll always be here
Try to think of my love without any fear
All I can say is I love you, my dear

The stars give us our future and
The moon shines on the waves on the water
My love will last forever
Like the waves on the water

Your touch brings me such a warming delight
Our love will take us to the greatest height
And my heart knows that it feels something right

The stars give us our future and
The moon shines on the waves on the water
My love will last forever
Like the waves on the water

My love will last forever
Like the waves on the water

"What a wonderful song," Hannah whispered. They exchanged small, playful kisses.

"He has a great voice, so melodic," said Devon. "And his piano playing is beautiful."

She rested her head against his shoulder. "And I've had a wonderful day on the waves on the Pearl River. Thank you for arranging everything."

"I've had a great day too."

They spent the next hour playing records and relaxing, with the doors to the terrace open. A breeze coming up the hill brought in the perfume of jasmine and freesia. When it was late, Hannah stood and closed the doors and went into her bedroom, silently brushing a hand across Devon's face as she passed. He sat still for few moments, but then rose to follow her in. She was lying on the bed. He lay beside her. They shared long, tender kisses and caresses. They did not disturb each other's clothes; they could easily have gone further but they knew that the time wasn't right. That would be something to enjoy in the future, something to keep as a precious understanding between them.

Nearing sleep, Hannah went to the bathroom and showered before dressing in her gold Chinese silk pyjamas. When she returned to her bedroom, she saw that Devon had taken a sheet and a pillow from the armoire and made a bed for himself on the settee in the living room. He was already asleep.

"Goodnight, my love. Sleep well," she said quietly.

THIRTY-EIGHT

True to their word, when Fitzjohn arrived at 7 p.m. sharp Pierre Fazil and Ahmad Kouri were waiting at the ferry terminal in Central beside a parked car, not just a taxi but a large limousine. Its door was being held open by a chauffeur.

"Good evening, Henry. It's a pleasure to see you again, sir." Fazil gave an obsequious bow and guided Fitzjohn into the rear seat, where Kouri was already installed.

"Hello again, Ahmad. Looking forward to the evening, I hope?" said Fitzjohn.

"Very much. Let us wish for good luck."

"How is business? Made any bargain purchases this week?"

"We have agreed some deals. The Chinese manufacturers are claiming the civil unrest is increasing prices. But we do the best we can, of course."

The car pulled up to the main entrance to Happy Valley Racecourse, where they were greeted by a thick-set Chinese man in a black suit, black shirt and tie, curiously wearing a traditional red fez with a gold tassel, and three women, very smartly dressed in European style. After handshakes and welcomes, the party was ushered into an exclusive bar where champagne had already been poured. More expressions of wealth from the Egyptians.

"Thank you, Jimmy, that will be all." Kouri dismissed the man in the hat. "Henry, let me introduce our companions for the evening: Zara, Layla and Amira."

Very exotic, very Levantine, thought Fitzjohn. Amira was a tall, striking thirty-something with long, tumbling black hair swept back over her shoulders. In her company, he felt that he would have a very pleasant evening.

"Delighted to meet you, ladies. Are you horseracing lovers?" Fitzjohn was at his most charming. Zara, probably the youngest of the three women, giggled and raised her fingers to her lips.

Amira smiled slowly. "Yes, we are all very keen. I have the race cards here. Perhaps if we are all ready we can go to the enclosure. The first race starts in twenty minutes."

The group strolled through the noisy, chattering crowd. A sense of anticipation filled the air as bets were placed and people moved towards the track. Fitzjohn selected his horse and rubbed his hands. "Just a few dollars to start with. The night is young!"

"A good choice, Henry, let's see how your horse goes. I'm backing the chestnut – looks to be in good shape," said Kouri.

The race was under way when Fitzjohn realised that Amira had disappeared. Shame, he thought. She's not a bad number to spend some time with.

Fitzjohn's horse came in second. With none of the men enjoying a win, they ambled back to the enclosure to consider their plans for the next race. Fitzjohn decided to play a cautious game and backed the favourite with a small bet. No joy, as his horse finished fourth.

"Time for a swift drink, Henry?" said Kouri. "It might bring us some inspiration."

"Splendid idea." Fitzjohn was all for someone else buying the drinks.

"Zara, would you be so kind as to request three whiskies from the bar? Talisker, if they have it."

They took their drinks outside and walked slowly back to the enclosure. As they did, Fitzjohn caught a glimpse of Amira with a group of what looked like racehorse owners, conversing in a close circle.

"It might be harder to pick the winner of the next race," said Kouri. "Maiden races are open to any good horse that has not won before."

"I like the look of the grey there. Let me see ... yes, Blue Hawk. Seems up for it," said Fitzjohn.

"A very nice horse, it but may not do so well tonight. Take a look at the brown horse, number fourteen." It was Amira, standing behind Fitzjohn. He glanced at the card. "Forest Lily, three years old. Got a good chance, do you think? The odds are pretty long."

"A good investment, I would say."

"Right you are, then. Let's get to the bookies."

The race was tightly fought; three horses vied for the lead. In the last fifty yards Forest Lily put on a dash and won by half a length. Fitzjohn was delighted: he had placed US$10 to win, at 12-1 odds. A very nice windfall.

"What made you choose the filly, Amira?" said Fitzjohn.

"Just a hunch." She looked across at the group she had been talking to and nodded to them.

As the evening progressed, Fitzjohn's luck continued and he made some good choices himself, with a little help from the mysterious Amira.

"Henry, perhaps we can retire now we are ahead. I would like to invite you to take a nightcap with us at the trade delegation offices in Wan Chai. Our cars are waiting."

"Thank you, Ahmad, that would be a pleasure."

There were two cars to take them the short drive to Wan Chai.

A security man greeted Kouri and the party walked across the office's lobby to a large boardroom that boasted a well-stocked bar. Zara poured the drinks, then she and Layla disappeared. The three men sat in comfortable armchairs. Amira sat opposite Fitzjohn and slowly crossed her long, slender legs.

"I hope you like our offices, Henry – we can show you around later. We have further rooms upstairs with views of the harbour. You might even see the lights across at Kai Tak," said Kouri.

"Very smart."

"Tell me, what are your plans for the future?" Kouri asked Fitzjohn. "We hear that the RAF is reducing operational squadrons and pilots are looking at new flying opportunities. Some are even taking jobs flying for other air forces."

"Well, my aim is to stay with the squadron. I'm helping out with operational planning at the moment, ready for any Chinese invasion. In the longer term, I might be interested in commercial flying, air taxi, that sort of thing. The possibility of the squadron being disbanded is the issue of the day on the base. Some servicemen have resigned to take up other opportunities – the squadron leader, for instance, has got himself a very nice little role at BOAC. Another is taking a bloody factory job at Avro. Several of the younger pilots are concerned about their future."

Kouri sat forward. "You will be aware that many foreign pilots have joined the Israeli Air Force and are operational right now. We know they are seeking others and they have agents here in Hong Kong, although we do not know who they are … at this stage."

Fitzjohn sat up, suddenly realising where the discussion was going. "I think I see what you're getting at. You boys are not in the slightest interested in Chinese silks, are you? You're here to recruit pilots for the Egyptian Air Force."

"That is not the case. We are not trying to recruit you or any other serviceman. We have all the pilots we need in Egypt."

"So why are you interested in me?"

"Because we want to know who the Israelis might be recruiting. Our aim is to stop them being successful. The first priority for us is to identify the Israeli agents here and to eliminate them. When it comes to pilots, we might also find it necessary to deal with them, to persuade them that they are making a mistake."

"I can't be much help to you, I'm afraid. I've no idea who these agents are. And what made you approach me?"

Kouri smiled. "We have some good friends here in Hong Kong, particularly in the Chinese community. Very vigilant people, able to follow and observe those who are important to us. You made a name for yourself at a certain gambling establishment recently and we realised we share many interests: a nice malt, perhaps a wager occasionally. All the pleasures of life."

Amira uncrossed her legs and, smiling, sipped her drink.

"What we want from you is information. Identify the pilots who may be talking to the Israelis, and we will find the agents. There is no risk to you, and of course you will not be doing any disservice to your country. Pierre, the packet, please."

The young Egyptian went over to a desk and took out an envelope.

"Henry, we would like you to accept this gift as a token of our friendship. We simply ask you to provide leads for us. If we are successful and find out who the agents are, then there will be another of these packages."

Fitzjohn nonchalantly opened the envelope and flicked through the wad of $20 bills. He thought there must be around $5,000 – enough and more to buy a new Jaguar Roadster back home. Almost laughing, he said, "I can't promise anything, but I would be very happy to help you if I can."

"Excellent! Now let us celebrate with another drink, then Amira will show you around our accommodation. As well as our offices and this boardroom we have a gymnasium and guest suites where we provide comforts for our visiting dignitaries."

After she had poured the drinks, Amira touched Fitzjohn's hand and tilted her head towards the corridor. "Come this way – bring your drink."

Fitzjohn followed as she opened an office door and walked in.

"Six members of staff work here on research and communications."

Fitzjohn noticed a large radio transmitter at the far end of the room – no doubt enabling direct discussions with their HQ. Back in the hall, Amira opened another door. "This leads to the gymnasium and massage room. We take the lift here to the top floor."

Alighting from the lift, Amira walked ahead of Fitzjohn, stopped at a door and turned a key. When they entered, Fitzjohn was stunned: they were in an opulent bedroom. The only light came from a small lamp on the dressing table. The scent of roses came from the en-suite bathroom, and candles glowed on the mirrored shelf. Amira closed the door behind them, kicked off her shoes and sat on the bed. She took Fitzjohn's glass from his hand and placed it on the bedside table, then lay back seductively.

THIRTY-NINE

Flying operations continued on a daily basis, with the usual mixture of assignments over the colony. Squadron Leader Wills didn't let up on his insistence of precise, textbook flying but introduced some changes to squadron roles and activities to provide more focus. He made some of the senior pilots squadron leaders for a day, to give them experience of planning and leading an operation. The younger pilots were given timed solo navigation missions, where they were to overfly and photograph checkpoints and return by a stated time. All pilots went through regular aerial combat practice: dogfighting exercises they all enjoyed as they had the chance to see what their Spitfire could do.

Fitzjohn sat at his desk in the adjutant's office and started to work through personnel administration – work he considered to be the most boring and mundane. Requests for leave, sickness reports, disciplinary records. Some resignations, men who had served through the war and now wanted to find a new life outside the armed forces, to try their luck with the new opportunities in Britain. He was surprised to see Pilot Corrigan, one of his men from his flight in Malaya, resigning

– surprised and annoyed that the man had not thought to discuss his desire to leave the service with him. His documents simply stated 'career progression' as his reason for resigning.

"Fools – all they will get is a council flat and a job on a building site," Fitzjohn mumbled. He separated the forms to be passed to the CO so they would be processed without delay; Fitzjohn did not wish to see any servicemen retained who did not want to be in the air force.

One request for leave caught his attention. It was from Devon. With less than a month until he left the service, why would he want a three-day pass? Fitzjohn leant back in his chair and looked up at the ceiling, pondering. He took up the little rubber stamp and carefully printed APPROVED on the docket. His Egyptian friends might help him to find out what Devon got up to in his own time.

As he processed the other documents, he yawned and decided he would take an early lunch, but after he had strolled across to the Officers' Mess to be one of the first to be seated, he realised he wasn't particularly hungry. A light snack and half a pint of bitter was all he needed. After lunch, he took a walk along the airfield perimeter to stretch his legs. Glancing back to the adjutant's office, he saw the three WAAFs who worked there leave together for their own lunch. They were not supposed to leave the office unattended, and Fitzjohn presumed they were taking liberties as the adjutant was away on leave.

Closing the door to the office firmly behind him, Fitzjohn went straight to the filing cabinet containing his own staff file. Sitting at his desk, he read through the most recent papers: a record of his interview with the CO and his grounding. Below that was a memorandum detailing the gambling club incident and his brief hospitalisation from the knife wound: copies of requests for leave, a summary of his flight tests. In a pocket on the front cover of the file was a handwritten note that read:

Note for file. Flt Lt Fitzjohn AWOL 18 September 1949 by overstaying late pass. Drunk and incapable. Returned to station by colleagues. No action taken but record of behaviour noted.

The note was signed by Squadron Leader Porter.

"That bastard Devon, he must have reported me to the skipper – that's how they came to know about the Green Lotus. Couldn't bloody well keep it quiet," Fitzjohn said to himself and thumped the desk with his fist. "Well, let's see what favour I can do him in return."

***

Fitzjohn took his preferred seat at the bar in the Peninsula that evening. He enjoyed the luxurious setting and the atmosphere of success and privilege. He was naturally at home with wealthy people. Feeling very pleased to have a couple of names to give to Kouri, he ordered an Old-Fashioned and waited to see if his Egyptian friends would arrive. The bar was busy with the usual mix of European businessmen with their smartly dressed women. After half an hour he thought he might ask reception to call Kouri's room, but he needn't have worried. He saw – in the mirrored wall opposite him – Kouri and Fazil come into the bar.

"Good evening, Henry, such a delight to see you here. I trust you have had a good week so far." Kouri shook hands with a powerful grip that Fitzjohn felt a touch uncomfortable with.

"Oh yes, Ahmad. Let me get you both a drink. Would an Old-Fashioned fit the bill?" He clicked his fingers. "Bobby, two more of these, please. No, make it three."

After making small talk about the local weather and the lack of activity on the Chinese mainland, the men took their drinks to a quiet corner.

"I'm concerned about the activities of two of our number who have resigned from the service. A terrible shame, as they're both competent pilots. Unfortunately they have declined to disclose their plans for the future, simply saying that they're returning to England. Seems odd, especially for my colleague Flight Lieutenant Adam Devon, who is the one said to be joining an aircraft manufacturer. The other party is Pilot John Corrigan – there's no apparent reason for him to jump ship."

"This is very interesting, thank you," said Kouri. "How can we best identify these gentlemen?"

"I'm afraid I don't move in the same social circles as these men, although I can say that Corrigan likes the dice tables and I dare say Devon can be seen here at the Peninsula from time to time. I'm sure it wouldn't take your contacts long to identify them and see what they're up to, if anything. But Devon has a three-day leave pass starting tomorrow. It would be fascinating to know what he does during that time – and with whom."

"Agreed, Henry. We will set the task to our contacts. Let us meet again in a few days' time," said Kouri, "but for now we shall wish you a pleasant evening."

"Perhaps another drink? said Fitzjohn.

"No, thank you, we have work to do."

FORTY

Hannah had taken Friday off work so they could enjoy a long weekend. She had mentioned she enjoyed the botanical gardens, so Devon suggested they take a walk there, have lunch and relax in the afternoon. Hong Kong's oppressive heat and humidity was tempered by the shade of the lush green gardens and secluded avenues. The winding paths around the gardens took them among an amazing array of tropical trees, including an ancient white jade orchid tree, where they lingered to enjoy the fragrance from the flowers. They walked among the garden's collection of camellias, admiring the various shades: several reds, a pale yellow and an orange. Devon held a branch of an intense crimson specimen against Hannah's long brown hair.

"You two go together so well," he said

"My hair looks like twigs, you mean?" Hannah smiled.

Devon had brought his camera, a new compact Olympus he had purchased in a store in Kowloon – he wasn't against the purchase of Japanese products, as some of the servicemen were. He took some pictures of Hannah by the camellias and a couple of shots of the more unusual trees. He asked a Chinese couple to take some pictures of Hannah and himself together. After an hour they found a bench in a quiet, shaded spot, away from most of the tourists.

"We haven't really spoken about your plans, Hannah, when I'm in Israel. What do you think you will do? Will you be released from the secret service here in Hong Kong?"

"I'm not certain of anything yet, but from the discussions I've had with David Hartman it seems likely that the Hong Kong operation will continue, looking for pilots, mechanics and maybe other military people. Recruitment efforts are to be expanded in other areas – the US, probably. But I want to move to Israel as soon as you leave here. I still have to think about where I can work and how I can be useful. A lot of the young people I met in London have joined a kibbutz. I also know that the orange groves near Jaffa are to be expanded – most of the oranges will be exported to earn foreign currency, which is so important. I could work there, although I'm really not sure that working in agriculture is what I want to do."

"Perhaps the bank would give you a job?" asked Devon.

"Yes, I hope so. In fact, I'm thinking of applying for a transfer to the new branch in Tel Aviv next week. I will have to talk all this over with Hartman and Mars."

As they walked they came to a long flight of steps that took them up to an open circle of ground with a huge fountain at its centre. The water seemed to cool and purify the area and the sound of spray on the stones around the fountain blended beautifully with the songs of the birds drinking at the edges.

"Such a lovely feature, Adam," said Hannah as they circled the fountain. "It brings the gardens to life."

They strolled down another avenue and approached the impressive bronze statue of King George VI.

"All part of the Empire," said Devon as they continued their tour.

They came upon a small zoo containing numerous animals and birds. Hannah walked past the enclosures. "I'm not a big fan of zoos. I don't like to see animals caged."

From this high position in the gardens they could look out towards the east and beyond that to the Chinese mainland. The humidity had been steadily increasing during the day and the wind was strengthening, coming in from the South China Sea. Devon was aware that a storm had been forecast but wasn't too worried, as he wouldn't be flying for a couple of days. The enormous grey clouds were moving inland and would soon be directly over Hong Kong Island. A few drops of rain were already falling.

"Perhaps we should call into the café," said Devon. "We can shelter there."

"Yes, let's do that."

The café was no more than a small wooden shed, but it was dry. It was just as well that they had found somewhere. Within minutes the light drizzle had turned to a downpour, with rain crashing down and splashing up in a chaotic spray of water. The noise was mesmerising. Devon held Hannah's hand as she cuddled close to him.

A strong wind soon drove the clouds on, and a crystal-clear sky followed. Devon bought two glasses of orange juice. "When it stops, why don't we continue through the gardens and walk down to Queens Road and find something to eat down there?"

They walked down the narrow streets, newly washed and sparkling, some so steep that the pavement was a series of steps. Small Chinese shops lined the streets, selling all types of goods: Chinese clothing and rolls of fabrics, pots and pans, brushes, mops and buckets. They stopped and looked into food shops selling strange-looking meat, so many kinds of mushrooms, every flavour of tea, green vegetables, and eggs from chickens, ducks, quails and geese. Bags of rice and noodles were stacked up on the steps.

"Look, Adam, there's a shop selling dim sum to take away. We could buy a couple of boxes."

"Good idea," said Devon. "Let's sit here to eat."

Hannah sat on a low wall under a cotton shade while Devon went into the shop.

They only had to wait ten minutes for their food to be cooked fresh. A young girl brought out the food, bowed graciously and handed the boxes to Hannah. She opened hers and inhaled the fragrant steam. "These smell so good. What did you choose?"

"My favourites, of course!"

Hannah smiled with pretend mockery.

"Prawn dumplings, pork buns, vegetable spring rolls and rice noodle rolls."

As they ate, using the short chopsticks provided, the girl from the shop returned with two paper cups and a small jug of sugared lemon juice and placed them on the wall.

"Thank you, that's very thoughtful," said Devon. "I forgot to order any drinks." He took out some dollars and held them out to the girl, who shook her head vigorously and bowed again before returning to the shop.

After their snack they continued to tour the shops, arm in arm. As the afternoon turned into early evening, Hannah suggested taking a taxi up to her house, as she was tired.

"Of course. I'm sure I can flag one down on Des Voeux Road."

Back at the villa they went through their now familiar routine of making tea and stepping out to the terrace to relax.

"Shall we go up to the New Territories tomorrow?" Devon suggested. "I can borrow a car and we could take a tour. I gather there are some lovely villages and beautiful countryside up there."

Hannah agreed readily and they decided to meet at the Kowloon clock tower at noon the next day.

Late that evening, Devon boarded a ferry back to Kowloon. He sat looking out across the water, down the full length of Victoria harbour, relaxed and happy, feeling a warm glow inside as he pictured Hannah's smile in his mind.

FORTY-ONE

Devon started Saturday morning with a run around the airfield perimeter. He wanted to loosen up before his trip to the New Territories with Hannah, and he wanted to get an early start to avoid the heat of the day.

After showering and dressing, he was cooling off in his room when Young entered.

"Good morning, sir, your tea." Young placed the tray on the sideboard and dropped a couple of newspapers at the foot of Devon's bed.

"Thank you, Young." Devon sat on the bed and picked up the *South China Morning Post* first. The front page was filled with pictures and commentary on the developments in China: half-factual and half-scaremongering the Hong Kong Chinese community, who perhaps feared an invasion the most.

By force of habit, Devon flicked the newspaper over and looked at the sports pages. Usually there were reports from county cricket matches – his home team Lancashire were not having a great season, and he hoped for better in 1950. This year New Zealand were touring

England. Although they weren't generating the same excitement as the Australian tour had the year before, the matches were well supported. The *Post* gave a short, factual report on what Devon concluded must have been something of a dull second test match, which had ended, like the first, in a draw.

Devon turned back to the main news of the day, the political position in China. He glanced through the stories before turning the page, where shipping reports and news of manufacturing orders won by Hong Kong businesses provided local interest. When he turned to the next page, a headline caught his eye.

Israeli Airforce Scores Victories Over RAF

His heart pounding, he read on, his eyes widening when he read a report of a dogfight near Tel Aviv between Israeli and British Spitfires. He was shocked to read that two British pilots had been shot down and killed. Two Israeli aircraft were also damaged in the action; they had crash-landed and both pilots survived. The report described how the Israelis had 'bumped' the RAF's Spitfires, attacking them without warning. A Canadian and a South African were cited as being part of the Israeli force.

"What the hell is going on? We're not at war with Israel!" he said to himself. He walked around his room, rereading the item in disbelief. "Bloody hell!" He threw down the *Post* and picked up the second newspaper. It reported fewer details but it had a photograph of a wrecked Spitfire, its RAF markings clear.

"Young, are you there?" he called into the corridor.

Young came at a run, concerned at his officer's uncharacteristic shout. "Yes, sir, what is it?"

Devon held open the *South China Morning Post*. "Have you seen this? Two RAF pilots killed in Israel?"

238 | MARK BUTTERWORTH

"I heard about it last night in the bar, sir. Arnold from the telegraph office mentioned it. Very unfortunate, sir – a tragedy, in fact."

"Certainly is," said Devon in a calmer voice. He realised that Young would find it very strange that he should have reacted in the way he did. "It would be very helpful to all concerned if the bloody British government would decide where they stood in the Middle East." Devon's anger rose again.

"I'm not sure I understand why we're still in Palestine, sir," said Young.

"Nor am I, Young, nor am I."

This news meant that Devon knew he could not fly for the Israeli Air Force. His conscience would not allow him to. He felt that Britain was not the enemy of the new State of Israel; it was supposed to be a peacekeeper. He knew there were diplomatic complications and that Britain did not wish to make enemies of either the Arabs or Israel.

How the hell did they come to engage the Israelis, let alone fight them? he wondered. Shooting down Arab-state aircraft or attacking their ground forces was part of the job he had agreed to, as he saw them as the aggressors, but he was not willing to kill people from his own country.

He had to see Hartman and tell him the deal was off. He found the emergency telephone number Hartman had given him and strode across to the telegraph office, where there was a phone he could use. He had to be discreet; he would probably be overheard. The number rang five or six times before a woman answered.

"Causeway Construction."

"I'd like to speak to David, please," said Devon.

"I'm afraid David is not available at the moment. May I take a message?"

"Yes, I would like to call in for coffee with David this morning at 11 a.m. I will meet him at his office."

"Very well, caller, I shall pass that message on."

As Devon returned to his quarters, Young emerged from his room.

"Get me a taxi, please, Young, to go to the Star Ferry terminal. Urgent."

***

The *Northern Star* was surprisingly crowded for a Saturday morning, with dozens of Chinese workers going over to the island to their jobs. As Devon took his seat he rested his arm on the railing and looked at his watch: 10 a.m. He had time to call at Hannah's house, explain his decision and go on to Causeway's offices. He was dreading the discussion with Hannah: how would she react? Would she see his point? Would she be angry? He couldn't see the trip to the New Territories going ahead.

There was a line of taxis at Central terminal, and Devon reached Hannah's house by 10.15. He knocked and waited, then knocked again. No answer. Before resolving to go direct to meet Hartman, a thought came to him. He squeezed through the bushes at the side of the villa and called Hannah's name. She responded with a "Hello?" and he found her sitting on the terrace having breakfast.

"Adam, what is it? Why are you here?"

"Hannah, sit down. I have some news." He wished he had brought the newspapers with him. "This morning I read newspaper reports about an incident – the Israeli Air Force have shot down two British Spitfires. The pilots were killed. This changes everything. I'm on my way to meet Hartman to tell him I'm not joining. I can't be involved with any action against British forces."

Hannah sat back, looking stunned. The colour had drained from her face. "I see what you mean, Adam. I had never thought you would be asked to fight your own people. But Hartman will go mad. He'll try to make you honour your commitment."

"Then he'll be out of luck. He'll have to find someone else to do this work. I had better go. It's a long walk down to Wan Chai."

"I'll come with you," Hannah said. "Give me a moment to dress."

The couple walked out onto Magazine Gap Road and started downhill. Fortunately a taxi was parked just ahead and they were able to ride down to Gloucester Road. They were dropped off right outside the Causeway Construction offices, and went into the lobby. A moment later the lift arrived, with Miss Walker holding the doors-open button.

"Please come this way," she said.

She ushered them into the boardroom. David Hartman stood by the window, and a man unknown to Devon sat at the head of the table.

"Come in, Adam. Let me introduce our senior officer here in Hong Kong. You will know him as Mars."

"Good morning," said Adam.

"Please come and sit, both of you. Adam, I think I know why you're here." Mars looked over at an open newspaper lying on the table. "These reports in the press are rather unfortunate, but of course it is very difficult to maintain secrecy in the world today."

Devon leant forward. "Perhaps, but the fact is that the Israeli Air Force is ready and willing to attack British forces, and that's something I can have nothing to do with. So, I will not be joining you. I'm sure you will be able to find mercenaries less concerned about who they shoot down."

"Adam, I can understand your anger, but think about the longer term: what you will be doing is for the greater good. Establishing the State of Israel is a cause that all people will see as right. We certainly do not seek to fight the British and we aim to live in peace with our Arab neighbours, but there are birth pains that must be endured."

Devon had not come to argue the morals of the situation. "Be that as it may, but I'm the wrong person for this job. I will not support an organisation or country that has willingly attacked and killed British people. There has been enough of it among your various factions in the past, and it seems no different at a state level." He got up to leave.

"Please sit." Mars waved his hand. "There is a problem we must address. You know about our operation here in Hong Kong. Any breach of security will put all our lives in danger, including Hannah's. We cannot simply say 'goodbye, have a pleasant day'."

"I've thought of that. You have my word that I won't mention any of this to anyone outside this room. Also, I will return as soon as I can to England by air and ship. Your security will be watertight."

"I'm glad to have your assurances. But please be aware: if you breach our trust, our secret service colleagues will seek to put matters right. And they are ruthless people."

"You needn't threaten me. I have no intention of betraying your operation; I just want out of here and to return home. Now, if you will excuse me." Devon rose from his chair, hesitated and looked at Hannah. "Will you come with me?"

Hannah wavered.

"Come on, Hannah. If you really want to be with me, now is the time to make the decision. Let's go," Devon pleaded.

"No, Adam, I can't. I need to serve my people and not think of my own feelings." She looked away. Tears welled in her eyes.

Devon was shocked. He would never have believed that Hannah would let him go. Slowly he walked across the room, feeling numb and utterly drained of energy. *So this is how it ends between us.*

Miss Walker escorted him down in the lift and let him out into the street. In a daze, he found the same taxi that had brought them down from Mid-levels to take him to the ferry terminal, then boarded the *Morning Star* to cross to Kowloon.

FORTY-TWO

The bar in the Peninsula was particularly busy – it wasn't surprising for a Saturday evening. Fitzjohn took a seat in a quiet corner of the lobby. He felt that discretion and privacy were more important than socialising with the barman and other drinkers. He didn't have long to wait until the two Egyptians came and joined him. He ordered drinks and young Pierre took a small black notebook from his inner jacket pocket, flipped it open and read from it like a policeman in a courtroom.

"We have been observing the people you kindly mentioned to us, Henry. First, Corrigan seems to be intent on joining BOAC after he leaves the RAF. He was heard discussing his plans in the airfield bar last night – we understand he has been in contact with David Porter, your previous squadron leader, asking for a reference. It seems a response has not come back yet, but our agent in the bar is unsure. In any event, we don't believe he's been in touch with any Israeli agents."

"How can you be so sure?" said Fitzjohn. He was aware that these people had spies among the civilian staff at the station – the pot washers and cleaners. The stewards in particular in the bars came from many countries. And many servicemen seemed to have forgotten the wartime maxim that careless talk costs lives.

"We can't be one hundred per cent certain, of course," Kouri stepped in, "but until we have positive news on that score, we prefer to assume there is no contact."

"Alright, what about Devon?"

"A different situation entirely." Pierre Fazil looked back at his notebook. "Mr Devon has spent quite some time with a young lady from the London and Hong Kong Bank – someone we have been interested in for a couple of weeks. They have been socialising and indeed he has spent some time at her house, including overnight. We think she could be acting for the Israeli Secret Service. A Miss Hannah Shaw."

"Bloody hell!" Fitzjohn nearly jumped out of his seat. "That bloody floozy!"

"You know her?"

"I certainly do, Ahmad – she made a play for me when we first arrived here in Hong Kong. Not my type, so I gave her the cold shoulder and I've been ignoring her since. She didn't come across as being a Mata Hari to me – a girl on the make. She didn't mention working for the Israelis or anything like that. Why do you think she's tied up in all this?"

"The bank has known connections with the Jewish community in Hong Kong. Also, she occasionally meets with another young man, name of David Hartman, but there is no apparent romantic connection between them. He is ostensibly employed by the Causeway Construction Company in Wan Chai. We believe this company is nothing more than a front for Israeli operations – there is undoubtedly construction work being undertaken, but not involving Hartman. We also believe there must be a senior-ranking secret service director involved somewhere. We're still trying to find out who he is."

Kouri continued, "We have many good friends on the island who are working for us to that end."

"Oh yes? Like who?" said Fitzjohn.

"There is no need for you to know who exactly. Émigrés from Egypt, mainly – some work on the Star Ferry docks, some drive taxis, some sit in the fashionable bars and talk to their fellow guests."

"Well, what are you going to do about all this? I think I have settled my side of the bargain. Another of your little gifts would be appropriate."

"That will be my pleasure, Henry. We shall honour our promises as soon as the enemy agents have been eliminated."

"Eliminated? Now hang on, nobody mentioned murder before…"

"My dear Henry, we do not use such language, but as a serving officer in the armed forces you must know that sometimes you have to take lives to save lives."

Fitzjohn had a pang of conscience. "That's as maybe, Ahmad, but no harm must come to Miss Shaw. She is, after all, a British citizen, even if perhaps a foolish one; she cannot be more than a pawn in this game. I'm sure you will appreciate that the fallout if anything happens to her will harm British–Egyptian relations. And you should expect a ton of trouble if you even think of harming a British officer, so I recommend that you put such thoughts out of your minds."

"Your wishes are noted, Henry. No intervention will take place until we identify the senior officer in question. In the meantime, please observe Mr Devon's movements and advise us of any useful information that might come your way."

FORTY-THREE

"It has taken us a few days, but we now know who our man is," said Kouri. "His cover is as a senior manager at Causeway Construction, but our agents in Israel tracked him from Tel Aviv to Hong Kong – they have such poor security, the Israelis. His name is Peter Kahn but he works under the codename of Mars. Do you know him? Has he ever approached you?"

Fitzjohn was impressed by the Egyptians' intelligence operation. He felt that now they had found the man they'd been looking for he could withdraw and leave Hannah and Devon's friends to whatever fate the Egyptians had in mind for them.

"Good show, but I've never heard of him. Now, if you don't mind, I will depart with one of your kind gifts. All being well, we shall not meet again."

"The gift will be forthcoming once we have eliminated the Israeli agents, as I promised. You can be sure of our reliability in this regard. In the meantime, please keep us informed should you hear of any further pilots being attracted to the Israeli Air Force."

Fitzjohn left the Peninsula with a high degree of self-satisfaction. He had received a very nice payment for the work he had carried out so far, but he doubted he would ever receive any further payment – he didn't trust the Egyptians an inch. But he didn't care. He would soon be back flying and would forget all about the Egyptians. He had no intention of continuing to work for them, no matter what the pay and benefits were.

***

But in the Officers' Mess over dinner that evening, Fitzjohn was troubled. His earlier elation had dissipated and he felt a growing unease at his association with the Egyptians, which left him with the bad taste of duplicity in his mouth. He had no desire to see either Israel or the Arab countries prevail, he couldn't care less, but he was anxious not to be responsible for Hannah's associates being killed. He was also worried that the Egyptians couldn't be trusted not to 'eliminate' Hannah or even Devon. Before going to bed, he suddenly realised that in the morning he might be able to prevent any harm befalling them, at no cost to himself. They would be grateful to him. His change of heart gave him a sense of pride. It would be a noble gesture, one that fitted well with his view of himself as an honourable English gentleman.

FORTY-FOUR

On Tuesday morning, just three days after Devon's meeting at the Causeway Construction offices, Hannah was shocked to receive a telegram from Devon, sent from the Peninsula Hotel. It simply said:

Confidential STOP Meet me Thursday evening at 6 p.m. Ming Lantern Restaurant Causeway Bay STOP M and H must be with you STOP Adam STOP

She phoned Hartman, hopeful that Adam had calmed down and changed his mind. Mindful of the poor security in the telephone system, she coded her call. "I have heard from our potential new customer at the bank. He might like to open an account after all." Hannah read out the telegram to Hartman.

"Hannah, this is not the way we operate. The manager does not associate with contacts outside our office. Why doesn't he want to meet us here?"

"I don't know, but he's obviously very sensitive about contact with us. I think he's trying to clear the air and perhaps confirm that he will join us after all." Hannah wasn't wholly convinced of this, but she felt they had to meet him to at least hear what he had to say.

Hartman was clearly less keen on meeting in a public place, but he had no choice. "Very well. I will ensure that the manager joins us at the restaurant tomorrow at six. I suggest you confirm back to your contact."

"No – I think he sent the telegram from the Peninsula to maintain confidentiality. He wants to keep his business affairs secret."

"Good point. Alright, leave it. We will meet him tomorrow."

***

Ahmad Kouri paced the lush carpet in his suite at the Peninsula, looking out across Victoria Harbour towards Hong Kong Island. The usual activity on the water continued, regardless of the politics being played out off the water.

"Has the telegram been sent? With exactly the wording I required?" Kouri tended to be obsessive when under pressure.

"Yes, sir, and I have had confirmation that it has been delivered."

"Excellent, Pierre. I'm relying on them not suspecting anything amiss, since we're setting up the meeting in such a public place. Have Omar bring his taxi to the trade delegation offices at six o'clock precisely."

"But sir, don't we need to be at the restaurant for six?"

"No, we shall arrive at six fifteen – I want the targets to be settled in before we get there. There should be very few customers in the restaurant, and they're not likely to give us any trouble. Remember, we're looking for two western men and a woman. I will call out a friendly hello to the younger man, Hartman, who will naturally respond to me, so we will know it's them. I will shoot Mars, you will shoot Hartman, and then I will take out the girl. We do it in that order – get the key man first."

"But, sir," protested Fazil, "we promised Fitzjohn that we wouldn't harm Miss Shaw. He was right about the potential repercussions for Egypt if we kill a British citizen."

"That is not your concern, Pierre. You seem to forget that she is an Israeli secret agent. Remember, when our work is done, leave it to me to deal with anyone who obstructs us. We will depart the way we arrived: the car will drop us at the Central ferry terminal for our return to the Peninsula. The British might suspect our country, but will have no proof. We will complete our purchase of fine silks and cottons this week and depart as successful businessmen."

"Yes, sir. Will we carry the Berettas on the mission, sir?"

"Yes, with silencers fitted. We don't want to attract any undue attention."

FORTY-FIVE

On a bright and sweltering Wednesday morning, Fitzjohn was at the telegraph room just after sunrise. "Arnold Ridgewell, isn't it?"

"Yes, sir. Can I help you?"

The room was empty; most men were still at breakfast or were out at the aircraft, readying them for the morning's patrols. Fitzjohn picked up a telegram pad and quickly wrote two lines of text. "I'd like this to go immediately. Can you arrange that?"

"Certainly, sir. Let me read it back to you. *To Government House, attention Miss Hetherington-Brown STOP Urgent meeting required STOP Will call at GH 1100 hrs today STOP Fitzjohn STOP.*"

"That's it. Thank you, Ridgewell."

"Not at all, sir."

After having breakfast, Fitzjohn walked out of the airfield gate. No taxis were around so he took one of the ever-present cycle rickshaws to the Star Ferry terminal. As luck would have it, the *Guiding Star* was about to leave. Fitzjohn hopped from the pier onto the deck.

Another rickshaw dropped him at the main entrance to Government

House, where two armed sentries stood. Fitzjohn knew they were more than just ceremonial. He was directed to a desk where he could make his business known. A trim British woman with blue-rimmed glasses and a Kensington accent made a note of his name and who he wished to visit before escorting him to a small meeting room off the main reception area. The room contained a table and two chairs, a jug of water and glasses.

Five minutes later, the door opened and Val Hetherington-Brown came in. Another soldier with a pistol at his side took up position outside the door.

"Good morning, Mr Fitzjohn. How can I help you?" Straight to the point, no niceties.

"Good morning, Val." Fitzjohn had resolved to be amiable and appeasing. Apart from the main reason for his visit, he wanted to rebuild relations with the colonial types. "I'm here to alert you to some … mischief that I believe might happen and that in all equity should be prevented. It's absolutely unrelated to that unfortunate business with the armoury keys."

"Be more specific, please," said Hetherington-Brown sternly.

"Of course. Let me relate to you some intelligence that has come my way in regard to my colleague, Flight Lieutenant Adam Devon."

Fitzjohn gave Hetherington-Brown an abridged version of his short-lived relationship with Hannah and how he had met two Egyptian agents and their friends and, through them, became aware of the Israelis' recruitment of pilots. Again, he left out certain details.

"Look, the Egyptians have no intention to recruit pilots," Fitzjohn said "they want to stop them being recruited by the Israelis, and this includes eliminating the Israeli agents and possibly Devon and any other pilot who might have signed up. Apparently the Israelis have a high-ranking officer here, trades under the codename Mars, plus a junior. And Hannah Shaw."

Fitzjohn's mention of the senior Israeli agent in Hong Kong had caught Hetherington-Brown's attention. "My department is already keeping a low-key watch over Miss Shaw and Hartman," she said. "This Mars character – have you met him?"

"No, nor Hartman," said Fitzjohn. "In fact, like I say, I really didn't engage with the Israelis, unlike Devon. The real problem is that our friends from Egypt are minded to take out these two chaps from Israel. It's not very helpful to British interests for this to happen on our territory, of course, but more importantly, when the shooting starts, Miss Shaw and Devon could well be in the firing line."

"Indeed," said Hetherington-Brown. "Let me have the names and descriptions of these Egyptians. You say they're staying at the Peninsula?"

"Yes, and they're using the offices at the Egyptian trade delegation in Wan Chai."

Fitzjohn dictated Kauri and Fazil's names and descriptions, and Hetherington-Brown entered them into a notebook she had brought with her.

"Stay here, Fitzjohn. I will not be long." She left the room, but the guard remained outside.

Twenty minutes later she returned. Behind her was a young Chinese woman, smartly dressed in a black and white maid's uniform, carrying a tray of coffee. A good sign, Fitzjohn thought.

"We have an agent at the Peninsula who is checking your story as we speak. We have to be thorough, you understand."

"Naturally," said Fitzjohn. "I should get a move on, if I were you. I don't think these Egyptians will waste any time. Shall I pour the coffee while we wait?"

FORTY-SIX

Their taxi dropped off Kouri and Fazil a short walk from the Ming Lantern. They had instructed the driver to continue fifty yards beyond the restaurant and wait for them there. The driver was a reliable secret service resource. Kouri wanted to survey the scene and make sure they would have no difficulty in getting away in a hurry.

They had chosen the Ming Lantern Restaurant as it was not large, seating around thirty people at most. It would be easy to identify their targets, kill them and depart without any interference. Both men wore suit jackets and had their guns in underarm holsters, specially adapted to hold a pistol with a silencer fitted.

Twenty minutes earlier Hannah, Hartman and Mars had arrived at the restaurant. They sat at a quiet table at the back. They had ordered drinks but declined food. Only two other tables were occupied: one by two expat businessmen and one by a young Chinese couple.

Mars had briefed Hartman and Hannah: until Devon arrived they were to discuss construction issues, in case they were overheard.

"He's late," said Hartman, glancing at his watch.

"Five minutes. It's difficult to be exact when you're coming over from the mainland," said Hannah. Nervous as hell, she listened intently for a taxi to pull up outside and for Devon to come in.

The Chinese couple were looking lovingly into each other's eyes and whispering sweet nothings. Their food was served, then the waitress went to the expats and took orders for more drinks. The restaurant fell quiet. Mars looked at his watch. "I'll give him five more minutes."

Then the door opened. Kouri and Fazil walked in slowly and looked around, as if choosing where to sit. They saw Hartman, Mars and Hannah and knew they were the targets. Kouri stepped forward and called, "David, good to see you!"

Hartman looked surprised. "Who the hell's that?" he said under his breath. But manners took over and he waved and mouthed a quick hello. Kouri and Fazil went for their pistols. Fazil was so nervous, he snagged the silencer on the holster and couldn't pull his gun out. Kouri drew his gun out smoothly and levelled it at Mars.

Hartman and Mars were experienced agents: with lightning-fast reactions, they dived towards the floor and went for their own guns. Hannah, who only had basic training in close-quarters fighting, threw herself to one side. Kouri fired at Mars, but he missed, and the bullet went through the wall behind him. Before the Egyptian could fire again, a double shot rang out. Kouri slammed forward onto a table, then slid onto the floor. The young Chinese man was standing, holding a smoking pistol in a two-handed grip. The two expat diners had also drawn pistols. One man called out to Fazil: "Stop! Get your hands away! Kahn, Hartman, hold your fire!"

Fazil held his hands high in the air. "OK, OK! Don't shoot!"

The restaurant door burst open and three more British agents dashed in. Leading them was Val Hetherington-Brown, her Walther PPK in her hand.

"Everyone, stay calm. Raleigh, good work," she said to the older expat, then turned to Hartman and Mars. "You two, get back into your seats. Put your weapons on the table and stay still."

The other agent with Raleigh collected their guns. Hetherington-Brown turned to one of the agents behind her. "Get the medics in. And have that taxi driver arrested."

Mars went to stand up.

"Stay where you are! No one is going anywhere before we've had a little chat," snapped Hetherington-Brown.

Mars slumped back in his seat. "Devon must have done this – only he knew we were here. These guys came to kill us and he set us up."

"Not true," said Hetherington-Brown. "He doesn't know anything about this. We had an informer. We've been watching these Egyptians. We knew they were likely to try to take you out, but we didn't know where and when until our agent at the Peninsula told us about the telegram that was sent to you, ostensibly from Devon. But it came from these two guys. Devon had nothing to do with it."

"I recognise you – you're from Government House!" said Hannah.

"Yes, I thought you might remember me, hence my late arrival. But I think we can say that my colleagues here have done a good job. You can't be surprised that you were targets? We know about your efforts to recruit pilots. These Egyptian fellows' job was to put an end to your activities, at any price."

Another agent came in and spoke to Hetherington-Brown. "The truck is ready, ma'am."

She waved her pistol at Mars and Hartman. "Right, you two, get up and out to the truck. We're taking you into custody for questioning. Miss Shaw, stay there."

"We haven't broken any laws here – you can't arrest us!" Mars, having recovered his composure, sounded indignant.

"That remains to be seen. For a start, you're carrying guns, which is not something we like to see in Hong Kong. If you're in the clear you will be released in a couple of days and deported as unwelcome aliens. Take them out, Raleigh."

One of the medics treating Kouri looked up. "He's still alive, ma'am, but we need to get him to hospital. We'll have to hurry – he's lost a lot of blood."

"Right, off you go then." Hetherington-Brown turned to another of her team and pointed at Fazil. "Thompson, cuff this young idiot and take him in. Report to me later." She turned back to Hannah. "Right. I think we should have a chat back at Government House."

FORTY-SEVEN

"How are you planning to return to England, sir?" asked Young.

"There are regular flights to Singapore, and I'll book myself onto a troop ship from there. There are plenty of servicemen returning at the moment, but I should have no trouble in getting a berth."

Young hesitated. "Sir, if I may, my uncle is a steward on the Orient Line steamship *Orcades*. It's a lovely new liner and it will be on its way up from Australia soon, stopping off at Singapore. I'm sure it would have a cabin you could book, so you could enjoy a cruise back home in comfort."

Devon reflected on the prospect of a cramped troopship or the luxury of a brand-new liner. "You know, Steven, that's a grand idea. Can you look into it, see what's available?"

"Right away, sir. I will go to the telegraph office and get them to send a message to the Orient Line office in Singapore. Should have an answer by tomorrow."

Devon had started packing his possessions, ready for shipping home. Young provided a pile of old newspapers for him to wrap his record collection. He also wrapped gifts for his mother and sister – two small Chinese plates painted with jasmine and lotus flowers that he had purchased at a store in Kowloon that sold genuine antiques. For his father he had bought a bamboo-handled paring knife and for himself a fountain pen, gold-nibbed with a black and red lacquered body.

Carefully he packed a small watercolour of a crimson-red camellia he had bought to remind him of the botanical gardens.

***

As Devon left the Officers' Mess after lunch the next day, Young hurried over towards him.

"What is it, Young?"

"I've heard back from the Orient Line, sir. They have reserved a cabin for you on the *Orcades*, but you need to confirm within the hour. I have the details here."

"Right, come into my quarters. Let's have a look."

Young unfolded a long telegram and placed it on Devon's desk. He read the salient parts out loud. "*Orient Line Singapore, passage for one person, Mr Adam Devon, 15 November 1949, sailing to London on SS Orcades via Bombay and Suez, one cabin first class, forward deck four STOP.*" Devon frowned. "But, Young, there must be a mistake. I can't afford first class."

"Well, sir, I mentioned that you were an RAF officer returning to England, and that my uncle is a steward on board. The Orient Line kindly agreed to provide a first-class cabin at the same price as a tourist-class ticket. I thought you would like to travel in style, sir. But we do have to confirm by return."

"Hell's bells, Young, good work! Yes, please go ahead and confirm."

"Straight away, sir. Later today, may I suggest you visit the tailor in

Nathan Road and have yourself a dinner jacket made? White would be customary. You'll need it to dine with the captain."

"Really?"

"Most certainly, sir."

***

Devon's departure from Hong Kong took place without ceremony. After his farewell drinks party the night before, all he had left to do was say goodbye to the senior officers and the rest of the squadron. Young had organised his baggage. Suitcases were marked 'required during voyage' and a large trunk that he would not require was to be stowed in the hold. Devon couldn't force out of his mind the wish, or perhaps the expectation, that Hannah would come to see him off. He knew deep inside that he was just being hopeful. She had made it clear where her loyalties lay, and she would be setting up a new life in Israel – without him.

The DC-3 sat at the small commercial terminal at Kai Tak, its silver and white colour scheme making the red lettering along the fuselage – Cathay Pacific Airlines – stand out. He looked across to the parking area for the RAF aircraft to see mechanics, armourers and the refuelling team milling around, preparing for the morning's patrols. He had no regrets at resigning, even though it happened the way it did. He was also happy that he had decided not to join the Israelis. It was the right decision, that he was certain.

As Devon strapped himself into his seat, a pretty Chinese stewardess brought him a copy of the *South China Morning Post* and a glass of orange juice. She gave him a warm smile. Devon looked at the newspaper. China's communist Chairman Mao Zedong and its new regime dominated the headlines and the editorial. China is going to be quite a power to reckon with, he thought, once they have sorted out their internal differences.

On arrival at Changi Airfield in Singapore, Devon supervised the transfer of his baggage and had time for lunch before heading down to the docks on a courtesy bus provided by the Orient Line. He decided not to call in to the RAF station to say hello to the few servicemen still there that he knew. It would only lead to the usual questions about what he was going to do next.

***

The Orient Line steamship *Orcades* sat in the Singapore Strait, dazzling with her corn-yellow hull and white superstructure. Little more than a year old, she represented the new world of post-war optimism, revival and excitement. Tenders ferried passengers, crew and supplies to the ship on a near calm sea under a blindingly hot sun. Even in November the heat of the tropics were both a delight and a curse to British travellers – those who loved the heat and those who reminisced about the fresh Spring days in England.

Devon was enthralled by the reception. He was taken up to deck four by a steward, where he was delighted to find he had been allocated a well-appointed single cabin on the starboard side of the ship. Two windows gave plenty of natural light, and a desk and seating would make life during the journey very comfortable. He resolved not to overuse the drinks on the silver salver placed on a walnut-veneered sideboard; they were all included in the ticket price.

On the desk was a welcome note, meal times, the daily schedule of activities for the first week and details of the voyage. The ship would call at Colombo in Ceylon, Bombay, then Aden before sailing through the Suez Canal. The route through the Mediterranean included stops at Naples and Barcelona. The ship would finally arrive in Tilbury, to the east of London. The list of entertainment, sports and events seemed to cover every day and every evening: Devon knew he wouldn't be bored for one moment on the cruise home.

The steward started to unpack Devon's suitcases and hang his clothes in the wardrobe. "That's OK, thanks. I'll do it myself." Devon was not used to travelling first class. He admired his new dinner jacket, realising now why Young had insisted on him acquiring one. He was also pleased that Young had included a black silk bowtie in his case.

Before dinner on the first evening, Devon explored the ship. He was delighted to see there was a deck where he could walk or run completely around the ship, and promised himself he would keep in good shape during the journey. More than three weeks on board ship, well fed and with plenty of drinks available, could play havoc with his fitness, he thought. When he arrived in the first-class lounge for pre-dinner drinks, a steward gave him a table number, where he would dine for the whole voyage. He took a gin and tonic from another steward and ambled around the lounge. The dining saloon was furnished with a mixture of round tables for six guests and rectangular tables for eight. He was pleased to see from the seating plan resting on an easel that he was allocated to a round table. He glanced at the names of his fellow diners: they looked to be two married couples, a woman and himself.

A gong sounded and everyone moved through to the dining saloon. The table was beautifully dressed with a starched white tablecloth and napkins. A bowl of fresh flowers, perfect silver cutlery, fine china, wine and water glasses, bread rolls and butter were already on the tables. Devon felt again a pang of embarrassment at the luxury of first class, but knew that it would help him enjoy the trip and put his RAF service behind him – and of course his thoughts of Hannah.

He was right about the married couples. The first couple were, he guessed, in their mid-thirties, well dressed, with the woman wearing more jewellery than Devon believed anyone could own. The man introduced himself as Justin White and his wife Alison. He explained he was a lawyer specialising in corporate law and had been to Australia to set up a new partnership in Sydney.

Devon turned to the single woman in her fifties who had been assigned to the place next to him. He immediately thought of Agatha Christie, she was so like pictures of the author he had seen. Her tweed suit, dainty hat with two feathers and fox stole seemed completely out of place on board a ship in the tropics, but suited her exactly. Devon introduced himself and found out in return that she was Lady Joanna Tredwen from Cornwall. She had been on a trip to Australia, looking at mineral mining and production. Lady Joanna said that tin mining on her estate was declining and she was keen to invest in the growing opportunities in the New World. She seemed a very powerful and formidable lady.

They all took their seats. To Devon's right were the other couple. Given the names on the seating plan, Devon was not surprised to hear the man's French accent when he introduced himself. Claude Verte was accompanied by his wife, Suzanna. They were probably in their fifties. Claude explained they had moved to Australia immediately after the war to plant new vineyards in land around Adelaide. They were taking their first holiday back to France.

Devon found the conversation around the table fascinating, opening his mind to aspects of the world that had never previously interested him. These were successful, sophisticated people, the wealthy upper classes: they were self-assured, well-mannered and welcoming to those they felt were of their class, and naturally this included a recently retired RAF officer. Devon was asked many questions about his flying career and experiences and the political position in Hong Kong, in a way that showed his listeners were genuinely interested. He was confident he would enjoy the company of his fellow travellers very much.

At the conclusion of the meal, Devon felt the need for a stroll on the deck. As he walked out of the saloon and turned towards an exit door, he felt a tap on his shoulder. He turned to see a tall, short-haired woman in a close-fitting black and silver evening dress. "How about that – Flight Lieutenant Adam Devon, isn't it?"

Devon remembered her instantly. "Yes indeed – Nurse Barbara Blake, the famous cricketer! How nice to see you. On your way home, presumably?"

"Yes, I've served my time in Queen Alexandra's. I have a job at Guy's Hospital in London. What better way to return than on this gin bucket? Shall we take a turn around the deck, and then perhaps have a drink?"

"That would be splendid. We have quite a bit to catch up on," said Devon.

They sat together until late into the evening, enjoying several drinks. Devon explained his decision to leave the RAF and go into avionics development, avoiding any mention of the Israeli flying job. Barbara told him of her desire to settle down and return to London. Her parents were both successful doctors. Devon felt this was how she could afford to travel first class. Barbara said she wanted to specialise in treating burns, which she explained she could do at Guy's.

Approaching 11 p.m. they said goodnight and agreed to meet the following afternoon – the ship's entertainment programme listed a badminton tournament.

***

Racket sports were not Devon's strong point, and he was quickly eliminated in the singles knock-out competition. Barbara was a natural and easily got through to the ladies' final. She was fiercely competitive, but cricket was her sport and she was up against a badminton champion from Australia. In the match Barbara was outclassed and lost by quite a margin. Nonetheless, Devon was impressed with her sporting prowess and the fact that she took losing in good spirits. It showed something of her character that he liked.

After the tournament they took afternoon tea together on the aft deck near the swimming pool. Being fair-haired, Devon burned easily and was always careful in the sun. Barbara loved to sunbathe. Thanks to her time in Singapore, her skin was deeply tanned and smooth. Devon could not see a pale part of her body, even in her singlet and shorts.

Each day they met and joined in with sporting events or simply walked around, chatting. One day Devon agreed to accompany Barbara to an afternoon of dancing on one of the wider decks. A quartet played upbeat melodies and everyone tried their best to dance as elegantly as possible on the moving ship. In the evening they attended a musical revue put on by the ship's crew in the ballroom, and enjoyed the slapstick and clowning.

Devon was becoming very attached to Barbara, but had made no move to show his affection. Nor had she given him any indication of her feelings. He knew it was only a passing holiday romance, but this new and unexpected relationship had helped him to overcome the anguish he felt at leaving Hannah in Hong Kong,

After a week at sea the ship docked at Bombay. A handful of new passengers joined – mainly civil servants glad to be on their way home after a period of service in India. The ship headed north, but without any respite from the heat. The prospect of a transit through the Suez Canal in a few days' time created excitement and expectation in the passengers. The gift shop did a brisk trade in postcards of the ship that would be sent by airmail from Port Said: an opportunity for passengers to give their families and friends news about the progress of the journey. Devon and Barbara bought their cards and spent an afternoon writing them out. When they were finished Devon offered to take them to the purser's desk for stamps and to be put in the mail.

On his way down to the desk, he couldn't help glancing at the cards Barbara had given him. They were notes to family and friends, and a couple to nurses at a hospital in London. One was addressed to someone called Sam.

Looking forward so much to seeing you, my dear. Missing you terribly. Ship is good fun – wait until you see my suntan! Love always, Barbara x

Devon wondered who Sam was and what he meant to Barbara. He dropped the cards into the post box and went to his cabin.

At dinner that evening Lady Joanna said, "Adam, you're very quiet tonight. Are you feeling well?"

"Is it perhaps a matter of the heart?" said Suzanna Verte, pursing her lips and looking over towards Barbara.

Devon snapped out of his reverie. "No, no, I'm fine, thank you. A little tired, perhaps, but otherwise in good shape. Have you had an enjoyable day, Lady Joanna? What have you been doing?"

The evening passed quietly. Barbara stayed with the people on her table and Devon joined the Whites for drinks in the Galleries bar. He pondered Suzanna's comment and asked himself if his languid state was because of Hannah or due to disappointment at knowing that Barbara seemed to have someone special in her life.

After breakfast the next day, Devon found a comfortable deckchair on the sunny side of the ship and relaxed with a book, but he found himself unable to concentrate. He sat there for a while, people-watching. Passengers were enjoying walks around the deck – a pastime undertaken by all on board. First-class passengers mixed with those from tourist class, all enjoying the fine weather. Mid-morning a steward offered to fetch a pot of coffee, which Devon accepted gratefully then gave the book another try. As the coffee arrived, one of the passengers stopped and stood in front of Devon, blocking out the sun. He squinted over his book to see who it was.

"Ah, good morning, Barbara. Would you like to join me for coffee?"

She smiled and nodded.

"Steward, would a pot for two be possible?"

"Of course, sir, right away."

"What plans do you have for today?" said Barbara.

"Not much, really. Passing the time being lazy!"

She smiled. "Shall we have lunch together? Then this afternoon there's a concert in the ballroom."

"I'd love to do both of those things. Thank you."

***

After Suez the ship sailed through the Mediterranean Sea, making good speed. The captain confirmed their expected arrival date of 7 December in London. After they passed Gibraltar, the ship headed north. Each day brought cooler temperatures. On the last night of the trip the entertainment staff excelled themselves with a gala dinner, music and dancing. Devon didn't realise that he enjoyed dancing so much – having a beautiful girl in his arms made all the difference, he now appreciated. He spent the whole evening with Barbara and as the night neared its close, he suggested they took a final drink out onto the deck.

Devon sighed. There was something so romantic about being on the deck of a ship at night, with only the sounds of the sea, a fresh breeze, and the moon shining down on the water.

"The waves on the water," he said to himself, and smiled at his happy memory. Barbara touched his arm.

Devon had prepared himself for leaving Barbara. For days he had wondered whether he should ask to see her after the cruise, but he didn't want to risk her refusing. And he didn't want to leap into another relationship solely as a way to replace Hannah. It wouldn't work. Throughout the voyage they had both, perhaps deliberately, avoided talking about their love lives or any partners back home.

Barbara broke the ice. "Will anyone be meeting you when we dock?" she asked.

"No. I will be staying a couple of nights in London and then go home to my parents. Next week I have a job interview with Avro. How about you? Will anyone special be waiting for you, emotionally waving a handkerchief?"

Barbara laughed, then became serious. "There is someone. Someone I will be starting a new life with, actually. Sam. We have been good friends – more than that – for several years. Sam's the reason I decided to leave Queen Alexandra's and return home. There comes a time when we all have to settle down, Adam."

"That's true. Does Sam live in London?"

"Yes, she has a flat in Putney."

"She?"

"Yes. Samantha."

Devon's face froze in surprise, and he was momentarily speechless.

"Don't look so shocked, Adam. We live in progressive times."

Devon smiled and linked his arm through Barbara's. "Ah, I see. I wish you all the happiness in the world, Barbara. It has been such a pleasure spending time with you on this trip. Perhaps one day we could meet for a drink? With Sam, of course!"

FORTY-EIGHT

March 1950

The air in London had a distinct feel of spring. A fresh westerly breeze had brought a welcome reprieve from the smog the city had endured during the winter months. Adam Devon walked south along Bishopsgate, looking for a right turn into Cornhill. The City of London still bore the scars of the Blitz: many buildings were shuttered while others had been demolished, leaving gaps along the roads. The church of St Peter-upon-Cornhill had a gleaming new roof.

It was lunchtime, and office clerks scurried to sandwich bars and cafes, luncheon vouchers in hand. As he turned into Cornhill, Devon could see right down to Bank and the imposing frontage of the Mappin & Webb shop, famous for luxury watches, wedding rings and silver picture frames, today thriving after the wartime constraints. Now that he was earning a good salary he had committed to saving enough money for the Omega watch he had promised himself, and made a mental note to call at the shop on his next visit to London.

A minute later he cut into Ball Court, a narrow alley that was a relic of old London, and found his destination: Simpson's Tavern. It was packed with businessmen, largely in grey suits, their bowler hats hanging on pegs, in earnest discussion on interest rates, insurance premiums and shipping costs. When he entered, a rotund, red-faced waitress called from behind the tiny bar, "Come in, dearie, I'll find you a table."

"I'm meeting someone," Devon called back. "Could I have a table for two, please?"

"Yes, my love, come this way." She led him to a quiet alcove at the far end of the tavern.

"Mug of ale while you wait, sir?" asked the waitress as she wiped her hands on a linen glass cloth.

"Yes, thank you." Devon took in the atmosphere. He felt like an intruder at a family dinner, the City men knew each other so well, but he smiled inwardly at their camaraderie, which was no different to that in the Mess. He checked his watch. It was almost 1 o'clock. A few minutes later, right on time, the door opened. His guest had arrived. The waitress brought him through.

"Steven, thanks for coming. It's great to see you again," said Devon.

"And you, sir. You're looking well."

"No more of that, we're not in the forces now. Call me Adam."

"Of course, er, Adam."

They sat down and the waitress brought over two mugs. "I recommend the potted shrimps and brown bread to start with, and today's Barnsley chop is very nice. Shall I bring these for you, sirs?"

The two men were not inclined to argue.

"So, Steven, tell me about your job."

"Well, sir ... Adam. You'll remember that I was offered an interview at the Great Eastern Hotel. After I arrived back in England I went to see them. I was given a two-week trial in the restaurant and I'm glad to say they took me on. It's a very pleasant place to work. As well as serving in the restaurant, the sommelier has taken me under his wing and I'm learning more about wines. Thank you again for sending the reference – it really helped."

"Excellent. Glad to hear that things have worked out so well."

"And what about you? What are you doing now?" asked Young.

"I'm pleased to say I'm still flying. I went for an interview at the Avro factory near Manchester but found that the work I would be doing was not at all appealing – essentially working at a desk analysing numbers from flight tests. I wanted something more challenging. Then I had a letter from an old pal from my Cranwell days asking if I was interested in joining de Havilland at Hatfield Aerodrome. So that's where I am, test-flying new versions of the DH104."

"The twin?" asked Young

"Yes, that's right – the de Havilland Dove. It carries ten or twelve passengers. De Havilland are hoping to sell it to commercial operators as well as air forces around the world. I was chuffed to get a flying job that involves aircraft development. The Dove has new avionics and radar, designed to be operated in all weathers."

"That sounds like it suits you very well. And do you now live in Hatfield?"

"Not far away, in a place called Welham Green. Very rural. I'm renting an ancient two-bedroom cottage there. It's an easy drive to work – and of course a short train ride to London."

The two men savoured the meal and each other's company as the lunch period passed and most of the diners left the restaurant. Devon ordered coffee.

"Have you heard how other chaps from the squadron are doing? I know most of them decided to stay on in Hong Kong after it was confirmed that 28 Squadron wouldn't be disbanded," said Devon.

"Well, some of the men came back soon after you and I left. You may remember Arnold Ridgewell? He now works for the GPO not far from here in the international telephone exchange."

Devon nodded.

"And do you remember Mackie, Fitzjohn's old orderly?"

"Sure – a good man, as I recall."

"He also has a job at the hotel. Works at the concierge desk. He's loving it."

"Good show.'

It was Young's turn to ask. "What about other pilots, sir – Adam? Any news there?"

"Yes, I had lunch with David Porter a couple of weeks ago. He's thoroughly enjoying working for BOAC. Next month he will be in Africa, planning new routes right down to Cape Town. John Corrigan joined Channel Islands Airways, flying out of Croydon Airport. And then there's Fitzjohn, of course – he stayed for a couple of months longer but David Porter told me that he was sent home. The OC Far East had enough of his antics and gave him the option to resign."

Young looked up at the clock on the wall.

"Are you on duty today?" Devon asked.

"Yes, I'm on the late shift, starting at 3 p.m. I have a bit of time yet. What are your plans for the rest of the day?"

"Nothing special. I have some time until my train leaves so I'll take a walk. I could do with stretching my legs to help digest that lunch. But we must do this again, and maybe get some of the other chaps together for a reunion."

"Good idea. I'll round up some of the aircraftmen who are back and living in London. Most are working at Ford's in Dagenham, so it would be easy to get a group together."

Outside the restaurant, the men shook hands warmly then parted at the junction of Bishopsgate and Cornhill. Devon crossed Gracechurch Street and stepped into the glass-covered arcades of Leadenhall Market.

A few men stood with their beer outside the Lamb pub, while the butcher was closing his shop and the florist was tidying the remaining flowers in her display. Adam looked in the window of a stationer's at the array of fountain pens and was pleased to see that his own one from Hong Kong had cost him about a quarter of the shop's price. Turning into Leadenhall Street he saw the entrance to Lloyd's of London, with brokers going in and out carrying leather document holders and looking more nonchalant, he thought, than Battle of Britain fighter pilots.

Devon turned right and strolled slowly along Leadenhall Street. Several of the offices were shipping agents and ticket offices, and he stopped and admired a model of the beautiful *Caronia* cruise ship in the window of Cunard's building. It brought back happy memories of his journey home from Singapore. Devon continued almost to Aldgate, then decided it was time to think of getting his train and turned back down Leadenhall Street. Towards the western end of the street a tall building made of Portland stone loomed above him. Its doors were open, and a uniformed commissionaire was saluting visitors. He was wearing a Brigade of Guards tie: no doubt a retired soldier now enjoying a new career in the City. It seems that every serviceman has to be prepared to adapt to changing circumstances, Devon reflected.

Devon suddenly saw, behind the commissionaire, the polished brass name plate, and stopped dead in his tracks. *London and Hong Kong Bank*, he read. He was immobilised for several seconds before the commissionaire spoke to him. "Can I be of any assistance, sir?"

"Ah, er … no, thank you. It's just that a friend of mine used to work here. Haven't seen her for a while."

The commissionaire moved towards him. "Do come in, sir, have a look around. Most people like to admire our banking hall."

He was right. Devon was entranced by the white marble floor, the sparkling chandeliers, the brass grilles on the teak counters and the ornate ceiling cornices. The few customers present spoke quietly to the tellers or sat with bank officials at desks around the hall.

"Very impressive," he said.

"What was the name of your friend, sir? I might have known her."

"Shaw, Miss Hannah Shaw." It felt exhilarating even to speak her name.

"Yes, of course, Miss Shaw," said the commissionaire. "But she still works here. I believe she returned from her overseas posting some weeks ago. I will call her and let her know you're here. Do come this way."

Devon was shocked. "No, no, that's quite alright, no need to disturb her."

But the man had stepped into a small cubicle, no more than a sentry box off the main hall, and picked up the telephone. He looked at Devon expectantly.

"Miss Foy, it's Arthur on the front door. Could you put me through to Miss Shaw, please?" He smiled at Devon. "Ah, Miss Shaw, Arthur here. There's a visitor for you in the banking hall." He hesitated, listening to her response. "Yes, I see. Very good, ma'am, I shall pass that on." He hung up and gestured towards a small leather-bound bench. "Please take a seat. She will be down in a few minutes."

Devon managed to control his breathing, but his heart rate he could not control. What the hell could he say to her? How would she react when she saw it was him? There was a pair of lifts at the far end of the hall. The doors to the left-hand lift opened, and she stepped out.

Devon saw Hannah as he had imagined she would look: her long brown hair was swept over her right shoulder. She wore a smart maroon suit that could have been by Chanel and a white silk blouse, with only a touch of make-up. And her pearl necklace, of course. When she saw him, her fingers flew to her mouth and she hesitated. But then she hurried over to him. "Adam, it's wonderful to see you. Such a lovely surprise."

"And you too. Look, I was just passing. I didn't know you were back in England. I heard about the shooting in Hong Kong, but I've no idea what happened after that."

They sat down on the bench, knees touching, Hannah's smile creasing her right cheek in the way Adam loved.

"The Hong Kong operation ended when Mars and Hartman were deported. My cover was blown so I was no further use to the service – I'm not sure I was really right for them anyway." Hannah smiled. "I decided against moving to a kibbutz in Israel and the bank gave me a new role here. I've been back two months. And you? What brings you to London? And what are you doing now?"

"I'm in London today to have lunch with my old orderly, Steven Young. I'm now working for de Havilland up at Hatfield, test-flying the new Dove aircraft."

"That's great. I'm so glad you have a flying job."

They sat for a few moments in silence, each with so much to say but unable to choose the right words.

"Hannah, what time do you finish here? Perhaps we could have a glass of wine somewhere?"

"I would love to, but are you sure you want to?"

"Yes, yes, I'm sure."

Half an hour later they left the bank. Hannah slipped her hand into Adam's and kissed him briefly on the cheek, her eyelashes brushing his temple.

FORTY-NINE

"Henry, how jolly nice to see you again. Come in, come in. What has it been – three, four years?" Julian Temple grasped Fitzjohn's hand and shook it vigorously, bending forward as if bowing to royalty. He was a small man with plenty of grey hair, wearing a suit of charcoal grey with a white chalk pinstripe.

"Yes, it must be, Julian – three, in fact. I think the last time we met was before I went out east in 1947, at a Party fundraiser at Audley End House."

"Ah yes, I remember, a fine occasion. Splendid host, Lord Benbrooke." Temple was an East Anglian farmer who had spent thirty years serving the local Conservative Party branch, and since the war had held the post of chairman of the Sudbury Conservatives. Fitzjohn had attended social occasions at the Party offices in the town centre many times with his father, but today he was here in a more official capacity. Temple directed him to a sparsely furnished meeting room, with a coffee tray set on a small cabinet.

"We will be meeting Amanda Spencer, our campaign manager.

Don't be frightened – she might look like a horse but her bark is worse than her bite!" Temple chuckled at his own humour. "We must remember that the decision about who the committee elects as our future candidate for Member of Parliament is strongly influenced by her."

Temple spent half an hour briefing Fitzjohn on the key issues that the Party was focusing on. After a short rehearsal of the likely interview questions, there was a knock at the door. A tall woman aged around fifty entered. Her classical good looks contradicted what Templar had said; she had a slim, lithe figure that Fitzjohn admired immediately. She wore a brown tweed suit and her glasses hung from a chain around her neck. An expensive stylist had clearly worked wonders on her blonde hair. Fitzjohn noticed that she was not wearing a wedding ring.

"Good morning, Amanda, do come in," said Templar. "May I introduce Henry Fitzjohn? Henry, Amanda Spencer."

"Delighted to meet you, Amanda."

"And you, Henry. We like our parliamentary candidates to be local people, and I think it's fair to say that you and your family are well known in county life. Now, shall we get down to business?"

The group sat at the table and Amanda opened her foolscap notebook. "As you know, we have three candidates to consider. I have already interviewed the other two. My aim this morning is to get to know a little more about you, Henry, why you wish to stand for election, and how you would serve the constituency. We fully expect the Labour government to call a snap election this year, and we have to be ready if and when it comes."

"Understood," said Fitzjohn.

"Tell me something about your education and military service. And what have you been doing since leaving the RAF?"

Fitzjohn related the story of his school days, humbly mentioning that his academic achievements were not the highest, then quickly moved on to talk about joining the RAF as a Spitfire pilot. Amanda seemed to be impressed, and made copious notes. Fitzjohn brushed his right index finger across his moustache, to the left and then the right. "As the squadron was likely to be marked for disbandment, I decided it was a good time to come home and start my own business. You may be aware that I have purchased two aircraft to use as executive air taxis, based at Duxford. When I was approached to consider standing as the parliamentary candidate I was delighted, given my long association with the branch and my fervent support for the future of Sudbury, and Suffolk more widely."

"And how would you convince the electorate to vote for you?" Amanda's tone was challenging, but no more than Fitzjohn expected.

"I believe that the people of Sudbury are not sold on the trend towards socialism. It's time to build a new Britain – one that will give us growth and wealth at home and the standing in world affairs that we deserve and need. Our strengths lie in our world-class education system, our agricultural prowess, and our skilled scientists." Fitzjohn took Amanda through the list of issues that Temple had briefed him on. He wanted to show her that he was a first-rate orator and that the electorate would find him engaging.

"Very good, Henry. You clearly have a good grasp of what the voting public want," said Amanda. "There is one further question I would like to ask. Give me three words that would capture the essence of your campaign."

"Ah well … perhaps 'Building Britain Great' would sum up my ambitions."

Glancing at Temple, Amanda smiled, closed her notebook and sat back. "Henry, that was excellent, thank you. I am pleased to say that my recommendation to the Party branch committee will be that you are chosen as the next candidate for Member of Parliament for Sudbury. Congratulations."

"Thank you so much, Amanda. I look forward to working together on the election campaign. I'm sure you and I will enjoy a fruitful relationship."

FIFTY

July 1950

"Your fiancé has such graceful hands, Mr Devon. Any of our rings will look beautiful on her. These diamond solitaires are some of our most popular engagement ring designs."

Devon knew the sales assistant was running through her flattering routine to butter him up, but he agreed: Hannah had the most elegant hands, with long, slim fingers and manicured nails.

"Do any of these appeal, darling?" Devon said.

"Yes, I think I like these two the most." Hannah took two rings from the royal-blue velvet tray. She slipped the first onto the third finger of her left hand and spread her hand out on the table. She turned her hand this way and that so the diamond caught the light, saying nothing. Then she took it off. Devon had the second ring in his hand. "Allow me," and he slipped the ring onto her finger.

"This one is so beautiful, my love, but I'm guessing it's very expensive."

Devon shrugged. "I'm sure it's quite affordable." He had accepted he would have to delay buying himself the Omega watch he had his eye on. "If that's the one you like, then you must have it."

Hannah touched the single diamond and ran her fingers over the plain gold ring. "I love it. Thank you so much, darling. It really is lovely." She leant across and kissed Devon on the cheek.

The sales assistant took out a small black leather box with a sky-blue silk lining.

"Oh darling, is it alright if I wear it?"

"Yes of course, it looks beautiful."

***

As the couple stepped out of the Queen Victoria Street exit from Mappin & Webb Devon glanced up at the huge clock on the front of the building. "Perfect timing. We should be at the restaurant just before 1 p.m. It's only about five or six minutes' walk."

"What is the name of the place?" asked Hannah.

"The Olde Wine Shades. It's one of the City's oldest restaurants. A bit of history will appeal to my mother."

"I'm so nervous about meeting your family, Adam."

"You're bound to be nervous the first time, but you will like them, I'm sure, and they will absolutely love you."

The pair walked slowly along Cannon Street before cutting downhill to the restaurant in Martin Lane. The *maître d'* took them through to the private room Devon had reserved. A few minutes later the door opened and Devon's mother and father entered. They were followed by his sister Joan and a squat middle-aged man with a permanent smile, very smartly dressed in a dark blue suit and black trilby.

Devon embraced his mother and everyone shook hands and sat down.

"How was the journey, Dad?" said Devon.

"Very pleasant. I think we shall see a much improved train service in this country now we have British Railways taking care of things."

"Great to see you again, Michael," said Devon. They had met when Devon had visited his parents at Christmas.

"Thank you, Adam, it's good to see you too. And of course to meet Hannah. We're in the same line of business, although banking in Manchester is not as glamourous as it is in the famous City of London!"

Hannah laughed softly. "I'm sure that's not true."

Mrs Devon couldn't hold her curiosity any longer. "Adam, dear, tell me how you two met."

Devon looked sideways at her. "Mother, you know that. It was in Hong Kong. But then we met again after we both came back, in London earlier this year." He turned to Hannah. "Darling, can we see the little present I bought you this morning?"

Devon took Hannah's left hand in his.

"Mother, Dad, we have some news for you. We're planning to get married – perhaps next summer. This is Hannah's engagement ring," said Devon.

"Oh, that's wonderful, Adam, Hannah! And the ring is beautiful," said Joan, taking Hannah's hand. "I hope you will be very happy, as Michael and I are."

Michael leant across the table to shake hands with Devon.

Devon's mother's initial smiles turned to a sour look of uncertainty. "I'm very pleased to hear this, Adam. But where will you live? I hope you'll find somewhere near the rest of your family in Manchester. Especially after all your years away with the RAF."

"We're not sure where exactly yet, Mother, but because of our jobs I expect we will live down here. Sorry but, as Dad said, there's a good train service and we will visit often. And Hannah's family are in Cambridge, so we won't be far from them."

"Splendid – congratulations to both of you," Mr Devon interjected quickly. "I'm sure you will make the right decision. Now, shall we order?"

ACKNOWLEDGEMENTS

When writing about service life the best place to go is to talk to those who have served. My thanks go to the retired RAF personnel now working and volunteering at the Imperial War Museum, Duxford for the advice they gave me on the development of Spitfire marks and the insight on relationships between officers and other ranks.

Jane Hammett carried out the text editing and development editing, and added more than a touch of creative writing advice. Thank you for your excellent guidance and patience.

Mike Duval (ably assisted by Lisa Duval no doubt!) carried out readings of early drafts of the manuscript and provided invaluable comments on the storyline.

To David Worsfold, journalist and author, many thanks for providing insight and guidance on the world of writing and publication.

There have been many contributors at Troubadour Publishing, each one professional and easy to work with. But I should mention in particular Hannah Makin who has helped me to understand some of the mysteries of the publishing industry.

I have been asked if the main characters are based on real people. My father was a Spitfire pilot, but Adam Devon is a combination of people. Fitzjohn is an entirely made up character, with many of those elements of people you might hate but secretly admire. The beautiful, pearl-wearing Hannah Shaw is very much a reflection of a good friend of mine.

ABOUT THE AUTHOR

Born in London, but now living in Essex, Mark Butterworth worked in the City of London in financial services for nearly 40 years, including as a Lloyd's underwriter and risk management consultant. Travelling widely on holidays and business, often the two combined, Mark developed his appreciation of the Far East, Australasia, North America, the Caribbean and Europe. Mark held a Private Pilot's Licence for 15 years, including flights from Kai Tak and over the Sydney Harbour Bridge and Niagara Falls. Mark has flown a two-seater Spitfire and made more than 50 parachute jumps. Mark enjoys running, country walking, golf and salsa dancing and has two grown up daughters and a Springer Spaniel called Arthur.

The Pearl River is Mark's debut novel. He has had two non-fiction (business) books published, both commissioned by the Chartered Insurance Institute as well as numerous business articles and opinion pieces published in journals.